"I have moved on!"

"Not far." Gabe touched her shoulder before she could move away. "It's not just you, Siddah. My parents are the same way. I know you loved Peter. Everybody did. But don't you think he'd rather see you enjoying life again?"

Siddah glared at him, but she waited to speak until a couple on the sidewalk had passed them. "You don't know what you're talking about," she said when they were alone again.

"I know my brother. I know how much he liked to laugh. I know how much he enjoyed life. Of the two of us, I was the serious one. So I know how much he'd hate seeing my mother so sad and my dad so angry. I'm sure he'd feel the same way about you and Bobby."

"We're trying," Siddah snapped. "Helene's already different since you've been back, but I can't just flip a switch on my feelings."

Gabe's expression remained kind. Too kind. "I'm not suggesting you should. But you wouldn't be betraying Peter if you rejoined the human race."

Siddah opened her mouth to argue, but the words wouldn't come.

Dear Reader,

Every once in a while, I'm lucky enough to stumble across a fully formed character in my imagination. In the blink of an eye I know about his hopes, his dreams, his sorrows, his joys, his deepest fears and his wildest dreams. It doesn't happen to me often—maybe once or twice in a decade—but it's a whole lot of fun to write a story when it does.

Other people keep a notebook and pen beside the bed so they can write down the flashes of brilliance that come to them in the middle of the night but, frankly, my thoughts in the middle of the night are rarely even coherent, much less brilliant. The night Gabe King popped into my head just as I was drifting off to sleep was a rare (and welcome) exception. Even half asleep, I know a good man when I see one, so I scrambled out of bed and spent the next hour or so writing down everything I'd learned about him between one breath and the next.

I'm endlessly fascinated by family dynamics, and the dynamics within the King family were especially interesting to me. Like all families, the Kings have places where they bump up against each other, but all relationships constantly grow and change, and theirs do, too. I hope you enjoy meeting Gabe and his family, and that you enjoy this visit to my home state of Montana!

Sherry Lewis

I love hearing from you! You can reach me by e-mail at sherrysbooks@peoplepc.com, via my Web site at www.sherrylewisbooks.com, or by regular mail at P.O. Box 540010, North Salt Lake, UT 84054.

High Mountain Home
Sherry Lewis

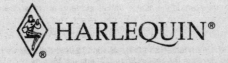

HARLEQUIN®

TORONTO • NEW YORK • LONDON
AMSTERDAM • PARIS • SYDNEY • HAMBURG
STOCKHOLM • ATHENS • TOKYO • MILAN • MADRID
PRAGUE • WARSAW • BUDAPEST • AUCKLAND

ISBN 0-373-71275-8

HIGH MOUNTAIN HOME

Copyright © 2005 by Sherry Lewis.

This edition published by arrangement with Harlequin Books S.A.

® and TM are trademarks of the publisher. Trademarks indicated with
® are registered in the United States Patent and Trademark Office, the
Canadian Trade Marks Office and in other countries.

www.eHarlequin.com

Printed in U.S.A.

For Troy and Emily

Books by Sherry Lewis

HARLEQUIN SUPERROMANCE

Don't miss any of our special offers. Write to us at the following address for information on our newest releases.

Harlequin Reader Service
U.S.: 3010 Walden Ave., P.O. Box 1325, Buffalo, NY 14269
Canadian: P.O. Box 609, Fort Erie, Ont. L2A 5X3

PROLOGUE

TOO FURIOUS TO TAKE the news he'd just been given lying down, Gabe King struggled to sit upright in his hospital bed. "Six months?" he demanded. "What the hell am I supposed to do with myself for half a year?"

"You'll figure something out." From the visitor's chair at his bedside, Professor Wes Buchi met his gaze and held it. Wes had been his teacher, mentor and friend for the past ten years. He knew more about Gabe than any man alive, which meant that he also knew just how much Gabe's career meant to him.

"I've spoken with the local doctor," Wes said, "and I know what he's told you. I've also spoken with the doctors from the university. They agree you're well enough to travel, but you're not going back into the field for at *least* six months. I don't want to see your face here in Ecuador before March."

"Be serious, Wes. I'll go crazy and you know it."

"Maybe so, but at least you'll be alive."

Gabe made a noise of derision and fell back on his pillow.

"I want you back in the States," Wes ordered. He grimaced at the patches of sweat staining his shirt. "Preferably somewhere without humidity. Later, when you're feeling better, we can get you an office at the university so you can catch up your journals."

"I'm not a scholar, Wes. I belong here."

"You'll be back here once you get clearance from the doctors." Wes must have felt Gabe's next protest coming, because he held up a hand to ward it off. "This isn't negotiable, Gabe. You've already been out of commission for over a year. Another six months isn't going to hurt anything."

"I've already lost *eighteen* months," Gabe argued. "If I don't get back out into the rain forest, I'll lose the Oxbow Grant. I can't afford to pay back the money I've already received from them."

Wes mopped his face with a handkerchief and hitched an ankle over one knee. "Oxbow's already pulled out," he admitted reluctantly. "The grant was re-assigned three weeks ago—before you were well enough to even think about this stuff. I know this isn't the ideal situation, Gabe, but it's the only thing we can do. The university won't accept the liability for letting you back out into the field, nor should they."

"They don't have to accept liability."

"As long as you're part of this research team, they call the shots. You know that as well as I do." Wes's expression softened. "As your colleague *and* your friend, I'm begging you to be reasonable. Take time. Heal. Come back to us when you're one-hundred percent again. A few months completely away from all of this might do you a world of good."

"And what am I supposed to do?"

"I don't know. Relax. Enjoy. Go see your family. How long has it been, anyway?"

Not even Wes knew the real answer to that. Gabe shrugged and raked his fingers through his hair. "It's been a while. A couple of years, maybe." *Or ten.*

"Then it's definitely time to go home. They must be worried."

"My family? Worried?" Gabe laughed harshly. "Not in this lifetime."

"I know you had problems with your father in the past," Wes said, "but your mother writes."

"Occasionally."

"So go see your mother. She's probably crazy with worry and she deserves to know how sick you've been. The fever nearly killed you."

"Seeing my mother means seeing my old man, and what happened here doesn't concern them."

"They're your *family,*" Wes insisted. "What concerns you concerns them."

Gabe had never liked talking about his family. Wes knew that. So why was he pushing this? "That's a nice platitude. Where did you find it, on a greeting card?"

Wes gave him a thin smile. "Look, Gabe, we're all away from our families too much. It's easy to let distance grow…"

"It's not just about a little distance." Gabe could feel the tremors starting again and he cursed silently. The fever's symptoms would pass in time—at least that's what everyone kept telling him. "My brother's there with them. They don't need me." His old man had made that abundantly clear the last time he'd been in Montana.

"Believe me, I'm the last person my father would want to see walking through the door."

Wes pulled an envelope from his inside pocket and held it out for Gabe. "I found this yesterday. It's been sitting in a box in the storage room for a while."

Suddenly wary, Gabe took the envelope and checked the handwriting. "It's from my mother."

"Maybe you should read it."

Gabe felt his pulse stutter. He checked the postmark, and saw that the letter had been mailed the previous spring. Eighteen months was a little long to remain silent, even for him. "Why wasn't this sent to me at the village?"

"It must have fallen through the cracks. I also found a notation in the records that your family tried to reach you through the embassy."

That brought Gabe's head up with a snap. "When?"

"About the same time the letter was mailed."

Gabe felt his chest tighten. No one from Libby would have gone to those extremes unless something was wrong. So what was it? Had something happened to his mother? No, she'd written the letter. So it must have been the old man. He ignored the sharp pang of regret and focused on Wes's narrow face.

"You were out there under some rather unusual circumstances, Gabe. Only a couple of us knew exactly where you were. I was out of the country, and VanPelt was called back to Virginia unexpectedly. We didn't know where to look."

Heat seemed to rush from the envelope into Gabe's fingers and, from there, to his entire body. He'd always known this day would come, and for that reason he'd promised himself to mend the rift between himself and his father. Had he waited too long?

At thirty-four, he'd grown tired of the anger, tired of pretending nothing was wrong and of telling himself he didn't long for closer ties with his family. He could have done something about it a long time ago, but old habits were hard to break.

A tremor shook his fingers and made it difficult to hang on to the envelope. Slowly, hesitantly, he tore open the flap and removed the single sheet inside. He read the words penned in his mother's cautious handwriting and felt the world he'd constructed so carefully come crashing down around him.

CHAPTER ONE

BATTLING SELF-DOUBT and second thoughts, Gabe stopped his Jeep on the edge of the winding two-lane highway he'd been driving for the past hour. Far below, a broad valley in the heart of Montana's timber country stretched between mountain and river. Spires of spruce and pine reached toward the deep blue sky, jockeying for their share of the late-August sunlight, leaving little for the undergrowth. In the distance, he could see rooftops from the town of Libby and the water of the Kootenai River sparkling in the noonday sun. A little beyond that the Cabinet Mountains, purple and majestic, stood watch over the valley.

It had been years since Gabe had seen this view, but little had changed in the time he'd been away. The valley, including the house barely visible directly below, was as familiar to him as it had ever been. Since graduating from the university he'd traveled the world over, yet he'd seen nothing that could top this combination of blue and green, sky, water and earth. But appreciation for the magnificent scenery warred with trepidation over what he was doing.

It wasn't too late to change his mind. His family

didn't need to know he'd come back. If he drove away, he wouldn't have to explain or apologize or—far more likely—argue. But he'd spent the past ten years running away, or at least avoiding what he couldn't change. He was here now. He wouldn't turn back.

Gabe fingered the letter in his pocket, fighting the impulse to read it again. He'd tortured himself with it a dozen times or more in the past two weeks, but the words never changed. Maybe he should have called to warn everyone of his impending visit, but that old fear had kept him from doing it. Now that he knew how fragile life really was, staying away was no longer an option.

Smiling grimly, he shifted into gear and pulled onto the road, sending a shower of dust and gravel into the air behind him. He followed the highway almost to the bottom of the hill, then turned onto the lane that led through an arched wooden gateway made from Triple Crown lumber, past a long split-rail fence, and finally into the front yard of the home where he'd grown up. Even after all these years, the house managed, somehow, to look haughty and humble at the same time.

He shut off the ignition and studied what had once been so familiar. Before he could take it all in, the front door banged open and a lone figure stepped onto the porch. Although his once-dark hair had turned to gray, and his shoulders were stooped instead of straight and proud, in every other respect Montgomery King looked much younger than sixty-eight.

Shielding his eyes with one hand, Monty walked to the edge of the porch and looked out at the Jeep. Gabe hesitated, but only for a heartbeat, before opening the door and stepping out. He stood there, unmoving, until he was certain his father had recognized him, then walked slowly toward the house. He'd played this moment in his mind a thousand times in the past two weeks but now, faced with the reality of his homecoming, he suddenly had no idea what to say.

His father remained silent until Gabe reached the bottom of the three short steps that led to the porch. Then, without a hint of emotion, jerked his head toward the Jeep. "You're going to have to move that thing. Your mother won't be able to pull her car in when she gets home."

It was so far from the reaction Gabe had expected, he couldn't even think of a response.

"Did you hear me?" Monty demanded. "Park that thing somewhere else. You're in the way there."

"Sure," Gabe sputtered. "Where would you like me to put it?"

"Wherever you want, long as it's not there." Without another word, the great Monty King stepped back into the shadows of the house and let the screen door bang shut between them.

Gabe wondered what he had expected. Not tears of joy, that was for damn sure. But the old man could have worked up a bit of anger if he'd tried. Gabe would have known what to do with that.

The one thing he hadn't expected, and wasn't at all sure how to handle, was complete indifference.

Telling himself he was lucky he hadn't been sent packing, Gabe slid behind the wheel of the Jeep and looked around for a parking spot his father might consider acceptable. He settled on a patch of mowed wild grass near the back fence, parked, and crossed the yard to the kitchen door, soaking in the almost-forgotten scents of pine and sweet grass.

He'd been away too long to act as if he'd never left, so when he reached the porch, he knocked, just as he would have at a stranger's house.

The old man kept him cooling his heels for a few minutes, but his burly shadow finally materialized behind the lace curtains in the kitchen doorway. Gabe could see a deep scowl on his dad's face, but Monty merely opened the door and motioned Gabe inside with a jerk of his head.

"There's a beer if you want one," Monty said with a nod at the refrigerator.

Gabe glanced at the clock—it was barely twelve-thirty. "Thanks, but I think I'll pass." He stuffed his hands into his pockets. "Mom's gone somewhere?"

"Just into town to see Siddah and the boy. She goes every Sunday, but she won't be long."

Gabe had only seen the name written in a couple of letters, so it took a second to place it when he heard it spoken aloud. "You mean Peter's wife?"

"I mean his widow." Some of the coldness Gabe remembered so well crept into his father's voice. "And don't pretend you didn't hear about that, because your mother tried everything to find you when it happened."

Almost unconsciously, Gabe's hand flew to his pocket. "I got the letter," he admitted, "but only a couple of weeks ago." He thought about telling his dad why the letter had languished for a year before he received it, but he wasn't ready to hand over proof that the career he'd chosen had turned out to be as dangerous and unreliable as Monty had warned him it would be. "I was in the interior when it came. Out of touch. I came as soon as I heard."

His father made a sound deep in his throat. "Well, isn't that just fine? You came as soon as you heard. I'm sure it'll make your mother feel a whole lot better to know that." Monty opened the refrigerator and pulled out two cans. Tossing one at Gabe, he resumed his journey into the living room. "You be sure you let her know that, Gabriel. You came just as soon as you heard."

When had his father started drinking in the middle of the day? Was it something he did often, or was today an exception? "I didn't come home to fight with you," Gabe said, setting the can on the table. "I came because I got Mom's letter. What happened? The letter just said it was an accident at the sawmill."

His father stared at him for an uncomfortably long time before speaking. "Are we going to pretend you care now?"

"I've always cared."

"You've always had an interesting way of showing it, then."

"Dammit, Dad—"

Some of the old, familiar anger flashed in his father's eyes. "I've let you in because your mother would never forgive me if I didn't, but that doesn't mean things have changed. You've made your choices."

Now *there* was the Monty King Gabe knew best. "Yeah, I have."

"Family never was important to you. I think show-

ing up a year and a half late ought to make it plenty clear
that nothing's changed, even to your mother."

"I would have been here if I'd known."

"Yeah?" Monty tilted his head to one side and pretended to consider that. "For how long, Gabe? Ten minutes? Two days?"

"I'd have stayed as long as you and Mom needed me."

Monty laughed harshly and turned away. "Yeah. I believe that, all right." He shuffled out of the room, leaving Gabe staring after him.

Gabe waited until Monty disappeared, then dropped
into one of the chairs flanking the large oval table in the
center of the room. He'd spent hours here doing his
homework while his mother bustled around the kitchen,
but the room seemed smaller now than it did then.
Smaller, and empty without Peter.

He couldn't help wondering how many other things
had changed in the time he'd been gone. Had he done
the right thing by coming back? Or was he about to
make everything worse?

GABE WAS SITTING in the same spot, staring at the
brass gelatin molds that had belonged to his grandmother, when his mother came home an hour later.
His father had driven off somewhere, leaving Gabe
alone in the house.

"Monty? Whose Jeep is that out there?" his mother
called as she let herself in the door. Like her husband,
Helene King had changed over the years. Though she'd
put on a few pounds, the new curves looked good on her.
But the blond hair she'd always worn shoulder-length

was now short and almost shapeless, and deep lines bracketed her mouth.

Focused on the bags in her hand, it took a few seconds for her to notice Gabe. When she did, her hand flew to her mouth. The bags slipped to the floor along with her purse and keys, and tears filled her eyes. "Gabe?" she whispered. "Am I dreaming, or is that really you?"

Gabe wasn't prepared for the depth of feeling that tore through him. He stood uncertainly, unsure whether she was glad to see him or merely shocked.

He didn't have to wonder long. She crossed the room and gathered him into her arms, sending a wash of relief through him so strong it left him speechless and frozen. At last, he got his arms moving and held on to her for dear life.

He didn't know how long they stood that way, but at some point one of them moved and he found himself at arm's length while his mother's hungry eyes traveled over him from head to toe. "It really *is* you, isn't it?"

With effort, he got a few words out around the burning lump in his throat. "In the flesh."

"I don't believe it." Helene pulled him close again and kissed his cheek, then led him by the hand to the table and motioned for him to sit down. "When did you get here? How long are you staying? What…? Why…?" Shaking her head, she wagged a hand in the space between them as if to wipe away all the questions. "Just tell me everything."

"I got back to the States three days ago," he said, taking her questions in order. "I drove straight through and pulled in about an hour ago."

"From where? Your place in Virginia?"

He nodded briefly. "I took care of a couple of things at the university while I was there and picked up the Jeep. I thought it would be easier to have it than a rental car." He'd ignored the doctors' advice again by driving across the country on his own, but he wasn't going to tell his mother that.

He couldn't make himself talk about Peter, so he pulled the letter from his pocket and laid it on the table. "I came as soon as I got this."

Her smile evaporated and her eyes misted over again. Sighing deeply, she dashed away the tears and made an effort to regain her composure. "I wrote that eighteen months ago," she said softly. There was more hurt than grief in her eyes. "I tried to reach you through the embassy."

"I know. I'm sorry I wasn't here. What happened, Mom? All you said was that there'd been an accident."

Her expression grew guarded. "It was at the mill. You know how dangerous the work can be."

Gabe waited for more, but she stopped talking and he didn't feel right pressuring her. "I would have come back for the funeral and stayed to help if I'd known. I hope you know that."

"I sent it to the most recent address I had."

Her stare made Gabe uncomfortable, but he didn't let himself look away. "It took nearly six months for the letter to reach me," he explained. "It arrived right after I left for an extended stay in a remote village in the interior." For the second time in an hour, he considered mentioning his illness, but it seemed heartless to tell her how close she'd come to losing both her sons in the same year. "I ended up spending more time there than I'd expected, but I started back as soon as I could book a flight."

"I see." Her shoulders grew stiff. Neither of his parents had ever understood the reasons he'd dedicated his life to learning more about other cultures and trying to make the world a better place. Obviously, time hadn't changed that.

"I came as soon as I could," he said again, but the explanation fell into the space between them like a rock in a pond.

His mother's lips curved slightly, but her attempt at a smile didn't fool him. She stood and crossed to the refrigerator. "And when are you going back?"

"I don't know yet. A week, I guess. Maybe two."

"That's all? You can't stay longer?"

"I should be back in Virginia by the end of the month."

"Well, we'll just have to be happy with what we get, won't we?"

We? Somehow, Gabe doubted that his father would be glad of anything, but his mother didn't leave him time to dwell on that.

Shifting gears abruptly, she started toward the stairs. "I'll get your room ready. I'm sure you'll probably want a chance to relax after driving all this way."

Startled, Gabe called after her, "Wait. Mom. I—I wasn't planning to stay *here*."

She turned back at the bottom of the stairs. "Don't be silly. Of course you'll stay here."

"You want me to spend a week under the same roof as the old man? I'm not sure any of us would survive that."

"That 'old man' you're talking about is my husband," she said. "He's also your father. No matter what's happened in the past, you can't change that."

"I don't want to change that, Mom. I just don't want to start arguing with him again. That's not what I came back for."

She looked directly into his eyes. "What *did* you come back for?"

"To see you and make sure you're doing all right. And to pay my respects to Peter." He looked around the kitchen and shrugged. "And maybe to prove to myself that it's true."

His mother turned again. "You'll need to be here to do all that, then, won't you?" And just like that, as if she'd settled something between them, she started up the stairs.

Feeling like a kid, Gabe trailed after her. "I'd stay here in a heartbeat if I thought it would work out, but are you forgetting? He kicked me out."

"Ten years ago."

"He told me not to come back."

His mother heaped sheets and a blanket from a hall closet into his arms. "But you did, and he let you in. Whether or not this works out is entirely up to you. Your father can't argue with himself, can he?"

She had a point, but Gabe wasn't sure he could resist the lure of a knock-down drag-out if the old man wanted to start one.

With a thin smile, she closed the closet door and turned toward him. "You're all we have left, Gabriel—besides Siddah and Bobby, of course. But Siddah's on her own, and there's no telling how long they'll stay. And since Bobby's not really ours, who's to say she'll let us keep seeing him if she eventually meets and marries someone else."

Gabe leaped on the chance to change the subject. "How are Siddah and the boy dealing with everything?"

"Siddah was devastated. It's taken a while to get back on her feet." Helene opened the door to his old bedroom. "Poor little Bobby was desolate. Still is, really. He lost interest in everything after the accident. He used to bring home As and Bs on his report card. Now, we're lucky if there's a single mark higher than a D. Poor boy even stopped playing football with his peewee team."

To Gabe's surprise, his old room hadn't changed in the past decade. Baseball and basketball trophies still sat on the shelves over the bed, pictures of the teams he'd played on hung on the walls. His favorite bat leaned against the wall in one corner, and his baseball mitt was hooked over one post of the headboard. His mother was already stripping old sheets from the bed.

With effort, he dragged himself back to the conversation. "He's changed because of Peter?"

His mother nodded. "We've all tried talking to him, but nothing we say makes any difference."

Gabe repressed a shudder at the memory of family councils where he'd been on the receiving end of advice. He'd adored his maternal grandparents, but his father's parents had been demanding and judgmental, full of opinions about almost everything he did. For Bobby's sake, he hoped his parents weren't following that example.

"How old is he now?" he asked when he couldn't immediately pull the answer from his own memory. "Seven? Eight?"

"Ten. He was nearly nine when Peter died. Bobby was always such a sweet boy. Always so willing to help and so loving. Now..." She broke off to shake a pillow out of its case. "Siddah's beside herself, of course. Bobby's all she has left. She's worried sick about him. We all are, but Siddah won't even consider the solution your father and I think is best."

Gabe heard his father's truck rattle into the yard and he stiffened in apprehension. "And what do you think she should do?"

"Spend more time at home, of course. It's not as if she needs to work. Your dad and I have offered to keep paying her Peter's salary. On top of the insurance and workmen's compensation settlements, that would be more than enough for anyone."

"She won't take it?"

"She won't even consider it."

Maybe his parents disapproved, but Gabe admired her independence. "Where does she work?"

"At the County Attorney's office. She started just a few months after Peter's accident, and now she won't even talk about leaving."

"She likes it?"

"She claims to."

Anger might be his father's trademark, but dismissing emotions she didn't understand was his mother's.

The old familiar frustrations began to churn, so Gabe turned the conversation back to the boy. "What's she doing to help the kid?"

His mother shrugged. "She takes him to a counselor, and they go to the grief and loss group. But the group only meets once a month and I'm not sure that's often enough. Bobby has no real interest in it, and some months it even seems to make him worse. Other than that, what *can* she do? She's up to her eyebrows just trying to get by." With another heavy sigh, she looked out the window. "Your dad is at his wit's end, I'll tell you. He thinks the world of Bobby. We both do, and we just want to help."

Envy Gabe didn't want to feel snaked through him. He wondered if Bobby had any idea how much Gabe would have given to have Monty feel that way about him. But what kind of man envied a boy such a thing? Especially a boy who was obviously unhappy.

"Where does he go while she's at work?"

"Siddah has a sitter. One of the neighborhood girls." There was no mistaking the disapproval in her voice, and Gabe wondered if she would prefer having Bobby stay here. "There's just so much your dad and I would like to do for him."

She fell silent for a moment, then said, "Losing Peter was the worst thing we've ever been through. For a while I wasn't sure either of us would survive. But life went on, even on the days when I wasn't sure I wanted it to. Now there's nothing I want more than to have life back to normal. As normal as it *can* be, anyway. Bobby might not have been Peter's natural son, but that didn't matter to Peter. It would break his heart to see Bobby hurting the way he is."

Obviously, Bobby wasn't the only one still hurting. "What about you and Dad? Did you get counseling?"

His mother took the bedding he'd been holding. "I had a few sessions, but your dad refused to go. He doesn't like to talk about the accident at all—even with me." She let out a sigh filled with sadness. "I don't know how to reach him, either. Sometimes he goes out to Peter's old work shed and stays there for hours, sweeping, dusting off the tools… I know he realizes that Peter's not coming back. He's not delusional. But he just can't seem to move on."

That didn't surprise Gabe. Suddenly uncertain, he looked around for something to do. Something he could put his mind to that might put a buffer between himself and the raw edges of his mother's emotion. "It just seems that somebody should be able to get through to the kid," he said. "Maybe not you and Dad, but *somebody*."

Shaking the folds out of the bottom sheet, his mother bent to the task of putting it on the mattress. "Your uncle Keith has tried, and so has your cousin Joey. Bobby just isn't responding to anyone."

"I don't want to sound rude," Gabe said, "but unless Keith and Joey have changed, that doesn't surprise me. Keith is about as cuddly as a cactus, and Joey's…Joey." His cousin had a good heart, but he'd always been rigid and a little cool. Peter, on the other hand, had probably been a get-on-the-floor-and-wrestle kind of dad.

Moving to the other side of the bed, Gabe slipped a corner over the mattress. "If I were trying to help him,

I'd get involved in the things he likes to do and try to draw him back."

His mother dropped her end of the sheet and clasped her hands together. "Oh, Gabe! Do you really think you could make a difference?"

"Me?" He gaped at her, astounded. "I didn't mean… that's not what I—"

"That's such a good idea, and it makes perfect sense." Dropping to the edge of the bed, she reached for his hand. "You're Peter's brother. Bobby's uncle, really. Who better?"

"That's not what I said, Mom. I—"

"Well, who else? Really, Gabe, everyone else has run out of ideas. And now here you are. It's almost like fate."

"Mom, no—" He cut himself off and tried to regroup. "I'm not going to be here more than a few days. I couldn't help even if I wanted to."

"You don't have to *do* anything," his mother argued. "Just meet him. Spend a few minutes with him while you're here. Connect."

With a kid? Was she joking? "And then what? What happens when I leave town?"

"Couldn't you call once in a while? Send him a letter now and then? An e-mail?"

"Sure. I guess." But, hell, he hardly did those things with his own family.

She looked at him hard. "You aren't refusing, are you? I thought you said you wanted to make things right."

"I do."

"You went through a rough time of your own when

you weren't much older than Bobby is now. I'm sure you'd understand better than most what he needs."

"My situation was a little different."

"Well, yes. But you know how a boy that age thinks. I certainly don't, and it's been too long since Monty was a boy. Times have changed."

"Don't expect him to say yes," his father said from the doorway. "He probably doesn't want to stick around that long." Lurching a little, Monty stepped back into the hallway and Gabe caught the distinct odor of beer.

Gabe watched his mother carefully, but her expression gave nothing away. "Instead of starting an argument," she called after Monty, "why don't you go downstairs and eat? I left a plate for you in the fridge. All you have to do is put it into the microwave."

That was certainly different. What had happened to the woman who used to scramble to do things for the old man?

Monty stepped back into the doorway. "You're wasting your breath. Gabriel never was one for commitment to his family."

As if his father had turned a key, Gabe went from hesitant to determined in one beat of his heart. "That was then," he said firmly. "This is now. If you really think I can help, and if Siddah agrees, I'll see what I can do."

His father growled his disapproval. "That boy doesn't need you worming your way into his life and then taking off again in a week or two. He's been through enough. Leave him alone."

Another change in Helene became evident as she put herself in her husband's path. "I'm warning you, Monty,

I won't have any arguing just because Gabe is back. If either of you wants to make hurtful comments to the other, you're going to have to do it somewhere else. And don't let me hear about it if you do, because you'll wish I hadn't."

His father's scowl deepened, but the explosion of anger Gabe expected never came. "It's my house, too, Helene. Remember that."

"Gabe is our son. Remember *that*. He's welcome to stay as long as he wants."

Monty grunted. "Don't get your heart set on a long visit. I'm surprised he's still here."

With a determination Gabe had never heard before, Helene said, "I'm warning you, Montgomery, if you drive him away again, I'll never forgive you."

But even that didn't get his father going. Shrugging off her warning, Monty peeled off the lightweight jacket he'd been wearing, tossed it over the banister and headed, stoop-shouldered, back down the stairs. "Do whatever you want, then. Just don't blame me if you end up with another disaster on your hands."

But she wouldn't, Gabe vowed silently. One way or another, he'd make sure of it.

CHAPTER TWO

BALANCING ON three-inch heels on a slick linoleum floor, Siddah King hurried after her boss as he pushed through the door of the County Courthouse and out into the bright summer sunlight. Offices on both sides of the corridor emptied as staff members from various county offices left for lunch.

Siddah had skipped breakfast and the aromas coming from the employee break room made her stomach growl. But as much as she wanted to eat, she wanted to talk with Evan alone even more.

As if in answer to her prayers, a new position had just been announced that morning—one with more responsibility and a significant jump in pay. It was fate. Siddah just knew it. And she intended to take advantage of it.

Evan was halfway across the parking lot before she made it outside, so she kicked off her shoes and carried them as she ran along the sidewalk after him. "Evan? Can I talk to you for a minute?"

He turned back at the sound of her voice, his eyes covered by sunglasses. At forty-nine, he was an attractive and vital man with dark hair just beginning to gray at the temples and only a hint of thickening at his waist.

He was determined to see justice done within the borders of his jurisdiction, but he was also intelligent and witty, a loving husband, devoted father and compassionate employer. After only a year, Siddah considered him a friend and a mentor, and it was that part of their relationship she counted on as she stepped back into her shoes and made her way across the parking lot.

"I know Francine is waiting for you," she said as she drew closer. "I promise this will only take a minute."

Evan slipped out of his suit jacket and slung it over one shoulder. "What is it? Something wrong at home?"

Hating that he'd naturally jump to that conclusion, she shook her head. "Everything's fine. This isn't personal." Though she'd worked hard to lessen the Arkansas drawl Peter had called "Southern honey," nerves always brought it back. Today, stress turned it from honey to molasses. "I heard about the new position, Evan. I want the job."

The reflective glass kept her from seeing his eyes, but it wasn't hard to read the plunge of his eyebrows. "That position is going to require a huge time commitment. Do you really think you're up to it?"

"I know I am."

Stepping sideways to get away from the glare of the sun, Evan tugged off his sunglasses and locked eyes with her. "You can put in extra hours if Chris and I need you?"

Chris Leta, the other attorney in their office, was notorious for putting in twelve- and fourteen-hour days, but Siddah would never be able to carve out the lifestyle she wanted or take care of the obligations Peter had left behind unless she made some changes. So many people had offered to help with money, especially Monty and Helene, but Siddah wouldn't take it. She'd spent the first sixteen years of her life living on charity. As a teenager, she'd watched Aunt Suzette approach one friend or relative after another for the money to get them through. She'd hated the humiliation and the pitying looks. The hand-me-down dresses, visits to the Food Pantry, and the Sub-for-Santa Christmases had all left her burning with shame, and she'd vowed to *never* put her son through anything like it.

So she pushed aside guilt at the thought of being away from Bobby more than she already was, and nodded. "Absolutely."

Evan's eyes narrowed. "I can't decide on the position for two months. I have to let the ads run in the paper and circulate through the government newsletters, and I have to give others an honest chance. You realize that, don't you?"

"Yes, but by then you'll know what I can do."

"I don't know," Evan said uncertainly. "What about Bobby? How's he doing?"

"He's fine. Much better. School will be starting in a couple of weeks, and that will make a big difference."

"And after school?"

"I have a great baby-sitter."

Tucking his sunglasses into his breast pocket, Evan glanced at the tops of the trees as if he might find the answer to her question up there. "And what about you?" he asked after a long moment. "How are you doing?"

"Me? I'm fine." She gave him a bright smile to prove it, but when the worry in his eyes didn't abate, she sobered again. "I know I was a wreck when I started working here, but that was over a year ago. And you know what they say—time heals."

"I know what they say. But the last thing I want to do is push you before you're ready."

At least he hadn't said never. "I appreciate the concern," she said, "but Peter's been gone for eighteen months already. Y'all really can stop handling me with kid gloves."

Evan started walking again and motioned for her to stay with him. "You can't blame friends and family for worrying."

"And I don't. Truly. I love the people here in Libby, and I don't know what I would have done without y'all after the accident." She matched her pace to his. "I'll probably never completely get over losing Peter, but I'm not as fragile as you think I am. I'm ready to move on. I just need somebody to let me do it."

Evan's lips quirked into a halfsmile as he aimed a keyless entry at his Denali. "Holding you back is the last thing I want to do, and I know everyone else in the office feels the same way." He tossed his jacket inside and leaned against the open door. "If you're sure you're ready—"

"I am."

"Then all right. I'll let you work on the Whitman stabbing case. If you do well, I'll consider you for the promotion. But only if you promise to say something if it gets to be too much. There will always be other cases, so don't put yourself and your boy in jeopardy over this one. And I'll reserve judgment on the promotion until later. Just make sure you get your application in before the cutoff so I can consider you. If all goes well on the case, we'll put you in the running."

Siddah grinned with satisfaction. "Thank you, Evan. I swear you won't regret this."

She was still smiling as he pulled out of the parking lot a minute later, narrowly missing a red Jeep as it pulled in. It was a small victory, but still a victory. She'd love to go out for lunch to celebrate, but celebrating alone wasn't much fun, and her best friend Ivy was working today getting her classroom ready for the start of school. Maybe later.

Sunlight glinted off the Jeep's windshield, momentarily blinding her. As the driver parked and slid out from behind the wheel, she froze mid-step. Everything from the set of his shoulders to the length of his stride screamed familiarity.

Her heart hammered in her chest, her hands trembled and she could scarcely breathe. She fell backward a step and tears burned her eyes. If she hadn't known it was impossible, she'd have sworn Peter was walking toward her.

Despite the assurances she'd glibly handed to Evan, the past eighteen months fell away and she felt herself drowning in pain. She'd been so sure it had faded enough to let her move on, but she had been so wrong.

She bit the inside of her cheek to stem the tears and told herself to stop dreaming. The Jeep's driver moved out of shadow into sunlight, but that only prompted another fierce argument with herself. He couldn't be Peter. Peter's straight hair had been light brown. This man's nearly black hair fell in lazy curls to his collar. Peter's eyes had been clear and blue as the sky in the spring.

Even from a distance she could tell that this man's were dark and narrow, set in a face that was deeply tanned from years doing who knows what.

Realizing she must look like a terrible fool, she pivoted away and hurried toward the office.

"Excuse me," the man called after her. His voice even sounded like Peter's, only deeper. Instinct urged her to flee, but common sense made her stop and turn around. Maybe he couldn't see the look on her face. Maybe he didn't care. Either way, he kept walking relentlessly toward her. "I wonder if you could help me?"

She nodded and actually croaked out a few words. "I can try."

"Do you work here?"

"I do."

"I wonder if you know where I can find Siddah King."

He was here to see her? Whatever for? Frantic to appear calm, she dug her fingernails into her palms and prayed that the discomfort would keep her grounded. "Are you here on business of some kind?"

He almost smiled, but not quite. "Maybe you could just tell me where the County Attorney's office is. I'll explain to Mrs. King when I find her."

She thought about sending him away until the shock of his resemblance to Peter wore off, but what good would that do? If he had business in her office, she wouldn't be able to hide for long. Eventually, he'd learn the truth. Then she'd not only suffer the embarrassment of having lied, but she might lose the chance she'd just worked so hard to get.

"As a matter of fact, I'm Siddah," she admitted. "How can I help you?"

His eyes widened slightly, but he held out a hand as if he wanted to shake hers. "Well, I guess that just proves that it's a small world, doesn't it? I'm Gabe. It's nice to meet you."

"Gabe?"

"Gabe King…Peter's brother?"

Somehow her hand found its way into his, and the touch electrified her. She jerked away quickly and backed up a step, trying to pull a thought from the fragmented pieces darting through her mind. She'd seen pictures of Gabe, of course, but they'd all been at least a decade old, and he was the last person she'd expected to see walking the sidewalks of Libby.

Gabe. The brother Peter had talked about endlessly. The brother who'd disappointed everyone in the family. The brother she'd resented from the first story she'd ever heard about him. Peter's almost naive belief in Gabe had been hard to witness, especially since Gabe had never given him reason to keep hoping. Her resentment had deepened over the years, and it had settled into something cold and hard inside her when he missed Peter's funeral.

Finding strength from somewhere, she lifted her eyes to meet his. "What do you want here?"

The question seemed to take him by surprise, though she had no idea why it should. "I just got into town yesterday, and I wanted to meet you. I wanted to make sure that you and the boy are okay."

His pretense of concern disgusted her. "Well, you've met me," she said, and started walking again.

"Wait a second."

"*The boy* and I are fine," she shot back over her shoulder. "You don't have to pretend to give a damn."

He caught up with her easily. "His name's Bobby, isn't it? I didn't mean to offend you."

His voice might be lower than Peter's, but his inflections were nearly identical. Her heart twisted again, but that only made her angrier. "Not using my son's name in conversation is hardly your greatest offense."

To her surprise, he actually smiled. "So my reputation precedes me."

"By at least ten years."

His smile faded. "Look, I—"

She couldn't bear to listen to him any longer, and she wasn't sure she could survive looking at him. She opened the door and paused on the threshold. "Let's be straight with each other, okay? I don't have anything to say to you and there's nothing I want to hear from you, so why don't you just leave?"

"I know how you must feel," he said, taking the weight of the door from her, "but if I leave without telling you why I'm here, I'm going to disappoint my mother—and you can't possibly imagine how much I don't want to disappoint my mother."

Only her mother-in-law's unfailing kindness over the years kept Siddah from stepping inside. "What does Helene have to do with this?"

"She's the one who suggested that I come to see you." He laughed a little and shook his head. "No, that's not entirely true. I wanted to meet you, and I would have made my way over here on my own. Mom just persuaded me to do it now instead of later."

"Why?"

"She's worried about Bobby."

"She's not alone, but what does that have to do with you?"

"She seems to think I can help."

In spite of her confusion, Siddah snorted. *"You?"* Had Helene lost her mind? "Just how does she think you can do that?"

Gabe shrugged. "She thinks Bobby's still having a hard time with Peter's death."

"That's no secret, but why does she think *you* can help?"

"Good question. Look, I know I haven't exactly been a model son, brother or uncle. I understand why you're reluctant to trust me."

"Reluctant?" Siddah laughed and stepped back into the heat so their voices wouldn't carry. "Try *not interested.*"

"Just hear me out, okay? Please?" Gabe raked fingers through his hair and shifted his weight the way Peter used to when he was nervous. He had no right to look so much like Peter. Or to sound so much like him. Or to touch that piece of her heart she didn't want touched. Ever. But she was a notorious pushover, and she'd never been able to resist Peter when he'd looked at her like that. It was almost as hard to look away from Gabe. Much as the similarities hurt, they also gave her a strange and unwelcome comfort.

With a quick check of her watch to see how much of her lunch break was left, she gave a curt nod and headed toward the side of the building, where a towering pine would give them shade. "You've got ten minutes."

"Thank you." He followed and stepped into the shade beside her, hooking his thumbs into the back of his waistband. "I know you've probably heard about what happened when I left town, but there are two sides to every story. I'm not going to bore you with long explanations, mostly because even I don't completely understand what happened, but I can tell you that things have changed. *I've* changed."

"Well, that's good news. Congratulations."

He went on as if she hadn't spoken. "I had a lot of time to think out there in the rain forest, and I'm carrying a load of regrets. I'd give anything for a chance to make things right."

"It's a little late for that, don't you think? You should have come home while Peter was still here."

"I—" His voice caught and he looked away quickly. "I'll never be able to undo the mistakes I made with Peter," he said after a long silence, "but Mom has told me how much Peter loved Bobby. If I can help your boy, maybe it will do a little to make up for everything I missed—" He broke off with another shrug, but Siddah heard his voice catch again. Whatever his faults, his emotion was genuine.

At least it seemed to be.

She had been fooled before. Bobby was proof of that. And even if Gabe *was* genuine, she wasn't ready to just open the door on her life and let him waltz through. "And what would you do to help Bobby?"

"I won't be here the way Peter was, but I can call. Write. See him when I am in town."

"The way you did with Peter?"

"Better."

"Well, it would be hard to get much worse."

"If you're trying to make me feel guilty, it's working. Then again, I already feel guilty enough."

"I doubt that. It would be physically impossible for you to feel all the guilt you should. And how am I supposed to know that I can trust you?"

"You don't. Neither do I. But I'm determined, if that counts for anything."

In spite of herself, Siddah felt a smile tug at her lips. "That's not the best sales pitch I've ever heard."

"It's not a pitch. It's the truth."

He made it easy to understand why Peter had never lost faith in his older brother, and why friends who'd known Gabe all those years ago still smiled when they talked about him. Some people called what he had "charm." Well, Siddah had stepped in enough charm in her lifetime to know that it wasn't always pleasant. Only time would tell whether he was genuine or not, whether this was charm or something that belonged in a barnyard.

How could she forget the hurt she'd seen on Helene and Monty's faces over the years? Or Peter's disappointment as holidays and birthdays passed with only a few meaningless gifts from the big brother he'd idolized?

Disappointed as he'd been, if Gabe *had* come back while he was alive, Peter would have forgiven everything. Knowing that made it hard for her to turn her back and tune Gabe out. "I don't know what to say. I'm going to have to think about it."

A grin illuminated his face and again her heart turned over. "I can't ask for more than that."

"At least there's one thing we agree on." She glanced at her watch, decided she'd given him enough time, and stepped into the sunlight. "I'll think about it," she said again. "I guess Helene and Monty will know where I can find you once I decide?"

"I'm staying with them, so you can leave a message if I'm not around. But I'll only be here for a few days. If I'm going to meet Bobby while I'm here, you can't wait too long."

She nodded, wishing she knew how to end the conversation. *Nice to meet you...talk to you later...see you around.* Not one of them applied.

As if he sensed her discomfort, Gabe glanced at his Jeep, then back at her. "I guess I'll just wait to hear from you, then." Stuffing his hands into his pockets, he moved a step or two away. Just when she thought the encounter was finally over, he turned back, looking straight at her with those deep, dark eyes. "Thank you, Siddah."

She shivered involuntarily and kicked herself for letting him get to her. "I haven't decided anything yet."

"No, but you've agreed to think about it. That's more than I expected." With that, he turned away and strode toward his Jeep. In spite of her relief, Siddah couldn't look away until he'd climbed inside and started the engine.

Ten minutes ago she'd assured Evan that she was ready to move beyond Peter's death. Now, with the past all around her, she wondered if that was true...or if it had ever been.

STILL RATTLED from her meeting with Gabe, Siddah closed her kitchen door with one hip and carried the groceries she'd picked up on her way home to the table. She tossed a handful of bills from the day's mail onto the counter and shoved her purse onto the top of the fridge.

With a glance at the clock, she put milk into the refrigerator and pulled out a cold Pepsi. She frowned when she realized that, once again, she was late. Sighing in frustration, she took a long drink and headed toward the living room, where she could hear Bobby playing his favorite video game.

How long had he been playing today? Had Whitney been able to interest him in something else? Had she even tried?

Sure enough, Bobby was on the couch, all slouched down like her Grandpa Carlisle used to sit after a few tugs on the bottle. His red hair was tousled as if he'd forgotten to comb it, and the clothes he'd worn yesterday hung off his bony shoulders and narrow hips.

Whitney bounded to her feet when Siddah entered, one finger marking her place in the paperback she'd been reading. Her pale cheeks bloomed with color and her normally thin, straight brows drew together over her nose in a frown. It didn't take a genius to figure out that she was eager to be on her way.

Smiling apologetically, Siddah bent to kiss Bobby's cheek. "I'm sorry I'm late. I thought I had time to stop by the store and still get here on time, but I misjudged."

Bobby grunted something Siddah couldn't understand, but she was growing used to that.

"I'm sure you're eager to leave," she said, "but you're welcome to join us for supper if you'd like. I'm going to grill some burgers on the patio."

The color in Whitney's cheeks deepened a shade. "Thanks, but I can't. Mom's making a special dinner tonight for my dad's birthday."

"Tonight?" Siddah felt about two inches tall. "I wish I'd known. I would have made sure I was home on time."

"That's okay. I…" Whitney shot a glance at Bobby and turned to Siddah. "I need to talk to you for a minute before I go."

Eager to make up for her tardiness, Siddah perched on the back of the couch. "Sure. What's up?"

"It's…" The girl moistened her lips and shifted her weight from one side to the other, and Siddah started to feel uneasy. "Look, I don't want to leave you hanging or anything, but school starts pretty soon and it's my senior year." Shifting again, Whitney chewed her bottom lip and made an effort to smile. "The thing is, I kind of need to stop baby-sitting."

The air left Siddah's lungs in a *whoosh,* and for the first time since she walked through the door, Bobby looked away from the television.

Something on the screen exploded, but he didn't look back. "You're not going to be here anymore?"

With a fond smile, Whitney tousled Bobby's hair. "It's not that I don't want to, squirt. It's just that I'm gonna have tons of homework to do…and other stuff." When she looked at Siddah, her eyes were filled with equal measures of regret and pleading. "You understand, don't you? It's my senior year."

Understand? That she was quitting? *Now?* Just when things were beginning to look up? Whitney couldn't have chosen a worse time to make this announcement if she'd tried. Somehow, Siddah got a couple of words out of her tight, dry throat. "How soon?"

"Like, right away." Whitney flashed another apologetic smile, for all the good it did. "A bunch of my friends want to drive over to Glacier before school starts, and I kinda want to go with them."

A dull ache pulsed behind Siddah's eyes. How could she work extra hours if she had no baby-sitter? How could she work at all? She couldn't leave Bobby alone all day.

Whitney flashed a concerned smile. "Do you hate me?"

Fighting panic, Siddah forced a shake of her head. "Of course I don't hate you. I'm just a little surprised, that's all. And it would have been nice to have some notice. Can't you please stay on for a couple of days so I can find another sitter?"

"If I do, I'll miss the Glacier trip. They're leaving tomorrow morning."

And God forbid she should stay behind, Siddah thought before she could stop herself. She remembered how it felt to be seventeen, and she could guess how important this trip was to Whitney, but all things considered, she had trouble rating it high on her own list of priorities. "If you can't sit with Bobby, do you know anyone else who can? A friend who isn't going on the trip, maybe?"

Whitney shook her head. "I already tried to find somebody, but everybody I know has plans."

Arguments rose to Siddah's lips, but she bit them all back. Obviously, Whitney had made up her mind. Siddah might be able to guilt her into changing plans, but her aunt Suzette had used that tactic on Siddah when she was younger, and she wouldn't let herself do it to anyone else. Wiping away the scowl she could feel creasing her face, she turned toward the front door. "Well, then, you go home and enjoy your dad's birthday dinner. I'll get busy making phone calls. I hope it's okay if I drop your check off in a few days."

Whitney looked relieved. "Sure. Mom's going to let me borrow the money for the trip, so I'll be okay." She glanced back at Bobby and wagged her fingers. "See ya later, squirt."

Without a word, Bobby flopped back against the couch and started a new game. Siddah couldn't tell if he was angry, hurt or indifferent. Even after she'd closed the door behind Whitney, Bobby didn't look away from the television.

She considered telling him about meeting Gabe, but decided she wasn't ready for him to know yet. She didn't even know what to make of Gabe's unexpected return, so how could she ask Bobby to deal with the news? Her heart broke at the slump of his little shoulders, the blank look on his freckled face.

Refusing to let Whitney's bombshell discourage her, she perched on the arm of the couch. "I'll be sad to lose Whitney, but I'm sure we'll find another great sitter for you. And I have a little good news. Want to hear it?"

He dipped his head.

"There's a chance I'll be getting a sort of promotion at work, and I thought it might be fun to barbecue tonight to celebrate. What do you say?"

One thin shoulder lifted in response. "I guess."

"We can invite Ivy and Rebecca over." Maybe Ivy would even have a suggestion or two about day-care options.

Bobby manipulated buttons on the remote for a few seconds. One of the animated figures on the TV screen exploded and he rolled his gaze toward Siddah. "Do we have to?"

"You don't want to?"

"Not really."

"Why not? You like Rebecca, don't you?"

"When she's not being stupid."

Siddah struggled not to let frustration creep into her voice. "I know you're a big, tough guy and it's probably not cool to be friends with a girl, but Rebecca is certainly not stupid. And nobody else will know that she's here, so you don't have to worry about your reputation."

Another explosion filled the screen. "You can invite her if you want. I don't care."

That was the problem. He didn't care about anything lately. Pretending enthusiasm she didn't feel, Siddah stood and smiled down at him. "Great. Want to help me start the grill?"

"Not really."

"Well, would you help me anyway?" She leaned into his line of vision. "It's not going to be much of a celebration if I have to do all the work myself."

With another roll of his eyes, he ended the game and tossed the controller onto the floor. "I'm not very hungry. Whitney made tuna sandwiches for lunch."

"What time did you eat?"

"I don't know. A while ago."

After spending the day assuring people that Bobby was fine, she felt the sudden need to prove herself right. She willed her small son to smile the way he used to. But he didn't. Not really. The expression that passed for a smile these days was a far cry from what it used to be.

His brow wrinkled and he scratched his belly. "How come you're late again?"

"I had a lot to do." Again she skirted the issue of Gabe's visit and focused on mundane every day things that would probably bore her son to death. "We got a new case today, and I had to file documents with the court on a couple of others. Evan was in one courtroom all afternoon and Chris was in the other. That left Amanda and me scrambling to handle everything else." She walked slowly, leading Bobby toward the kitchen as she talked.

He stuffed his hands into his pockets and scuffed his feet along the carpet. "Grandma came over."

Siddah's smile faltered. "She did?" Had she told Bobby about Gabe? Smiling as if a thousand questions weren't racing through her mind, she passed Bobby the drink she'd opened. "What did she want?"

"Nothing much. She said she'd take me shopping for school clothes if I wanted, but I told her I didn't need anything."

Siddah cast a wry glance at the pants that had grown too short over the summer and the T-shirt she'd patched twice already. "It's nice of Grandma to offer," she said, "but we'll make do. I'll bet we can find a couple pairs of jeans and some new T-shirts at the Ben Franklin for not much, and we can pick up more things from my next paycheck in a couple of weeks."

He shrugged again—his response to everything these days—and pulled ground beef from the bag on the counter. "Okay."

"Okay then, that's what we'll do."

With Gabe back in town, she and Bobby weren't the strongest link to Peter, and the fear that Helene would eventually grow tired of pretending to be Bobby's grandmother loomed large. And what if Gabe stayed in Libby? Got married and had a family? Produced biological grandchildren for Monty and Helene to bond with? Siddah's heart sank as she realized that potential hurt loomed around every corner. Even the most determined mother couldn't keep it away from her child.

"How about tomorrow after work?" she suggested. "We could even stop by the Sports Center to check out football equipment if you want to."

Bobby's head lifted, and for an instant she thought maybe she'd lit a spark. She didn't care if he got excited about rejoining his friends or angry with her for pushing him. She'd have welcomed any show of emotion. But Bobby merely rolled his eyes away again and lifted that shoulder in a gesture so lifeless she wanted to scream.

She sat so she could look him in the face. "Bobby, honey, you used to love to play with the team, and I know Coach Russert is eager to have you come back. I'll bet if you just tried, you'd start getting into the swing again real fast."

As if she hadn't spoken, her son picked up the ground beef and looked at the patio door. "If Ivy and Rebecca want to eat, they'd better come over pretty soon. It won't take very long to cook some burgers."

Hope faded as quickly as it had flared. "You're right. I'd better call right now." She managed a smile, but her heart wasn't in it, and it wasn't easy to hide the tears of frustration that swam in her eyes. Grabbing a box of matches and the cordless phone, she headed outside for a breath of fresh air and a chance to pull herself together. She'd been so certain that Bobby would recover from Peter's death in time. But time only seemed to be making him worse, and the security she longed for seemed more elusive than ever.

CHAPTER THREE

Two HOURS LATER, Siddah pushed through the kitchen door with her shoulder and stepped out onto the patio carrying two glasses of lemonade. She'd made a few phone calls already, but so far she'd had no luck finding a replacement baby-sitter. Between Bobby's mood, Whitney's decision to quit, and Rebecca's excitement over starting fifth grade in a week, their quiet celebration dinner had left Siddah more tightly wound than she'd been before.

In the backyard, Rebecca wandered around the flower beds while Bobby sat listlessly on the swing set, drawing patterns in the sand with the toe of his shoe. Ivy had curled into one of Siddah's new padded chairs beneath the spreading branches of an elm tree, where she could keep an eye on the kids. A slight breeze ruffled her short blond hair and a smile played on her lips.

She looked up as Siddah approached, and held out a hand for one of the glasses. "Bobby's quiet tonight."

"Bobby's quiet every night." Siddah sank into a chair beside Ivy's and put her feet up on a planter filled with petunias and marigolds. "Does he seem worse to you than usual?"

"A little, I think. Is he worried about starting school?"

"If he is, he's not saying anything to me." Siddah kicked off her sandals and arched her feet. "I think I'm more worried about it than he is."

"Oh? Why?"

"Whitney quit tonight."

Ivy's blue eyes grew wide. "No!"

"Yes. So here we are celebrating this great opportunity at work, but I have no way to take advantage of it."

"Don't be silly. There's always a way, we just need to think of it. Why did she quit? I thought she liked the job."

Siddah shrugged. "I thought so, too, but she's a senior in high school and she has better things to do."

"Hmm. Well, I guess I can understand that. I probably would have felt the same way at her age, but she sure has lousy timing. What are you going to do about the promotion?"

"I've worked too hard to give up now." High overhead, the wind chimes Peter and Bobby had given her for Mother's Day sang out in a whisper of breeze. Usually, Siddah found the sound soothing, but tonight it torched her already frazzled nerves. "I hate to ask this, Ivy, but do you think Bobby could spend the day with you tomorrow? He'd be a big help getting things set up at the school, and I just can't leave him home alone."

Ivy's expression sobered. "I wish I could say yes, but I'm scheduled to be in meetings with people from the district offices all day. Rebecca's not even going with me."

"Who's watching her?"

"Estelle from next door. I'd ask her about Bobby, but…well, you know. She's nearly eighty and I'm afraid two kids might be too much for her. How about Helene? I'm sure she'd take him."

"I can't ask Helene. I don't want Bobby over there right now."

"Why not?"

Siddah checked to make sure Bobby hadn't come closer, then brought up the subject that had been tormenting her all afternoon. "How well did you know Peter's brother?"

Ivy pulled back with a sharp laugh. "Gabe? What does he have to do with this?"

"What would you say if I told you he was back in town?"

"Gabe? Here?" Ivy laughed again. "I'd say you were nuts."

"Well I'm not."

Slowly, Ivy uncurled her legs. "Are you serious? Gabe King is back in Libby?"

"I'm afraid so. I met him this afternoon, but I don't want Bobby to know yet."

"You're sure it was Gabe?"

"That's what he said."

"But what…" Ivy shook her head and sat back hard in her chair. "Start from the beginning. Where did you meet him?"

"He came to the office looking for me. Apparently, Helene thinks he should try to help Bobby."

"And you're just getting around to telling me this *now?*"

"Like I said, I don't want Bobby to know yet."

Ivy nodded and dropped her voice a few decibels. "Have you talked to Helene?"

"Not yet. I was too busy at work, and when I got home, Whitney delivered her news." The enormity of the situation hit her, and she shivered in spite of the warm evening. "I just can't figure out what Helene is thinking. After everything he's done, why would she think Gabe could help Bobby?"

"Maybe he can."

Siddah gaped at her friend. "Be serious!"

"I am. Let's be logical for just a minute, okay?" Ivy reached across the space between them and touched Siddah's hand. "Maybe this would be good for Bobby. It won't cost you a dime to let him get to know his uncle."

"Gabe isn't his uncle."

"Peter would have said he was."

"Peter was an optimist," Siddah reminded her. "I'm a bit more realistic."

"You're always saying that you're worried about Peter's parents losing interest in Bobby, but you're the one who's pulling back. Can't you see that? You should be doing everything you can to cement his place in the family."

Siddah shot to her feet and rubbed her arms against a sudden chill. "Including letting him spend time with Gabe?" Filling him with the same strange mix of emotions she was feeling?

"Come on, Siddah, you weren't even around when Gabe left. All you know is what people have told you. You can't judge him on that."

"I'm judging him on a whole lot more than that," Siddah shot back. "I was married to Peter when Bobby was just a year old. In all that time, Gabe hasn't been here once. He's never met me until today, and he hasn't even seen Bobby."

"Here's here now."

Siddah let out an angry laugh. "So you're saying I should just ignore the warnings? Don't you think that's a little irresponsible?"

"Normally I'd say yes, but I know Gabe…at least I did." Ivy sat back. "He's a good guy, Siddah. You should give him a chance."

"A good guy who deserted his family for ten years."

"If he's staying with Helene and Monty, obviously things aren't as bad as Peter made them sound."

"We don't know that."

"So call Helene and ask what's going on," Ivy suggested. "You have to move on with your life, and you have to do what you can to help your son."

Siddah nodded miserably. "I know. And if I really thought it would help, I'd probably agree. But how do I know?"

"You don't." Ivy sent a pointed glance at Bobby, who still hadn't moved from the swing. "But you need to try. What's going on right now isn't good for either of you."

"I'm fine," Siddah insisted. "It's Bobby I worry about."

"And I'm worried about you. You've withdrawn from everyone since Peter's death."

Siddah gaped at her. "How can you say that? You and Rebecca are here tonight. I have a job. I'm going after a promotion. It's not as if I'm sitting inside the house with the blinds drawn, feeling sorry for myself."

Ivy swatted away a gnat and smiled gently. "You don't laugh anymore, and you haven't been to any of our progressive dinners since Peter died. You've stopped doing anything with the community theater, and I've hardly even seen you in church. Working all the time isn't exactly living."

Siddah sighed. "How did we switch from talking about Gabe to picking on me?"

Ivy quirked a smile. "I've been wanting to talk to you for a while now. Tonight just seems like the right time. And before you start telling me all the reasons I'm wrong, you need to know that I'm not the only one who's worried. I don't think a full week goes by that somebody doesn't tell me how concerned they are."

Stunned, Siddah sank into her chair. "Who?"

"Friends of yours. Ann and Cody. The Jamisons. Mrs. Pritchett from the theater."

"Why don't they talk to me?"

"How can they? You're either at work or home."

"They could call."

"Yeah, but you know how it is." Ivy ran her fingers through her pale hair. "Look, Siddah, summer's over. Our progressive dinners are going to be starting up again, and tryouts for the first play of the season are in just a couple of weeks. At least think about getting back to the things you used to do."

Stung by the mild criticism, Siddah shook her head. "Were you not paying attention before? I don't have day care worked out for the hours I'll be working, much less baby-sitters lined up so I can have a social life. And I don't think that my being gone even more is going to help Bobby."

"Having a mother who's living her own life might."

"I *am* living my life," Siddah argued. "Life's just different now than it was before and it's unrealistic to think I can simply go back to living the way I was."

"It's unrealistic for you to think you can lock yourself away and be happy."

Siddah laughed in disbelief. "Are we really having this conversation? I invited you over here to celebrate what I thought was a victory. Instead of congratulations, I'm under attack."

Ivy leaned up and put a gentle hand on her arm. "I'm not attacking you. I'm your friend and I'm concerned. Somebody needs to be since you don't seem to care." Before Siddah could argue, Ivy gripped her hands and held on tight. "I'm really thrilled that Evan's going to let you work on a big case, Siddah. Honestly, I am. But can you blame me for wanting to see you smile again? To hear you laugh? You used to love doing stuff with the theater group, and our dinners were one of your favorite parts of the month. Just think about coming back, okay? That's all I ask."

A dozen arguments rose to Siddah's lips, but even she couldn't deny the truth. She had loved the theater group once, and she'd found great joy in preparing her part of the progressive dinner, making sure the house sparkled, and setting the table just-so once a month.

But that was then. This was now. She wasn't the same woman she'd been back then, and her life wasn't her own. She'd find time for herself later...after she built the life she wanted for Bobby.

SUNLIGHT BEAT down on Gabe's head and shoulders and perspiration ran down his back in rivulets. He swung the ax high overhead and brought it down, finding again the rhythm that was buried deep inside. A rhythm he thought he'd forgotten.

He wiped his face with the back of his arm, grimacing at the pull of his muscles. Physical pain he could handle, but he'd never been good at dealing with his emotions. Peter had been much better at voicing his feelings aloud, processing them, making sense of them. To Gabe, emotions had always been something to run from. Something to be locked away.

The song of a meadowlark danced across the clearing and memories drifted all around him. The sound of Peter's laughter mixed with his own floated in and out of his head, and Gabe swung the ax once more in a vain attempt to escape it. Every muscle in his body ached and a chill traced through him.

Gritting his teeth as if sheer force of will could keep a recurrence of the fever away, he split another log and sank onto the stump to catch his breath. He didn't want the old man to catch him resting. He'd never hear the end of it.

The fever had changed him, and not for the better.

He'd spent too much time in the past day thinking about Siddah. Frankly, she'd been a surprise. A wave of shimmering brown hair, and eyes that fluctuated between gray and blue…

She was a beautiful woman. No surprise there. Peter had always been attracted to beauty, in nature, in wood, in women. But when they were younger, Peter had been attracted by women who had a little less bite. Gabe had been the one drawn to women who knew what they wanted and knew how to get it. And if ever he'd met a woman who fit that category, Siddah did.

Apparently, Peter's tastes had changed.

Not that Siddah was all fire. Behind the blaze in her eyes was a veil of sadness. He'd seen the shock on her face that afternoon and he knew that she'd mistaken him for Peter, if only for an instant. Watching the emotions play across her face had been hard on him, too. He wasn't eager to put either of them through another meeting, but if he didn't make an effort with Bobby, he'd lose this battle before it ever got started.

Setting aside the ax, he picked up an armful of wood and carried it toward the house. He wondered whether the old man would find fault with his efforts or if, just once, Monty would simply thank him.

"Gabe?" His mother appeared in the kitchen doorway, holding open the screen with one hand. "You have a phone call. Someone named Randall Hunt?"

Suddenly alert, Gabe dropped the wood against the wall and wiped lingering bits of sawdust and bark from his chest as he walked toward the house. He'd worked with Randy many times over the years, and he respected him as much as he respected anyone. Contacting Randy had been one of the things he'd done as he passed through Virginia, and he'd been more than grateful when Randy had offered to call in a few favors to help Gabe get on his feet again.

Inside, he snagged the phone from the counter where his mother had left it. "Randy? What's up?"

Randy didn't answer his question and asked instead, "How's Montana treating you?"

Small talk? That didn't bode well. "So far, so good. How are things at your end?"

"Busy, as usual. It's been one thing after another since I talked to you last. Hayley's got her driver's license, you know, and we decided to get another car for her to drive, so we've spent far too much time on that."

Gabe's mother hovered near the sink, obviously eavesdropping. He shifted so she wouldn't notice the slight tremor in his hand and tried to sound interested in Randy's story. "You found a good car, I hope?"

"Finally. Now we just need to get her some experience using the clutch."

"She'll get it," Gabe said. "She's a smart kid."

"Yeah, she is." Randy fell silent for a moment, then, "Listen, Gabe, I've been making those calls we talked about."

"And? What have you found out?"

"I don't have good news for you, I'm afraid. Nobody's willing to put up the backing you need to return to Ecuador."

Stunned, Gabe sank into a chair at the table. "Nobody? Who did you talk to?"

"Everybody I could. Problem is, word's out. People know you've been ill and they know the university's doctors have warned you about going back to work too soon. Nobody's willing to put up that much money when the risk of you having a relapse is so great."

"It's not great," Gabe growled. "I'm fine."

"Not according to Dr. Rawson. The university is skittish, and that's making everyone else skittish."

"There has to be somebody with some common

sense. Let me meet with them. Let them see me face-to-face. That ought to convince them."

"It's not going to work, Gabe."

"Then we'll try somebody else."

"There *isn't* anybody else. These people were my last resort. I wouldn't even know where to begin."

Gabe felt his stomach knot, and a sense of dread settled over him. "So you're giving up?"

"For the time being." Randy let out a deep breath. "I hate to say this, Gabe, and I know it's not what you want to hear, but maybe you should take the doctor's advice. Spend a few months recuperating here in the States. Rest. Build up your strength. Let's see where we are in six months or so."

"Six months?" The words shot out of his mouth before he could stop them. He caught the quick turn of his mother's head and tried to soften his voice. "I can't do that, Randy."

"I'm afraid you're going to have to. The university doesn't want to touch you until Dr. Rawson gives you the all-clear, and neither does anybody else."

And how was he supposed to live in the meantime? Gabe stood quickly and paced from one end of the kitchen to the other. "There has to be another way."

"If there is, I can't find it. If you want my advice, I think you should just stay where you are. Relax. There's no place like home, you know."

Except that this wasn't home. It hadn't been home for a long time. But Gabe didn't want to say that with his mother listening. "Yeah," he grumbled. "Thanks."

"I'm sorry, Gabe. I'd really hoped to have better news."

"You tried," Gabe conceded. "I can't ask for more than that."

Still numb and uncertain, he disconnected a few minutes later. The last thing he wanted was to spend six months or more in Montana. But with his bank account empty and his career in shambles, what choice did he have? At least here he had a roof over his head and three squares a day. That was more than he'd have if he left.

"How about potato chips?" Siddah asked as she slowly wheeled a grocery cart down the aisle. "Should we get some of those cheddar cheese ones you like?" It had been a long day at work, and Chris's never-ending demands had left her short-tempered and out of patience. Or maybe it was thinking about her conversation with Gabe that had put her in such a sour mood. She was going to have to give him an answer soon, but she still didn't know what would be best for Bobby.

What she really wanted was to forget about everything unpleasant and just curl up at home with a good book, but she had to do her weekly shopping. They were out of almost everything at home.

Bobby walked beside her, head down, shoulders slumped. "If you want, I guess."

She couldn't tell if he was tired or bored, but she sure could have used a little enthusiasm to help her get through the evening. "I thought maybe I'd make sloppy joes for dinner tomorrow," she said, keeping her tone light. "Sound good?"

"I guess so."

"Is there something you'd like better?"

He shook his head and scuffed his feet as the reached the end of one aisle and started up another. "I don't care, Mom. You decide."

"You mean that?" She grinned wickedly. "Okay then, how about liver?"

Bobby's attention shot to her and his lip curled. "I don't like liver."

"You don't? Well, for heaven's sake, I thought you did. Maybe I was confused. What should we have instead?"

Bobby rolled his eyes at her lame joke and worked up a halfhearted smile. "Anything. Chili-cheese dogs are good. So is macaroni and cheese." He let out a heavy sigh. "Shopping is boring. Can I go play the video games instead?"

Siddah hesitated before nodding reluctantly. Having Bobby's company might make the job easier on her, but she couldn't blame him for not being fascinated by the varieties of canned vegetables or the nutritional value of cereal. She dug a few quarters from her wallet and handed them over. "Play just until the money's gone, then come and find me, okay?"

"Sure. Okay." Clutching the coins tightly in one hand, Bobby loped off toward the front of the store. Siddah watched until he disappeared, then turned back to her cart with a sigh.

For the next ten minutes, she worked her way through the store, keeping track of how much she'd spent to make sure she didn't go over budget. Battling a yawn, she reached for a package of bow-tie pasta just as a chance piece of conversation drifted toward her from somewhere nearby.

' "Gabe? Is that you, or am I seeing things?"

Instantly awake, Siddah froze. Gabe answered too quietly for her to hear what he said, but the low timbre of his voice made her heart stop beating.

Scarcely daring to make any noise herself, she tried to figure out where they were. The next aisle over? The dairy section up ahead on the left or the meat department on the right?

She glanced around quickly to make sure Bobby wasn't coming back, then pushed her cart resolutely toward the end of the aisle. It had never occurred to her that they might run into Gabe at the grocery store or pumping gas for his car, but now that she'd been jolted out of *that* fantasy, she had to make sure Bobby didn't see Gabe tonight.

There he was, in front of the dairy aisle talking to a tall woman with graying hair. Gabe said something Siddah couldn't hear, but the woman's delighted laugh made Siddah wonder if Ivy was right. Was there more to Gabe's story than she'd heard?

This wasn't the time to find out.

Thinking only about finding Bobby before he came looking for her, she wheeled her cart around.

"Siddah?" Gabe's voice made her stop short again. From the corner of her eye, she saw him excuse himself from his conversation and start toward her.

Everything inside told her to ignore him, but she could feel the woman's curiosity and she didn't want to start gossip about the family. Monty, Helene, and Bobby had been through enough already.

"This is a nice surprise," Gabe said as he drew closer. "I was just thinking about you."

"About me? Why?"

"I wondered if you'd had a chance to think about our conversation the other day."

"It's been hard to think about anything else," Siddah admitted, "but I haven't made a decision yet if that's what you're wondering. I'd rather Bobby didn't see you until I've had a chance to tell him about you."

"He's here?"

"Up front playing video games."

To her surprise, Gabe actually looked concerned. "I don't think this is the best place for us to meet, either. Too public. I should go." His smile sent a shiver through her, but she couldn't say it was an unpleasant feeling. "Before I go, I should probably tell you that there's been a change in plans. I'm going to be staying around for longer than I originally thought."

That might be good news for Helene and Monty, but Siddah wasn't sure what it meant for her. "Can I ask why?"

"I'm not needed back at the university right away, so I might as well stick around here. That is, if you don't mind."

"If I—?" She laughed in disbelief. "Does that mean you'd leave if I wanted you to?"

He grinned almost boyishly. "Well…no. But it means I'll do my best not to bother you if that's what you want. It also means that you can take a little longer to decide what you want to do about Bobby if you need to."

Not at all sure what to make of him, Siddah tightened her grip on the shopping cart. "How long are you planning to stay?"

"Six months if I can find a temporary job. Less if I can't. But since I don't need to get back to work right away, I'd like to stick around and make sure Mom and Dad are really doing okay."

Six months? That meant he'd be here for Thanksgiving and Christmas. Even if she wanted to keep Bobby away from him she wouldn't be able to.

"Is that a problem?"

Did he really care? Yes, Siddah realized with a start, she thought he did. But she didn't have time to explain all the reasons why his staying in town wasn't a good idea. She wasn't even sure she understood them all, herself.

She forced a smile, but she knew she wasn't fooling him. "No, of course not. I'm sure Monty and Helene will be thrilled to have you around for so long."

With a shrug, Gabe hooked his thumbs in his back pockets. "Mom is. Dad's barely speaking to me."

"That won't last long. After all, he invited you to stay."

Gabe laughed softly. "The old man is tolerating my presence because of Mom. If he had his way, I'd be back in Ecuador."

He might have been smiling, but his eyes told a different story and an unwanted pang of sympathy shot through Siddah. She'd been a member of the family for nine years. She knew how intractable Monty could be. But, she reminded herself firmly, Gabe had brought this on himself. He'd known where to find the family. He could have come home any time he wanted to.

"Well," she said, checking over her shoulder once more for Bobby, "I'm sure it will all work out once Monty realizes you're serious about staying. I'm going to find Bobby before he comes looking for me. Give me five minutes before you come to the front of the store, okay? I'll keep him distracted while you leave."

Gabe nodded and took a step backward. "Sounds good." He lifted his head and his eyes locked on hers. It only lasted a second before Gabe looked away, but it was a second too long and the odd feeling of awareness left Siddah feeling uncomfortable.

She mumbled something about calling him with her decision when she finally made it and escaped up the frozen-foods aisle, but she could feel him watching her as she walked, and she had the strong feeling that the next six months were going to be a challenge.

She just hoped she would be strong enough to face it.

CHAPTER FOUR

GABE WAITED until dinner was over the following evening to put the first step of his plan in motion. He'd been in Libby for just two days, but already it was painfully clear that he couldn't just show up and hope the old man would let the past die. Judging from the monosyllabic grunts that passed for dinner conversation, and the speed with which his father left any room Gabe walked into, he'd have to wait a lifetime before that would happen. But something had to change or Gabe wouldn't last one month here, much less six.

He stood outside on the back porch, adjusting to the dry western air and the cool mountain evening, grateful that the symptoms he'd experienced the day before had disappeared and wondering how long it would take Siddah to reach a decision—or if she ever would.

He'd been surprised to see her at the market, and more than a little uncomfortable to find himself thinking about her wide dark eyes at odd times during the day. *That* was something he'd better get a grip on or the next six months would be miserable.

A scuff of footsteps in dirt brought Gabe's attention back to the moment just in time to see his father walking across the yard. Without even a backward glance, Monty let himself into the small wooden building that had been Peter's work shed and closed the door behind him.

Gabe had never been one to drag his feet when something needed doing, so he waited for a minute or two, then gathered both his courage and his patience, and followed.

Inside, Monty was plying the concrete floor with a wide push broom, his face a mask of concentration as he maneuvered around the table saw and router. Remembering his mother's assurances that the old man wasn't delusional, he searched his father's expression carefully.

Why did he come out here? Was it just a space to think? A need to feel closer to Peter? His brother's tools still hung in their designated spots on the walls, and a half-finished bookshelf stood in one corner as if someone expected Peter to come back and finish it. The scent of sawdust, once nearly overpowering, was now a faint memory.

Peter would have been just thirty now. He should have been here, working with his tools, singing along to the radio, frowning as he focused on a particularly tricky cut.

Gabe steeled himself against the thumping of his heart and tried to ignore the burning moisture in his eyes. He'd spent countless hours here with Peter, teasing his younger brother about his love of wood while secretly admiring his undeniable talent. Even as a teenager, Peter had been gifted. As a young man of twenty— the age he'd been last time Gabe saw him—the world could have been his for a song. But Peter had never been interested in leaving the valley.

What Gabe wouldn't give for just five minutes to tell Peter how he'd really felt.

His father turned slightly, realized Gabe was standing there, and looked away again. "Come to gloat?"

The question hit Gabe like a well-aimed spear. Shaking his head, he leaned against the workbench and ignored the memories living in every corner. He couldn't bring himself to ask about Peter's accident, so he focused on his other purpose. "Actually, I came to ask for some advice."

His father glanced at him and followed it with a laugh of disbelief. "You want advice from *me?*"

Okay, so it had been a while. Gabe smiled anyway and crossed one foot over the other. "I came back to make things different, Dad, not to stir things up again."

"You're not stirring up anything," his father said with an emphatic push of the broom. "They've been stirred since you walked out on us. Nothin's changed while you've been wherever the hell you've been, taking care of folks more important to you than your own mother and brother."

The old man knew how to dish out the guilt, that was for sure. Always had. But, of course, he'd learned from the master. Though it would be hard to convince someone who hadn't known him, old Calvin King had been even more harsh and less forgiving than his son.

"Nobody was ever more important than my family," Gabe said.

That only earned another harsh laugh from his father. "Actions speak louder than words, boy. If Helene and Peter had meant a damn thing to you, you'd have been here." He stopped sweeping and leaned on the broom handle while his expression turned from merely angry to hostile. "You'd have known your mother would rather have you here for Christmas than any of those fancy presents you sent. You'd have given a damn about your brother's wedding. And at the very least, you'd have interrupted your precious life to be here for his funeral."

Gabe had no excuses for the first two complaints, so he ignored them and zeroed in on the one he could answer. "I told you yesterday, I didn't know about the accident until two weeks ago. I came back as soon as I could after I got Mom's letter."

"You think that's an excuse?" his father thundered. "That you were off in some godforsaken place taking care of people who probably didn't even want you, while your mother was here suffering and your brother lay in a cold, dark grave? That doesn't make it all right, boy. Not even close."

Gabe recoiled from the force of his father's anger. Though he wanted to believe that Monty hadn't meant what he said all those years ago, the fact remained that he *had* ordered Gabe out of the house and warned him never to come back. Monty had always loved control, and he'd had no tolerance for anyone or anything that stepped outside the clearly defined box of what he found acceptable. Gabe's refusal to stay locked in Libby, letting the old man pull his strings, had driven Monty around the bend.

It had taken years for Gabe to make himself get over that. He wasn't sure he'd completely succeeded, even now.

"I'm not saying I haven't made mistakes," he said.

"But I can't undo those. The only thing I can do is to change the future, and that's what I'm trying to do. All I'm asking is that you give me a chance."

His father wheeled away and began working the broom again, but the shoulders that had seemed stooped and old just minutes before were now rigid with aggravation.

Gabe concentrated on the rhythm of the broom as his father worked from one side of the room to the other. He waited, as patiently as he could, for his father to speak again. The ball was in his court. Gabe was ready to make amends, but he wouldn't beg.

When he reached the opposite corner, Monty stopped sweeping. He didn't actually look at Gabe, but said, "You said you wanted advice. What about?"

It was just one small victory, but Gabe would take it. "I've decided to stick around for a while, but I don't want to hang out all day doing nothing, so I might as well get a job. I figure if anybody knows who's hiring in Lincoln County, it's you." It was a huge concession after the arguments they'd had over Gabe's career choices, and he hoped like hell his father would realize it.

Monty's brows knit. "You want my advice about where to work?"

"While I'm here."

"And just how long will that be?"

"At least six months, through the end of February."

His father swept a few more inches of concrete, frowning as if the floor had done something to offend him. "You expect somebody to give you a temporary job?"

"Why not? There are plenty of them available around here."

"In the summer months. Tourist season's almost over."

"And ski season is just around the corner."

Monty made eye contact without warning. "What do you have in mind?"

"I'm not sure."

"You think you can make enough to live on with a temp job?"

Gabe shrugged. He didn't expect or need to earn a fortune. Just enough to help with expenses and maybe enough to put a little aside. "I don't need much. I'll be all right if I can find the right job."

His father stopped sweeping again and leaned the broom against the silent bandsaw. "You want a decent job, come by the mill. I'll see what I can do."

That offer was the last thing Gabe had expected. He couldn't have disguised his surprise if he'd wanted to.

"What's the matter?" his father snapped. "An honest job with your old man's still not good enough for you?"

"I didn't say that." Gabe pushed away from the workbench. "I'm surprised, that's all. I didn't think you'd want me there."

"Wanting you there was never the problem."

Gabe couldn't exactly argue with that. "It's been a while since I worked with the equipment," he said. "I'm pretty rusty."

"I said come by. Do it or don't."

Though he couldn't imagine how he and the old man would work together on a daily basis, he forced a nod and a smile. "All right, then. First thing in the morning?"

His father gave a brisk dip of the head, picked up the broom and hung it back on its nail. "All right, then."

With one last glance in Gabe's direction, he walked out the door into the gathering twilight.

Gabe watched through the window, wondering when Monty's stride had shortened and his gait had become uneven. Gabe and Peter had called him "the old man" for years, but it had never been true before. With a twinge, he realized that his parents wouldn't be around forever. Like it or not, he had to stay in Libby until he'd mended all his relationships. He couldn't risk losing another loved one with things left unsaid.

GRINDING HIS TEETH in frustration, Gabe drove through the gates at Triple Crown Lumber just as the sun crested the mountains the next morning. With a look at his watch and a muttered curse to make himself feel better, he parked between a mud-splattered pickup truck and a rust-spotted Suburban, then headed across the parking lot toward the cavernous metal building that housed the sawmill's business offices.

Somehow he'd managed to screw up already, even though he'd set his alarm clock for five o'clock and checked it twice before finally drifting off to sleep. He'd bounded out of bed and stumbled into the shower before his eyes were fully open, then clambered downstairs for breakfast before the sane residents of Libby had even stirred from their pillows. But despite all his precautions, his father had been gone before Gabe poured his first cup of coffee.

Now he was scrambling to catch up.

He drained the last of his coffee, shook the remaining drops onto the ground as he walked, and steeled himself for the stern look of disapproval he knew was coming as he opened the metal door.

Inside, a short woman with chin-length salt-and-pepper hair glanced up from her desk and smiled when she saw him. Joan Halverson had been his father's right hand almost as long as Gabe could remember. He figured she must be close to sixty now, plumper than he remembered, but still as warm and welcoming as ever.

When things had been at their worst in his family, Joan had been a voice of reason. A haven in the storm. A confidante, not only for Gabe but for Monty and even Helene. She'd never betrayed a confidence, even when the tempest was raging. It did his heart good to know she still had a smile for him.

Perching on the corner of her desk, he tossed off a greeting as if he was still young and cocky and sure of himself. "Good morning, beautiful."

Just like old times, she swatted at him with a file folder. "Plunk your behind somewhere else, Gabriel. I'm right in the middle of something here."

"Aw, come on now. You know you've missed me." Absently, he picked up a stack of order forms and fanned through them.

She bolted from her chair and tried to grab them away. "If you mess those up, I'll whomp you good. It took me half the day yesterday to get them in order."

With a grin, Gabe returned them to the plastic tray where he'd found them. "You know I'd never do anything to make your life harder. I'm just happy to see that you haven't changed."

She pushed at the air between them, but he could tell

that she was pleased. "I'm still as ornery as ever," she said, rolling her chair back from her desk and making herself comfortable. "Just ask your dad if you don't believe me."

Gabe shook his head and held up a hand in protest. "Not on your life."

He'd meant it to sound lighthearted, but there was too much history stored in these walls, and Joan had witnessed it all. Her smile faded and a cloud passed over her eyes. "You've been gone a long time."

"I have."

"Keeping busy?"

"You could say that. I've been working with a native tribe in Ecuador. There are only twenty-four of them left in the world and their culture needs to be preserved."

"And you're the man to do it, I suppose."

"Letting them die out would be globally irresponsible."

Joan's smile didn't make it to her eyes. "I'm sure it's important work, Gabe. You always were determined to save the world."

Gabe's smile slipped. "Nothing wrong with that, is there?"

"No, but sometimes you have to look closer to home. Your family has been in crisis for the past two years. They've needed you."

The reminder wiped away his grin. "I'm here now. I came as soon as I got Mom's letter."

Joan studied his face for a long moment, then shrugged away his answer and stood. "I'm not trying to give you a hard time. I'm just worried about your mom and dad. Things have been rough around here, and they've been good to me over the years. They deserve better."

"I thought Peter was here with them."

"They had two sons, Gabe, not just one."

Before Gabe could defend himself, the door to his father's office opened. Monty burst into the room wearing a hard hat and steel-toed boots, and carrying the clipboard he took with him everywhere on the job. The mood was shattered, the time for confidences gone.

It didn't matter that Gabe was a grown man with a successful career of his own, seeing his father in that getup brought him to his feet like a soldier facing inspection.

Monty tossed a file into Joan's in-basket and skewered Gabe with a glance. "You're here, are you?"

"I said I would be."

"So you did." Monty turned his attention back to Joan. "Try to get Archibald on the phone. I'll be back in half an hour. And I want that letter to Senator Gibson to go out today. We can't let that wait." Ignoring Gabe, he crossed the office and stepped through the door.

Gabe put himself in gear and followed. "It was too late last night to pick up safety equipment," he said to his father's back. "But I can get it today and be ready to start tomorrow."

Monty glanced over his shoulder, but he didn't respond until he'd thoroughly checked the two logging trucks waiting near the gate. Gabe stood by, watching, remembering. He wasn't sure what his dad expected of him, but he was ready for anything.

After making the necessary notations on an inspection form, Monty flipped the page and motioned for the drivers to get started. "You won't need safety equipment," he said as he set off toward a nearby building. "You won't be doing anything dangerous."

It took half a second for Gabe to realize that Monty was speaking to him. Another to process what he'd said. "What does that mean? You want me to work in the office?" *Just kill me now and be done with it.*

Monty climbed a set of metal steps, stuffed foam plugs into his ears and handed a set to Gabe before opening the door. "You don't turn your back on the family business for ten years and walk into a cushy office job," he shouted over the roar of equipment inside. "Life doesn't work that way."

Feeling a little lost, Gabe trailed his father through the door and along a narrow concrete walkway overlooking the massive planer on the floor below. The smell of sawdust was thick inside, and the air slightly hazy with it. His father had something up his sleeve, probably expected Gabe to fold when he delivered the punch line.

Well, Gabe had news for him. He wasn't going to fold. Not this time. While his father engaged in a pantomime conversation with the crew-lead, Gabe watched the men working. He admired the economy of movement, the confidence and courage required to work around equipment that could take a man's life in a heartbeat.

So many of these men had been born with logging in their veins. Why hadn't he? It sure would have made life a lot easier.

He spotted a couple of guys he knew and grinned in response to their nodded hellos. He lifted a hand to wave at his cousin Roger on the crew, and earned only a reluctant dip of the head in greeting. One of the crew shouted something at a man wearing a bright yellow hard hat and a red plaid shirt at the end of the line. Even after the guy looked up, it took a second for Gabe to recognize Carlos Pino, his longtime friend, in the brawny lumberjack.

With a shout of displeasure, Monty jerked his head toward the door as a signal for Gabe to follow him, then plunged out into the sunlight. "Don't distract the men," he shouted as the door clanged shut behind them. "People can get killed that way."

Old habit brought a protest to Gabe's lips, but he swallowed it. Whether or not he'd intended to, he *had* distracted the crew. "It won't happen again," he promised.

The flash of surprise in his father's eyes was almost good enough to make him smile, but grinning right now might just ruin everything. He descended the steps first so he could take a second to disguise his reaction. "Where to next?" he asked when he trusted himself to look at his father again.

His dad came down the steps more slowly, the clipboard tucked under one arm, his hard hat pushed back on his head. "The Ben Franklin."

"Pardon me?"

"Head over there now. Buy yourself a heavy-duty flashlight, a pair of gray slacks and a white shirt—button-down collar." Monty tucked his pen into his shirt pocket. "You'll also need some steel-toed boots and a supply of pens."

Uncomprehending, Gabe could only stare.

"Report back here at ten-thirty tonight. I'll have Slim

show you the ropes and work with you for the first few nights. Once he thinks you can be trusted, you'll be on your own."

Monty had put a little distance between them, so Gabe was forced to follow him again. "Doing what?"

"The only job around here I think you're capable of doing." With a cool smile, Monty readjusted his hat. "I've been needing a night watchman for weeks. Now I've got one."

"Night watchman?" The words popped out before Gabe could stop them.

"You want the job, or don't you?"

There weren't even words to describe how much he *didn't* want it, but he was determined not to let his father push him away. Clenching his teeth, he nodded. "Yes."

"Okay, then. Be back here at ten-thirty."

"All right, I will."

"Have everything you need with you. If you can't find something, let Slim know. Joan can give you his number."

"I'll have what I need," Gabe vowed.

Monty regarded him for a long moment, and, in his expression, skepticism fought with something else for the upper hand. When he finally walked away, Gabe told himself to be grateful. Not only did he have a job, he'd spent fifteen whole minutes with his father and they hadn't had an argument.

He just hoped his luck would hold.

HOLDING A STACK of paper still warm from the copy center, Siddah pushed open the door to her office.

She'd only been working on the Whitman case for two days, but already she was running behind. The shopping trip she'd promised Bobby had been put off twice, and she had no idea when she'd actually find time to take him.

Organizing police reports, taking messages from opposing counsel and scheduling hearings with the court had taken up most of her morning, and there were still a dozen things Chris needed before the end of the day. Thank goodness she'd found a solution to her day-care problem. Janie Toone, a neighbor down the street who ran a day-care center, had a week-long opening while one of her regular kids was on vacation. It was only temporary, but it was something.

"Siddah?" Evan's voice floated through the door connecting their offices. "Is that you? Have you seen the Lundgreen file? I can't find it, and I need it for court in an hour."

Had she? She'd looked at so many files in the past two days, she couldn't remember. Leaving the copies on the corner of her desk, she poked her head into Evan's office. "It may be in that stack I gave to Amanda so she could bring the filing current. I'll check."

Evan nodded absently. "Make sure the judge's order from the dismissal hearing is in there, will you? I have a feeling opposing counsel is going to try to pull a fast one."

Hoping Amanda had the file, Siddah turned to leave, but the phone on her desk rang before she could get out the door. She crossed to her desk impatiently and lifted the receiver. "Evan Jacobs's office."

"Siddah? It's Janie."

Siddah glanced toward Evan's open doorway and dropped her voice. "Is something wrong?"

"Well, I'm not sure. I sent Bobby out to play with the other kids about an hour ago, and now I can't find him."

"What?"

"He was sitting here staring at the walls," Janie said defensively. "I thought it would do him good to get some fresh air."

Siddah sank into the chair behind her desk. "Are you sure he's not there?"

"I'm sure. I've looked all around the yard, and I sent one of the kids to your house to see if he'd gone there. I don't know where he is."

"And he's been gone *how* long?"

"I don't know for sure. The last time I saw him was an hour ago."

"An hour? But it's not like Bobby to just wander off. He never does things like that."

"Well, it looks like he's done it today. We've searched everywhere. There's no sign of him."

Struggling to remain calm, Siddah tried to think of places Bobby could have gone. "Have you checked next door at the Clarks? Bobby used to play with Travis all the time. And what about the Andersons?"

"I've looked around here, and I've checked at your place, but I can't leave the rest of the kids to search for him. That's why I'm calling you."

Evan walked past the connecting door and Siddah dropped her voice another notch. "Can you send one of the older kids to check? I'll leave here if he's really missing, but I'm seriously behind as it is. I'd like to make sure he's not just sitting in a neighbor's backyard before I leave everybody in the lurch."

"Kaitlin was the only older kid I had here today," Janie said, "but her mother picked her up about five minutes ago. I'm really sorry, Siddah, but I just can't go looking for him. He was in a pouty mood for most of the morning, so I'm sure that's all it is, but I have two babies here and a couple of toddlers. You understand, don't you?"

Oh, sure. Siddah understood. But would Evan? And Chris… She shuddered just thinking about his reaction. She'd have to track Bobby down and then come back. It was the only thing she could do. "Yeah," she said. "Sure. I won't be able to leave for a few minutes yet, so if you see him, please call. Tell Amanda to find me, no matter where I am, okay?"

"Of course. I'm sorry, Siddah. I've never had a child wander off like that before, and I certainly didn't expect it of Bobby."

But that was the problem, wasn't it? Since Peter's death, Siddah didn't know what to expect from Bobby anymore.

NEARLY AN HOUR LATER, Siddah pulled into the driveway at home. She'd looked every other place she could think of, but nobody had seen any sign of Bobby. What had started as mild annoyance had built to an almost mind-numbing fear. What if he wasn't just pouting? What if something had happened to him? What if—?

She stopped herself before she could finish the thought. Bobby was all she had left in the world. The alternative was unthinkable.

With her heart in her throat, she yanked her key from the ignition and bolted around the house to the backyard. Bobby didn't have keys and Siddah had never liked leaving a spare key where just anyone might find it. But he wasn't sitting on the patio or in a swing or even in the shade beneath his favorite old oak tree. Growing more frantic by the minute, she hurried back out to the front of the house, shouting his name. She'd exhausted every other possibility. If he wasn't home, she couldn't even think where to look next.

Tears burned Siddah's eyes as she jogged back to the street. She tried to keep them from getting the best of her. Tears wouldn't help find Bobby. Neither would panic.

Struggling to breathe, Siddah raced through her remaining options. Maybe she should call the police, and she should probably check with Helene and Monty, too. Neither of them would have just taken Bobby, and both would have phoned her if they suspected trouble of some kind, but maybe they'd heard from Bobby earlier in the day. Whatever she did, she couldn't just stand here and wait for Bobby to show up.

Eager to change from the skirt and heels she'd worn to work so she could move faster, she raced back to the house and onto the porch. But she was too nervous and her hands were shaking. She fumbled with the key for a few seconds before she managed to slip it into the lock, then let herself inside.

Her imagination was racing as she closed the door behind her. She even thought she heard the high-pitched music from Bobby's favorite video game. But that was impossible.

Wasn't it?

"Bobby?" she called, "is that you?"

The music stopped suddenly and a rush of relief swept over her, followed closely by a wave of anger. Tossing her keys onto the table, she strode into the living room, where Bobby sat slumped down on the couch, the game control clutched in his two small hands.

"What are you doing here?" she demanded. "You're supposed to be at Janie's."

Bobby slid down a little farther, obviously aware that he was in big trouble. "I don't like it there. I don't want to go there."

"So you just left?"

"I came home."

"Without telling Janie what you were up to. How did you get in, anyway?"

Bobby sent her a sidelong glance. "The basement window doesn't lock tight. I found out one time when me and Dad were playing catch."

"And you never told me?"

"I forgot until today."

Siddah sank to the arm of the couch and tried to stay focused on the real issues. "Do you have any idea how frightened I was? I didn't know where to find you."

"I'm okay. I just came home."

"Yes, but I didn't know that. You aren't supposed to be here."

"Why not?"

"Because I made arrangements for you to be at the baby-sitter's. I'm paying for you to be there so I don't have to worry about you while I'm at work. Not only did you make both Janie and me worry, I had to leave work to come and find you, and my boss isn't happy."

Bobby put both feet on the coffee table and glared at the toes of his shoes. "I don't want to go to Janie's house. I don't like it there."

"You haven't even given it a chance. This was your first day."

"Yeah?" He lifted his head suddenly, and the determination she saw on his face surprised her. "Well, all she has there is a bunch of little babies. There's nothing for me to do and nobody for me to play with."

"You'll make friends."

"With who? Everybody else is a baby, Mom. And Janie won't even let me stay inside. She says I need fresh air."

"Well, she's right," Siddah told him. "You do need fresh air. You need to do something besides sit in this house all day long playing that stupid game." Her voice rose with every word, and she realized that she was losing her temper. Dragging in a steadying breath, she sat on the floor in front of him and tried to regain control. "Bobby, I'm worried about you. Grandma and Grandpa are worried about you. You don't do any of the things you used to do, and that's just not good for you."

"But why do I have to go to Janie's house? Why can't I go to Grandma and Grandpa's?"

Siddah sat back hard against the coffee table. "You can't go there, Bobby."

"Why not? Grandma said I could come anytime."

"I know, buddy, but—"

"And Grandpa said he'd take me fishing, just like Dad used to. And there's lots of fresh air there."

She couldn't argue with that, but she still couldn't make herself agree. "Honey, I know Grandma said that she'd be happy to let you come, but—"

"But what, Mom? Why can't I go there? Why don't you want me to?"

"It's not that I don't want you to, sweetheart. I just don't want to take advantage of Grandma."

"But she *wants* me." His little face was filled with such sadness, Siddah felt all of her defenses crumble.

She wants me.

Closing her eyes, Siddah nodded slowly. "Okay, buddy, I'll call Grandma and see what she says, okay?"

"You will?"

"Yeah. I will. But if Grandma's busy tomorrow, you'll have to go to Janie's okay? Just until we can work something else out."

Bobby made a face, but he nodded grudgingly. Siddah stood and brushed off the back of her skirt. Hard as it was to admit she needed help, that was only the first problem this was going to cause for her. She'd have to let Bobby meet Gabe now. She had no choice.

CHAPTER FIVE

THURSDAY MORNING bright and early, Siddah loaded Bobby into the car and headed out of town. Not surprisingly, Helene had been delighted at the idea of having Bobby around. She'd even chided Siddah gently for not calling sooner, but Siddah didn't know if it was the prospect of having Bobby's company that made Helene happy or the chance to get him together with Gabe.

Personally, Siddah was torn between wanting to avoid Gabe completely and wanting to be there to supervise his first meeting with Bobby. But after leaving work early yesterday, she couldn't be late this morning. She'd just have to trust Helene to keep a close eye on things while she was at work.

That wasn't her biggest problem this morning, anyway. She still hadn't found a way to tell Bobby about Gabe, but time was running out. Gabe would probably be there when she and Bobby arrived, and she couldn't blindside Bobby with a new uncle.

As she left the city limits behind and drove into the forest, she glanced across the seat at Bobby, whose attention was riveted on a handheld game. "Hey, buddy. There's something we need to talk about before we get to Grandma's, okay?"

Bobby looked away from the screen. "What?"

"You and Grandma probably won't be alone today."

"Why? Is Grandpa going to be there?"

"Not Grandpa." Bobby had heard Peter talk about Gabe, so why was this so difficult? She steered around a sharp curve in the road and silently begged Peter to help her get through this. "You remember Daddy talking about his brother, don't you?"

"Sure."

"Well, he's here. In town for a little while." She tried to check Bobby's reaction. "He's staying with Grandma and Grandpa."

"Uncle Gabe is here?" For the first time in months, Bobby actually looked interested in something, and her heart plummeted. But that only made her angry with herself. Maybe Helene was right. Maybe Gabe could help Bobby get over this rough patch. Why couldn't she just embrace that idea and be grateful?

Was she jealous? If so, of what? That the mere mention of Gabe—who dropped in and out of people's lives as the mood suited him—might be able to do for her son what she couldn't? Or was she angry that men like Gabe and her own father could play fast and loose with their family commitments and get away with it?

She'd only met her father three times, and as far as she was concerned, that was three times too many. Though her mother had kept him at arm's length each time he drifted back into town, her grandmother had always killed the fatted calf for the return of her very own prodigal son, and she'd expected everyone else—especially Siddah—to be thrilled that he'd deigned to notice them for a few days.

Well, she hadn't gone hog wild over Oliver Carlisle's visits, and she wasn't about to lose her head over Gabe's, no matter how nice he seemed. Forcing a nod and a smile, she said, "He's here for a little while, anyway. I don't know how long he'll be staying."

Bobby turned off his game and put it on the seat beside him. "What's he doing here?"

"He just heard about Daddy's accident, so he came back."

That earned a grunt. "How come it took so long?"

"I guess he was in the jungle where there's no mail delivery."

"Really? Cool."

Cool? Siddah's heart twisted with equal parts of fear and hope. "I don't know how cool it is," she said, trying not to sound bitter, "but that's what he says."

She could feel Bobby staring at her. "What's the matter," he asked after several seconds. "Don't you like him?"

How was she supposed to answer that? She slowed to make the turn onto her in-laws' driveway and decided to stick with the truth. "I don't know him well enough to like him or not like him, but I don't understand why he spent so much time away from his family. Your dad would have given anything to see him again while he was still alive."

"Maybe he couldn't come back."

"I think he could have found time at least once in ten years."

"But you don't know."

"No," she admitted reluctantly, "I don't know." They fell into silence as the car bounced along the lane toward the house, but there was an edge to the air between them now.

Helene met them at the door with a bright smile for Siddah and a warm hug for Bobby. "I've made orange juice and French toast for breakfast," she said as Bobby squirmed away. "I hope you haven't eaten."

"Mom made me have some cereal," Bobby said, "but I'm not full."

"No, of course you're not. I swear, you get a little bigger every time I see you." Helene ushered them both inside, leaving the door open so the cool morning air could come through the screen. "I'm so glad you're going to spend time with me," she said, crossing to the griddle. "I've been thinking up things to do all morning."

Bobby sat at the table but, still mindful of the time, Siddah remained near the door. "I don't want you to put yourself out," she cautioned.

"Put myself out?" Helene laughed as if she'd never heard such an outrageous suggestion. "Siddah, sweetheart, having Bobby around is pure pleasure for me." She sent a grin along with her protest and added, "And you, too, of course."

From their first meeting, Helene had been like this with her. Warm and friendly. Accepting. Loving. She'd opened her arms wide and taken them in as if they'd always belonged. Maybe if she'd been a little less welcoming, Siddah wouldn't feel such deep pangs of regret over the possibility of losing them.

And maybe she wouldn't feel such guilt over accepting help from them. "I appreciate this more than you know," she told Helene. "I'll keep looking for a regular sitter, of course. Someone who can come to the house when school starts so Bobby can be home."

Helene moved the French toast onto a serving platter and carried it to the table. She shooed Bobby from the room to wash his hands and smiled at Siddah while she worked. "There's no need to rush, you know. Bobby can keep me entertained while he's here. And, of course, he'll want to meet Gabe and spend time with him."

"Yes. Well…"

Helene looked up sharply. "You did tell him, didn't you? He knows Gabe is here?"

"I told him on the way here, but I'm still not sure how much time he should spend with Gabe. What if connecting with Gabe while he's here makes things worse when he leaves again?"

Helene poured a cup of coffee and held up the pot in silent question. When Siddah waved away her offer, she leaned against the counter to drink. "That won't happen if Gabe stays in contact this time."

"Yes, but do you really think he will?" The flash of hurt on Helene's face made Siddah feel terrible for placing doubt in her mind. She glanced into the hall to make sure Bobby wasn't on his way back, and lowered her voice to make sure she wouldn't be overheard. "I'm sorry, Helene, but surely you know what a risk it is to rely on Gabe for anything." Or was she really so blind to his faults?

"Now you sound like Monty."

"I don't mean to," Siddah assured her quickly. "You know Gabe far better than I do, of course, but it's hard to believe that he cares a whole lot when he lets ten years go by between visits."

Helene's expression puckered with disapproval. "As you said, you don't know him."

"I'm certainly not saying that you and Monty shouldn't welcome him home and hope for the best," she said carefully, "but Bobby's just a boy. He can't process hopes and disappointments the same way you can."

"Maybe he won't have to."

And maybe the sun would rise in the west tomorrow. Siddah had the uncomfortable suspicion that if Gabe said it would, Helene would believe him. The roar of an engine caught her attention, and a few seconds later she saw Gabe striding toward the house carrying a lunch pail and thermos.

Her throat grew dry at his similarities to Peter—the length of his stride, the tilt of his head...

"Is that him?" Bobby's voice sounded close behind her.

She forced a nod, angry with herself for being so focused on Gabe that she'd missed hearing Bobby come back into the room. "That's him."

"He looks like Dad."

"Yes he does, a little bit." Her voice sounded high and tight, so she tried to get it sounding normal again. "I guess that's only natural, huh?"

"I guess." Bobby sidled closer to the door just as Gabe stepped onto the porch. The mixture of hope and fear in his eyes hit Siddah squarely in the chest, and she wondered why she'd ever agreed to this. But it was too late to back out now.

GABE DIDN'T SEE the kid standing inside the door until a split second before he opened the screen. He'd been too busy studying the strange car parked near the door, wondering who could be here this time of morning. The instant he saw the boy, he had his answer.

Bobby was at an awkward age—all legs and arms, no chest or shoulders to speak of. Red hair, teeth that would soon need the attention of a good orthodontist, and an unfortunate thick smattering of freckles on cheeks, nose and arms that probably earned no end of teasing from the kids at school.

Just like that, Gabe knew why Peter had taken the kid under his wing. Just like that, he felt a strong urge to follow in his brother's footsteps.

Siddah hovered behind the boy, her expression hard, cold, suspicious. A she-bear waiting for the chance to shred anyone who messed with her cub. Behind her, his mother watched all three of them with hope shining in her eyes.

No pressure here.

Gabe held out a hand to the kid and pasted a smile on his face, trying to look like someone the kid might like. "You must be Bobby. It's good to finally meet you."

The kid put a limp little hand in his and pulled it away almost immediately, but he studied Gabe for a long time without speaking. "You look kinda like him, I guess."

"A lot of people say that," Gabe admitted, then fell at a loss for words. He'd love to return the compliment, but finding a physical resemblance between this kid and Peter would be impossible. Truth was, Gabe had to struggle even to find a resemblance to the kid's mother.

After way too long, his mother seemed to collect herself and waved them all toward the table. "Why don't we sit down for a few minutes? Siddah, you have time, don't you?"

Anything was better than standing around looking like a dope. Gabe took a seat gratefully, but he was aware of Bobby's eyes on him the whole time.

Siddah glanced at her watch, frowned and shook her head. "I wish I could, but I'll be lucky to make it on time as it is." With a warning glance at Gabe, she gathered Bobby to her for a quick hug. "You listen to Grandma, okay? Help her out while you're here. If you need anything," she said to Helene, "call me. I can run out on my lunch break if I have to. And I'll get here just as soon as I can after work."

"There's no hurry," Helene assured her. "Bobby's always welcome. In fact, the two of you should plan to stay for dinner."

Siddah's expression froze. "Oh! I—" Her eyes darted around the room, making her look like a wounded animal. "I don't think——" She took a deep breath, pulled herself together and tried again. "That's too much, Helene. Bobby and I can eat at home."

"Too much? To have all of my family together?"

In the wake of her question, Peter's absence seemed to fill the room. Gabe felt it, and he was certain Siddah did.

Her cheeks flamed. "Another time, maybe." With one last, pointed look at Gabe, she let herself out the door. A wave of tension followed her outside, but both Bobby and Helene seemed oblivious.

The kid sat across the table from Gabe and cupped his chin in his hands. "How come I never met you before?"

Trust a kid to get straight to the point. "Because I've been away. Out of the country."

"Doing what?"

"I'm an anthropologist. Do you know what that is?"

"Grandpa says you mess around with dead people and their stuff."

How like his father to pay so little attention. "No, that's an archaeologist. I'm the kind of scientist who works with people who are still alive."

Bobby looked him over for a few seconds, probably trying to make a scientist out of him. "Doing what?"

"All kinds of things. For the past few years I've been helping one village learn how to grow crops and make shelter."

"They don't know how?"

"Well, yes, they do. They just need help learning how to do it better."

Bobby gave him another long, slow look, then turned his attention to breakfast. "Do you like to play video games?"

Gabe glanced at his mother, but she'd gone back to work at the stove. "I don't know," he admitted. "I haven't done a whole lot of it."

"How come? My dad used to play with me all the time. He was good."

Of course he was. Peter had excelled at everything he tried. "I'm not like your dad, but if you don't mind playing with somebody you can easily beat, I'm your guy."

He couldn't tell if the quick curve of Bobby's lips was a smile or a grimace, but the desire for it to actually be a smile surprised him.

"If you want," Bobby offered, "I could teach you."

"I might need an awful lot of teaching."

"That would be okay. I don't have anything else to do."

"So you'll take pity on me?"

Bobby slathered butter on his toast, reached for the syrup and poured way too much onto his plate. "I'm pretty good. I could probably teach you to be almost as good as me."

"But not quite, huh?"

Bobby shook his head solemnly. "I don't think so."

Gabe met his mother's amused expression over Bobby's head, and the approval on her face left him feeling warm all over. Grinning at Bobby, he helped himself to the French toast. This was going to be easier than he'd expected. "You don't, huh? And why not?"

"Because." Bobby sopped a piece of pancake in syrup, creating a sticky trail on the table as he wedged it into his mouth. "Grandpa says you never stick with anything, and Mom says you probably won't stay around for very long." He wiped his chin with his sleeve and looked at Gabe steadily. "So you probably won't ever beat me."

Gabe couldn't tell if Bobby made that announcement innocently, or if there was an accusation hidden in there somewhere. The old man's opinion of him was no surprise, but Siddah's pricked uncomfortably. Not that he'd earned anything different, but he sure didn't like being judged and found wanting by someone he'd met twice.

He accepted a cup of coffee and stacked another piece of French toast on his plate. And he made a silent vow to make sure the old man and Siddah ate their words before he left town.

AT A FEW MINUTES PAST FIVE that evening, Gabe parked his Jeep and pushed through the door into the Hungry Moose Lounge. Since his return, Gabe had run across a number of changes in the town. While change was to be expected after a decade, the differences in Libby weren't all for the better.

According to his mother, governmental restrictions had hit the logging industry hard and the sawmill had felt the impact. His father had been forced to lay off a number of longtime employees. The town's other large employer, the vermiculite mine, had closed down completely a couple of years back, leaving a number of people without jobs, and the economy in a tailspin. One after another, Gabe had driven past empty buildings where once there'd been a thriving small business, proof that his mother was right.

He was surprised to see the old watering hole still open for business. And not just open, but thriving. The town might be struggling, but the people still faced life with courage and spirit.

Pocketing his keys, he paused inside the door to let his eyes adjust. Back when he'd lived here, the Moose had been a favorite after-shift hangout for the guys who worked at Triple Crown, so he wasn't at all surprised to see Carlos Pino and a few others from the day shift stacked up against the bar.

As if Gabe had been here just yesterday, Carlos waved him over. Gave saw him get the bartender's attention and order a beer before he could even make it across the room.

Now that he was closer, Gabe realized that Carlos hadn't changed as much as he'd first thought. He was obviously older and a little more bulky. A few strands of gray showed in his jet-black hair and fine lines creased the skin around his eyes, but he still wore the broad grin that had landed him in trouble more than once as a kid.

"Bottom's up," Carlos said, sliding the bottle toward him. "Long time no see."

"It's been a while," Gabe conceded.

"You could have knocked me over with a feather when I looked up and saw you at the mill the other day. Never thought I'd see that again."

"You're not the only one," Gabe said with a laugh. "I hope you enjoyed it. You're not going to see it again for a while."

"You're leaving soon?"

"Not for a few months, but the old man has me working the graveyard shift."

One of Carlos's eyebrows winged upward. "I didn't know we ran a graveyard shift anymore."

Gabe took a pull on his beer and leaned onto the bar. "It's a shift of one. Very elite."

"The old man's playing favorites, is he?"

Gabe laughed. "You know it. From respected anthropologist to night watchman overnight. Nepotism at its finest."

Carlos studied him silently for a minute. "Why are you working at the mill at all? I thought you said you'd rather die first."

Gabe wondered what Carlos would say if he admit-

ted how close he'd come to doing just that. He turned
so he could look out at the crowd. "I'm taking a little
break from the university. A few months, just to make
sure the folks are okay."

"And they're okay with that?"

"My mother's thrilled."

Carlos belted a laugh, but sobered again quickly.
"Hey, man, I'm sorry about Pete."

"Thanks."

"You doing okay?"

"As okay as I can be." Gabe took a long pull on his
beer and hitched himself onto a stool. "I guess it will
get easier in time."

"That's what they say. I haven't seen much of your
mom. How's she holding up?"

Gabe shrugged. "About like you'd expect. She's getting by, but losing Peter took something out of her and
the old man." He shifted to look at Carlos. "Tell me
something, is he different at work?"

"How do you mean?"

Gabe didn't want to mention his suspicions about his
father's drinking. What if he was wrong? "I don't know.
He just seems changed."

Carlos swept the change from the bar into his hand
and slipped it into his pocket. "Well, sure he's changed.
He's had a rough time. It's to be expected."

"I suppose so." Gabe turned the bottle in his hands
and tried to shake off the mood. He was here to forget.
"Don't take this the wrong way, but do you mind if we
talk about something else?"

Carlos shook his head. "Naw, that's fine. Whatever,

man." That had always been the great thing about having him as a friend. No pressure. "What's up in…wherever you've been?"

"Ecuador."

"Still determined to save the world?"

"Trying."

"And you still think the rest of us are soulless devils just trying to make money?"

"That's a little harsh, isn't it? You're putting words into my mouth."

Carlos laughed and held up both hands to ward off Gabe's irritation. "Sorry, man. I didn't know it was still such a touchy subject. Just don't lump me in with the old man, okay? I'm just a poor working slob doing his best to get by."

Consciously relaxing his shoulders, Gabe nodded. "You and the old man? Not a chance. How long have you been working at the mill, anyway?"

"Just about ten years. I started a couple of months after you left."

Gabe swiveled on his stool to see Carlos better. "What happened to working with the forest service?"

Carlos laughed. "Marriage. Kids. Life."

For some reason, that surprised Gabe. "You're married? With kids? How many?"

"Four. Three boys and a girl."

Four kids? Unbelievable. Obviously, the world hadn't stood still while Gabe was away. Carlos married with kids. Peter married with a stepson. If anyone's life had remained stagnant, it was Gabe's. He didn't like that realization at all.

"So who'd you marry? Anyone I know?"

"Diana Boel. You remember her, don't you?"

"Sure. We were friends in high school. But when did the two of you start dating?"

"Six months before we got married." Carlos snagged a handful of quarters from the bar and jerked his head toward the electronic dartboard. "Want to toss a few?"

Gabe tossed back the rest of his beer and stood. "Sure, but I haven't played since I left here."

"That won't make any difference," Carlos said with a grin. "I could always kick your ass at this game." He fed quarters into the machine, pulled a set of custom darts from his pocket, and handed it over. "Toss a few practice shots so you don't whimper when it's all over."

Gabe fell into the easy banter gratefully. "I think you're mistaking me for someone else. *I'm* the one who used to kick *your* ass, and I've never whimpered in my life."

"No? What about the time Mikey Everall knocked you off the monkey bars?"

"I was six!"

"Doesn't matter. I distinctly remember whimpering."

Gabe laughed, amazed at how good it felt to joke around, how comfortable he felt being around someone who knew and accepted him, warts and all. He noted Carlos's empty glass and turned back toward the bar. "You drinking draft?"

"Was," Carlos said, "but one's my limit these days. Diana doesn't mind if I stop in for one beer with the guys once or twice a week, but my kids aren't going to grow up with a dad who smells like a bar."

Gabe grinned and turned back to the dartboard.

"Sounds like a smart decision to me. So what do we have, time for one game?"

"Just about." Carlos straddled a chair and settled in to watch him warm up. "You should come to dinner. Get reacquainted with Diana, meet the kids."

"Sure," Gabe said as he sighted in on the target. "Sounds great." He was surprised to discover how much he meant it.

"What nights do you have off?"

"Fridays and Mondays."

"How about this Friday then?"

"You sure Diana won't mind?"

"Mind? Are you kidding? She'll be thrilled."

"Yeah? Well, you'd better check with her and make sure. If this weekend doesn't work, I can come another time."

"She'll be fine," Carlos insisted. He glanced toward the crowd behind them at the bar. "It'll give us a chance to catch up without the whole town listening."

Gabe's laughter faded. "Is there a reason we need to do that?"

Carlos gathered his darts and took his place at the line. "Friday," he said again. "Come hungry."

CHAPTER SIX

BOBBY WAS SITTING at the kitchen table when Gabe got home from work the next morning, his little cheek propped up in one hand and one foot banging rhythmically against the chair. Some half-eaten oatmeal cooled in front of him and he dropped globs of it from a spoon back into the bowl.

Looks like they had at least one thing in common, Gabe thought as he let the door shut behind him. Of all the breakfasts he'd eaten over the years, oatmeal was still his least favorite. Trying to ignore the flicker of disappointment over having missed Siddah, Gabe left his lunch pail and jacket on the counter, brushed a kiss to his mother's cheek and headed for the stairs.

"Gabe?" Helene called after him. "Where are you going? Breakfast is ready."

He turned back slowly and put one hand on his stomach. "Yeah. I know. I'm just not hungry this morning. Too much junk food at work, I guess. I'll grab something later."

His mother's smile morphed into a scowl. "It's oatmeal."

"Yeah, I see that."

"With cinnamon and raisins."

Gabe could feel Bobby watching him, so he tried not to grimace, but it wasn't easy. "Sounds great, Mom, but really, I'm not—"

"Gabriel King! I know exactly what you're doing, and I don't find it one bit funny. Sit down at the table and eat your breakfast. I didn't spend time making it just to amuse myself."

Feeling ten years old, Gabe turned back to the table and dropped into a chair across from the kid. There weren't words strong enough to tell his mother how he felt about oatmeal. The texture alone was enough to make him gag, but no one should have to suffer through it alone.

He caught Bobby's attention on him, nodded toward the bowl and grimaced. "Any good?"

Bobby glanced at his grandmother and leaned closer to whisper, "Yeah, if you like eating paste."

Gabe choked on a laugh. "You got raisins in there?"

Bobby nodded, lifted another spoonful and dropped it into his bowl. "They look like mouse poop."

"Very funny," Helene said, sliding a bowl of paste and mouse droppings in front of Gabe. "If I hear one more word out of either of you, I'll give you double."

Bobby looked horrified, but when he saw Gabe wink reassurance, he relaxed and sent back a snaggle-toothed grin.

Cute kid, Gabe told himself. Good sense of humor. At least *this* part of his stay wouldn't be tough.

BY THE TIME Friday evening rolled around, Gabe was more than ready to hear what Carlos had to say. They didn't get a chance to talk until after dinner was over, the kids had raced off to play and Diana had retreated to a lounge chair with a paperback novel.

Only then did Carlos lead him across the lawn toward the garage so they could speak privately. Carlos lifted the door to let in the rapidly cooling evening air and rolled a motorcycle that had seen better days toward the daylight. The sounds of children's laughter drifted inside through the open doorway, reminding Gabe again of how much things in Libby had changed.

While Carlos set to work removing a worn clutch, Gabe found a seat on an upturned box and tried to hide the shortness of breath that had been plaguing him all evening.

"So now that you've been back for a few days," Carlos said, "what do you think?"

"There's a lot that's changed, that's for sure." Gabe nodded toward the hillside, where a ski trail of pale green grass cut through the trees. "That new ski lift almost makes this place look like the big time."

Carlos glanced toward the chairlift and nodded. "We've lost a lot, too. Businesses have closed. People have moved away. We even had to close one of the elementary schools a couple of years back."

"My mom mentioned that." Gabe looked at the kids on the lawn and tried again to connect them to Carlos. "Were your kids affected?"

"Not directly, but they had to put those kids somewhere. Class sizes got bigger all at once." Carlos loosened a bolt and dropped the parts into a upturned hubcap at his feet. "Things around here aren't what they were, that's for sure."

"I suppose that's only natural."

"I suppose." Carlos glanced at him over the cycle's seat. "Speaking of changes, how's the new job going?"

"Different from what I'm used to," Gabe admitted. He didn't want to offend Carlos by elaborating about just *how* different it was. On the days when he felt healthy and strong, the job didn't bother him. It was a temporary comedown. A way to connect with the old man. But when the fever came back, even slightly, a deep fear clutched at his chest. What if he never fully recovered? What would he do then? Shaking off the fear, he forced a grin and added, "The toughest thing I do all night is try to stay awake."

Carlos laughed. "You gonna stick with it?"

"That's my plan."

"You don't think it's going to make you crazy?"

"It's only for a little while," Gabe said firmly. "I'll be out of here again in six months at the latest. I think I can stand it that long."

Nodding, Carlos fell silent for a few minutes as he worked. "So what happens in six months?"

"If all goes well, I'll get back to Ecuador. If not, I'll be traveling around trying to find a new sponsor."

Carlos tossed aside one tool and reached for another. "So why wait six months?"

Gabe could have told him about the illness, but he didn't want word to filter back before he had a chance to tell his parents. He stood and pretended an interest in the tools hanging on the garage wall. "It's complicated," he said over his shoulder, "and not very interesting."

"Diana will be disappointed. She's hoping you'll decide to stay around." Carlos grinned. "I told her not to get excited. Everybody knows how much you hated it here."

"It wasn't the town I hated," Gabe said. "Or the people."

"You stayed away for a long time."

"Yeah, but that was a mistake."

Carlos nodded. "Everybody makes 'em, I guess."

"Not you." Carlos was one of those lucky guys who met the woman he loved early in life, knew just what he wanted and got it without ever having to search for it. Like Peter. A little surprised by the flash of envy, Gabe sat again and crossed one ankle over his knee. "Things seem good between you and Diana. You don't regret getting married so young?"

"Hell no. I'm too smart to let her go, and she's too sweet to kick me out. We're a perfect pair. What about you? Did you ever bite the bullet?"

"And get married?" Gabe shook his head. "That was never high on my list of priorities. Not sure if it ever will be, either."

Carlos reached into a cooler at his feet, tossed Gabe a soda and cracked open one for himself. "You're missing out, buddy. A wife. Kids. A place to call home… there's nothing better in the world."

"Now how would you know that?" Gabe asked with a laugh. "This is all of the world you've ever seen."

"You find anything better out there?"

He wanted to say yes, but the words stuck in his throat. "I've found plenty that's just as good," he said, but he sounded defensive, even to himself. He tried to laugh it off. "I hate to tell you this, but 'father of four' makes you sound pretty damn old."

Carlos chuckled. "What can I say? We had Mikey when we were twenty-three, and the rest came along like clockwork. Mikey's nine, and the baby will be two in October."

"And you're happy."

The screen door banged shut and Carlos checked over his shoulder for his wife. With her spiky brown hair and trim figure, Diana didn't look like someone who'd given birth to a handful of kids, but then Gabe wasn't exactly an expert on that, either.

"Yeah, I am," Carlos said with a smile. "Go figure." He let out a sigh full of contentment and turned his attention back to Gabe. "So what *have* you been doing with yourself?"

"Exactly what I left here to do. I did my postgraduate work at the University of Virginia, got an internship to help pay the bills, joined the professor down in Ecuador the following year, and the rest is history. The people down there got under my skin, I guess. It's where I spend most of my time."

"So then why'd you come back?"

"I heard about Peter."

"That happened a while ago."

"Yeah, I know, but Mom's letter just caught up with me a couple of weeks ago. I came back as soon as I could."

"And your father? How has he been handling having you back?"

"Better than I expected him to," Gabe admitted. "I'm

not under any delusion that he's glad to have me around, but Mom's determined to make sure we don't fight. He gets around her edict by refusing to speak to me." Gabe picked up a nail gun and turned it slowly in both hands. "Like I said the other night, he's different than he was. I thought maybe you'd know why."

"It's been a while," Carlos said with a shrug. "Nobody stays angry forever."

"It's more than that," Gabe said. "It's like the life has gone out of him."

"Well, it probably has. His kid died. How do you expect him to react?"

"Is it just that?"

"That's not enough?"

"More than enough," Gabe agreed. "I'm just trying to figure out how to approach him, that's all. I know how to deal with him when he's angry, but this sadness is something else. I don't know how to get past it."

One of the kids, a little girl of about five, let out a howl and raced across the lawn toward them. Without missing a beat, Carlos scooped her onto his lap and did daddy things—checking where she was hurt, nuzzling her with his forehead, and finally teasing a reluctant smile from her. When she raced off again, Carlos returned to their conversation.

"I don't know that you *can* get past what he's feeling. Your dad's grieving. It might take a while."

"It would help if I knew more about Peter's accident, about what led up to it, how it happened…"

"You don't know how it happened?"

Gabe shook his head. "I guess everybody figures

somebody else has told me. Neither Mom nor Dad seems ready to talk about it, and it doesn't seem right to ask Siddah."

Carlos looked up from his work. "You know Siddah?"

"I've met her."

"And? What do you think?"

"What do you mean, what do I think?"

"I mean, what do you think?" Carlos abandoned his tools and stood. "Diana thinks I'm crazy," he said, lowering his voice slightly, "but I never did think she and Peter were right for each other."

That surprised Gabe as much as anything he'd heard since he came back. "Why not?"

"Uh-uh. Answer my question first. What do you think?"

"I think she has a lot of spirit, why?"

"That's it?"

"I've barely met her. I haven't had time to think anything else." When he recognized the expectant look on his friend's face, he protested, "She's my brother's wife. What else can I think?"

Carlos barked a triumphant laugh and leaned closer. "I knew it!" Realizing how loud his voice was, he lowered it and said again, "I *knew* it. Look, don't get me wrong. You know how I felt about Pete. He was like a kid brother to me. But she wasn't right for him. From the minute I met her, I knew it. Nobody else did, though."

"I thought they were happy together."

"They were. She was just with the wrong guy, and sooner or later, Pete would've figured that out."

Gabe recoiled as if he'd been gut-punched. "Are you saying there was someone else?"

"No. Not at all!" Carlos leaned closer, resting both arms on the picnic table. "It's just that I always thought she was more…your type."

"My type? Are you crazy? Don't even think a thing like that."

Carlos waved off his objections with a wrench. "Look, I'm not saying you should do anything about it. Just that she always seemed more like someone you would have dated than Pete, that's all."

Gabe checked the open door to make sure nobody was listening and dropped his voice even lower. "She's *not* my type," he insisted. "And you can't go around saying things like that. The old man would have a stroke if he heard you."

"He's not here."

"No, but your kids are, and Diana…your neighbors…" Gabe took another look around and satisfied himself that no one seemed to be paying attention. "Look, maybe your dad would find that funny. He'd understand that you're just talking hypothetically. Making a point. But mine could hear something like that and decide that I'm planning to move in on Peter's territory. Being back here is tough enough without adding that."

Carlos actually looked regretful. "Sorry, man. I didn't mean anything by it. I didn't realize things were still so touchy at home."

"Like I said, I can count on one hand the number of words the old man's spoken to me since he gave me the job. We're not arguing, but the silence is deafening."

"It'll get better," Carlos predicted. "Just give it time."

Carlos had always been an optimist, but Gabe had never wanted to believe him as much as he did tonight. "I hope so. I want things better between us before I leave again."

With a sly grin, Carlos reached for his soda. "I still want to know who says you have to leave?"

"You're full of it tonight, aren't you? You know as well as I do, I can't stay here."

"Why not?"

"And do what? Be a night watchman the rest of my life?"

"Your dad isn't going to keep you in some dead-end job forever. If you'd just make a commitment, he'd make you my boss in a month, maybe less."

"Now you're dreaming." Gabe tried not to let himself become irritated. "Nothing's changed since I left here the first time. I still feel the same way about what the old man does. It's globally irresponsible."

"Maybe so, but it's a godsend here in Libby. It pays my mortgage and puts food in my kids' mouths. That's all I care about."

They were on dangerous ground. Gabe returned the nail gun to its hook and tried to steer them back on course. "I didn't come here to dig up old arguments. The fact is, there's still nothing here for me."

"Except friends and family. Or aren't those important to you?"

The question cut. "Of course they are."

Carlos gave his head a shake. "No offense, but it's kind of hard to believe that, all things considered."

Heat rushed to Gabe's face. "I realize that," he said evenly, "and that's why I'm here—or did you miss that part?"

"I didn't miss it. But I didn't miss the past ten years either. All I'm saying is, it took a long time to get your life where it is, and you can't expect everything to change overnight. It may take a while for people to figure out they can trust you."

"Including Siddah, I'm sure."

Carlos stopped working and quirked one eyebrow. "I thought we weren't going to talk about Siddah."

"We're not. Not the way you want to, anyway. But Mom tells me that Bobby's been having a tough time since Peter died, and she thinks I can help him. I've spent a little time with him out at Mom and Dad's, but I don't think Siddah's very happy about it."

"Yeah? Well, that doesn't surprise me, either. She's great, don't misunderstand me. I like her a lot. But she's… Well, it's like she's always holding something back, you know?"

"Some people are more private than others."

Carlos shook his head thoughtfully. "Yeah, I know. But that's what I mean about her not being right for Peter. You can deal with that. I don't think he could have. I'll bet if they'd stayed together a few more years, things would have gone sour."

Feeling disloyal to his brother, Gabe hung the nail gun in its place and glared at his friend. "That's a helluva thing to say."

"It's just the truth."

"It's speculation. It's gossip. And it's ugly."

Still blissfully unconcerned, Carlos shrugged. "All right. Whatever you say. When you get to know her better, *then* you can tell me what you think."

Again, Gabe struggled to keep his irritation in check. "Why don't you just tell me what I came here to find out and forget about all that?"

Carlos's smile faded. "Okay. Sure. You want to know about Pete's accident?"

"Yeah. All I know is that it was an accident at work."

"That's right." Carlos looked away and mopped his face with one hand. "It was one of those things, you know? They happen. It's a dangerous business."

Between the equipment, wood dust, and exposure to other noxious elements, foresting was one of the most dangerous jobs around. That didn't make it any easier to hear. "Where was he?"

"Right in the yard. They were unloading a shipment of logs and something happened. Chains broke. Whatever. The whole load came off that truck." He stopped, letting Gabe fill in the rest on his own.

Bile rose in his throat, and his eyes burned. "Was anyone else hurt?"

"Bill Wiley ended up with a broken leg. Thatch Granger had a couple of crushed ribs and lost a finger. A couple of others were hurt, too. They all survived, though. But Pete…well, he was right there, front and center. No matter what anybody says, he never asked anybody to do anything he wasn't willing to do himself, and that included taking the risks."

Gabe swallowed around the lump of emotion in his throat. "And the old man? Where was he?"

"In the office, but he came running as soon as the shouting started." Carlos wiped the corner of his eye with the back of a hand. "I've never seen anything like it, and I hope I never see it again. He went crazy, Gabe. Threw himself on that pile of logs like he was going to pull every one of them off Pete himself. Took three guys just to restrain him. We were hoping Pete was still alive and we didn't want the logs to shift." He lifted his eyes and the sadness there almost matched the ache in Gabe's heart. "It was too late, though. The coroner said he died instantly."

Gabe knew he should find comfort in knowing that Peter hadn't suffered, but it would be a while before he could do that.

"I don't think things are going well at the mill," Carlos said after a few minutes. "One of the families filed a lawsuit. They eventually settled, but I think it cost your dad a sizable chunk."

"A lawsuit? For what?"

"Negligence is what I heard. Some people are claiming that Peter was careless."

"Peter? That's nuts. He was always a perfectionist."

"Yeah, but he was also into trying new things. He'd been reading trade magazines, doing research, talking about changing things around the mill..." Carlos shrugged and turned his attention back to his bike. "I don't know, man. Things have been quiet for a while, so maybe they're starting to forgive and forget."

Maybe. But something was bothering his dad, and Gabe wanted to know what it was.

He looked away out over the yard, at the kids shouting and laughing together, oblivious to the pain he felt and to the horrors of the world. He and Peter had been like that once. They'd been just as carefree and happy as Carlos's kids were now. Their biggest problem had been a scraped knee or a cut finger, and a little attention from their parents had fixed everything right up.

It had been a long time since Gabe had looked back on his childhood with longing, but since coming home it seemed that's all he did. He'd have given anything to turn back the clock, to undo the wrongs and make everything right again. But maybe there were some things that just couldn't be made right.

No! He refused to believe that. He knew the whole story now. The healing could begin. And, by damn, he intended to make sure it did. His family had grieved enough. They'd hurt enough. He wanted to see his mother smile again. God only knows if it was possible, but he'd love to hear the old man laugh.

As for what Carlos said about Siddah... Gabe made a silent vow to make sure that never became an issue in the family. She was his sister-in-law. That's all she'd ever be. It was for damn sure all he wanted her to be. And he wasn't about to let Carlos's stupid suggestion make him start feeling uncomfortable around her.

The next time he saw her, he'd treat her just as he'd treat a sister. And he'd do it again, and again, and again until it felt normal.

A WEEK LATER, Siddah still hadn't found a permanent sitter for Bobby, and she still wasn't sure how she felt about him spending so much time at Helene's. She had nothing to complain about, really. Every time she picked him up, Bobby seemed a bit more animated, a little more interested in the world around him. He even shared stories about things Gabe did and brilliant things Gabe had said as they drove back to town.

Slowly but surely, Bobby was crawling out of his depression, but why did it have to be Gabe who brought about the change? And why did she still have such trouble accepting Gabe's presence in their lives? Helene was changing before her eyes, too. She smiled more. Laughed sometimes. Siddah had even heard her singing as she approached the door at the end of the day. What kind of person was she to resent that? Not the kind of person she wanted to be, that was for sure.

Maybe she just hadn't had time to really deal with Gabe's return. She'd been buried with the new case at work, putting in long hours, even taking work home with her. She was short on sleep and even shorter on patience, and her protective instincts still warned her to keep Bobby from growing too close to Gabe. She just wasn't sure she could stop it from happening.

Since walking away from her aunt Suzette's house back in George's Creek, she'd thought of herself as strong and decisive. As a child with a child of her own, she'd had to be if she wanted to get anywhere. But Peter's death had opened her eyes. She'd lost something during her marriage. She'd started relying on Peter too much, letting him make decisions for both of them, and she'd put herself and her future in his hands.

Well, look where that had gotten her.

Devastated by the disloyal thought, she hitched her

purse onto her shoulder and pushed through the door into the office-supply store just down the street from the County Complex. Amanda, whose job it was to pick up the office supplies, had gone out of town for a wedding. Siddah, in a burst of enthusiasm to show what a team player she was, had volunteered to take care of the order while she was on her lunch break.

She had no idea whether this would help her cause or hurt it. Evan seemed pleased by her efforts so far, but she couldn't say the same for Chris. His lack of confidence in her only made her more determined to prove him wrong.

Stepping back into the late-summer afternoon, Siddah glanced up the street toward her favorite Mexican restaurant. She didn't often splurge. Money was just too tight. But maybe just this once, she could treat herself to a nice lunch—and some quiet time to think.

Just as she stepped onto the sidewalk, someone came around the corner too fast and directly into her path. Giving a shout of warning, Siddah tried to sidestep him and dropped one of the sacks she was holding.

The man's head came up and his hands shot out instinctively, gripping her arms and trying to propel her out of his way. Too late, Siddah recognized Gabe, and all coherent thought flew out of her head.

His expression went from irritation to shocked recognition. "Siddah?"

"Hello, Gabe."

"I'm sorry. I wasn't paying attention, I guess. Are you all right?"

She stepped away and bent to retrieve her bag, but

he moved at the same time and she met him halfway down. He looked into her eyes and something inside cracked wide open. She had the brief, crazy urge to lean forward and kiss him, but that was insane.

She straightened abruptly and tried to pull herself together. She was tired and overworked and responding to his resemblance to Peter, that's all. But it was hard not to notice the perfect fit of his jeans or the way his pale green shirt lightened his eyes.

"Sorry about that," Gabe said, grinning up at her as if the tension between them wasn't as thick as her grandmother's corn chowder. Straightening, he handed over the package and nodded toward the end of the block. "I should have been watching where I was going, but I had my sights set on the Mexican restaurant down the street."

Making sure their fingers didn't brush, Siddah took the package from him. "There's no harm done. I wasn't paying attention, either."

"So are you on your lunch break?"

"I—" The words caught in her throat, but that only made her angry with herself. She wasn't a child, and he *wasn't* Peter. "I am now," she said. "I had to pick up a few things for the office first."

"Well, that's perfect timing, then. Can I talk you into joining me?"

"For lunch?" Sit at a table with him? Alone? She shook her head quickly and backed a step away. "I don't think so. I really… I need to get back."

Gabe's brows creased. "I thought you said you were just starting your lunch break."

"Well, I did, but—" She cut herself off and tried to figure out a way to explain. She certainly couldn't be honest. If she told him about the crazy thoughts flying through her head, he'd probably hate her. "I just don't think having lunch together would be a good idea."

"Oh?"

She clutched at the only excuse she could think of. "There's no reason for it, is there? Peter's not around any longer, so it's not as if we need to pretend to like each other for his sake."

Gabe's smile never even faltered, but she could have sworn she saw the determination in his eyes grow stronger. "Peter's not around, but Bobby is and so are my parents. And how do you know you won't like me unless you give me a chance?"

How did she know what would happen if she did? Wanting desperately to keep a safe distance between them, she managed a cool smile. "How many chances do you think one person should get in life?"

He did a little aw-shucks thing with one shoulder and hooked his thumbs through his belt loops. "I guess maybe one more than I've already had."

Siddah didn't know whether to smile or swear at him.

And obviously he could tell. "Come on. I know you don't like me, but Bobby does. And don't you think he's worth giving me a chance—even knowing I don't deserve one?" When she didn't immediately agree, he touched her arm as if he intended to guide her. The shock of his touch burned her, but she wasn't the only one to pull away. She could have sworn he looked a little less sure of himself. "At least give me an hour. Get to know me a little before you decide I'm really not worth the powder it would take to blow me to hell."

She knew she should refuse. Really, she did. But behind the sparkle in his eyes there was something she couldn't read—something that reached right out and connected with the part of her that had once been frightened and uncertain.

"I only have forty-five minutes left," she said. "I'm scheduled to be in depositions this afternoon, so I can't be late."

Relief flashed across his face a split second before that smile returned. "We can set the alarm on my watch to make sure you get back on time. If after forty-five minutes you still think the worst, then at least I'll know I've tried. I'm not the complete waste of humanity my father would like you to believe I am."

It was hard not to be affected by his easy smile, his self-deprecating outlook, his easy acceptance of the bad things she'd heard. She let out a sigh and chewed one corner of her lip as she looked him over. "No lunch," she said firmly, "but I'll give you the rest of my lunch hour. We can walk. You can talk."

Gabe grinned like a kid with a new toy, and her heart did another little flip in her chest. If he did that very often, she thought with sinking heart, she was going to have a tough time keeping him at arm's length. But the longer she spent around him, the more convinced she was that keeping a safe distance between them was absolutely necessary.

CHAPTER SEVEN

THE FIRST FEW MINUTES were taken up with small talk as Siddah and Gabe strolled through Libby's streets. They talked about the town and how much it had changed, about the people and their hardy pioneer spirit. But eventually, those subjects ran dry and Gabe linked his hands behind his back and tackled the topic they'd both been avoiding. "So what do you want to know?"

"What do *I*—?" She laughed and tucked a stray lock of hair behind one ear. "You're the one who wanted to talk."

"You're worried about Bobby, right? Concerned about what kind of influence I'm having?"

"Well, yes, but—"

"So ask me what you want to know."

His directness surprised her, but she liked it. "Okay. Suppose you tell me what you're *really* doing back in Libby after all this time?"

He looked surprised. "I told you. I got Mom's letter, and I came as soon as I could."

"But why now? Why not last year? Two years ago? Why not while Peter was still alive?"

Gabe shrugged eloquently. "I wasn't sure I'd be welcome. I'm not sure I'm welcome now either, but losing Peter opened a door that had always been closed before."

"You closed that door when you left."

"I left because it was closed for me," he said, "or didn't anybody ever bother to tell you that?"

Was that true? Siddah felt certain she'd never heard that. Or had she just forgotten?

No, surely she would have remembered. "If that were true," she said firmly, "Peter would have told me."

Gabe's lips curved gently. "Peter and I didn't exactly have the same experiences growing up. We might have shared a father, but he was like two different men with us. Besides, if you know Peter at all, you know he had a hard time believing the worst of anybody."

If Siddah had been granted her wish for more children, would she have treated them differently? She liked to think not, but maybe that was just wishful thinking. She tried to ignore the perspiration snaking down her back, but maybe she should have said yes to an air-conditioned lunch, after all. "It's true about you, anyway. He never did stop believing that you'd come home someday."

"He probably never stopped believing that the old man didn't mean what he said the night I left, either. I always thought of that night as hell on earth. Peter probably thought everybody was just in a bad mood."

Siddah had always loved Peter's optimism, but surely he hadn't been that naive. "Are you serious? You left because Monty made you leave?"

Gabe stooped to pluck a blade of grass. "I left because the old man strongly suggested I get the hell out of his sight and never show my face to him again." He sent her a wry grin. "Apparently, I wasn't supposed to take him seriously. Who knew?"

"According to you, Peter did. And I'm sure he would have told you if you'd ever asked him."

Gabe rolled the blade of grass between his fingers for a long time. "I never said I was blameless," he said at last. "Just that I'm not the only one who owns some of the responsibility for what happened." He tossed the grass to the ground and stuffed his hands into his pockets. "So what else do you want to know?"

A thousand things and nothing, all at the same time. "Why don't you tell me where you were when Helene's letter reached you?"

"I was in Ecuador," he said. "A city called Riobamba. Before that, I was in the interior working with a tribe called the Zaparo. There are only a handful of them left on the planet, and I'm trying to help."

"And how do you help them?"

"We've helped them plant gardens, provided medical help to keep their children from dying young, showed them how to build structures that are safer for their children out of their own raw materials. We've taught them any number of things that we believe will improve their quality of life without changing their culture in any meaningful way."

His eyes lit when he talked, just the way Peter's had when he worked with wood. "Why do you do it?"

Gabe looked away at the mountains visible over the tops of the buildings. "I grew up in these hills," he said. "All my life, I heard stories about the Sioux, the Crow, the Blackfeet, the Nez Percé…dozens of tribes chased off their land, relocated to worthless places in the desert, even murdered because white men wanted what they had. I hated hearing the stories, and I wanted to change things." He shrugged eloquently. "It's a little late here, but it's not too late in other parts of the world."

"That sounds like a worthy ambition. Why does Monty object?"

"Because he thinks I'm siding with the enemy, I guess. His ancestors were part of the problem. They drove the natives from their land and then claimed it for themselves. The Kings have made their living off that land for generations and, until I came along, they were all proud of it."

"But surely that's not a reason to kick your son out of the house." She stopped walking and folded her arms across her chest. "I know Monty. He's not heartless."

"I told you I wasn't blameless," Gabe said. "One argument led to another. Things were said neither of us could ever take back. The arguments stopped being about what I wanted to do with my life and started becoming personal—on both sides. I said things I regret deeply. Things about my father, about his father…" He grinned. "By the end, I was saying some pretty harsh stuff about Kings all the way back to Adam, and I was saying it to anybody who'd listen. I went public, and that was unforgivable."

"But you're his son."

Gabe shook his head and stared down at the toes of his shoes. "You never met Grandpa King," he said after a long silence. "He died before you met Peter. But he was about a thousand times worse than the old man. Grandpa figured me for a bleeding heart the first time I said anything about how I felt. I was ten, just Bobby's age, when I heard the story of Chief Joseph and the Nez Percé for the first time. They were trying to escape the reservation by crossing into Canada but, of course, the government wouldn't just let them go. I never understood why they herded them back and forced them onto land on the other side of the continent. I never understood why they felt it so necessary to kill so many human beings who only wanted to hold on to their homeland. I still don't."

He took a deep breath and let it out slowly. "Anyway, Grandpa badgered the old man about it for a couple of years. Dad wasn't all that happy himself, but Grandpa really pushed him around the corner. After a while, Dad decided that Grandpa was right and I was wrong. Dad told me that a career in any other field was out of the question, and the war began."

"Peter described your grandfather as a completely different man."

"I'm not surprised, but Peter never bucked the system, either."

Siddah started walking again, slowly. "Peter always was more of a peacemaker than a rule breaker."

"And I was just the opposite," Gabe said, falling into step beside her. "Anyway, I promised myself that I'd spend my life giving people back their dignity and helping them keep their land. It was a little late to do anything here, but there were places in the world where a guy like me could make a difference, so that's where I went."

Though she'd never met Peter's grandfather, she knew how bullheaded Monty could be, and Gabe's story had the ring of truth to it. The urge to touch his arm in a gesture of comfort swept through Siddah, but she clenched her hands tightly and willed it to pass.

"So what happened the night you left?"

Gabe didn't answer immediately. When he did, his voice was low and soft. "I'd been away at the University of Montana in Missoula. The old man had been after me to change my major by offering to pay my tuition and books. Accepting his money might have made getting my education a little easier, but it would have locked me into a life I didn't want."

"So you turned him down."

"Yeah. I turned him down." Gabe's face twisted at some memory. "My grandfather went ballistic. Told the old man to give me an ultimatum. Either I had to shape up and do what he wanted, or he'd write me out of his will. What old Calvin never could understand was that the money meant nothing to me. Less than nothing."

"Why did it matter so much to them? Why couldn't he just let you make your own decisions? You were an adult, weren't you?"

"Yeah, I was. And the old man would probably have to answer that question. Calvin was from the old school, where a man was the king of his family, and the patriarch made the decisions for everyone. He saw nothing wrong with clear-cutting forests and destroying natural resources, as long as there was a profit in it. The old man went along with everything he did."

Siddah shook her head in confusion. "It's hard to imagine Monty being submissive to anyone."

"Yeah? Well, only to his father." Gabe watched a car drive past before he spoke again. "The whole thing came to a head when I found out they were planning to cut up on Smoky Ridge. A group of us had been trying to get that area protected by the government. Calvin decided to clear-cut before we could succeed. I drove home that weekend and confronted them. Told them I hated what they were doing and tried to get them to listen to reason. Neither one of them would listen to me. No surprise there. I guess I didn't listen to them, either—until Calvin told the old man that getting Mom pregnant with me was the biggest mistake the old man had ever made."

Siddah gasped in horror. "He *said* that? In front of you? What did Monty do?"

"He said he knew, but it was too late to undo the damage." Gabe tried to smile, but remembered pain twisted his features. "I said I'd rather be dead than related to either one of them, and the old man told me to get the hell out."

"Where was Helene during all of this?"

"She was there. Trying to get us all to stop. She tried to keep me from leaving, but I was too pissed. And hurt. This was the last place I wanted to be."

"And you went, just like that."

"Not exactly." The grin crept back into his eyes. "I'm leaving out all the screaming, shouting, swearing, name-calling and fighting. That's where the story gets boring."

Siddah stopped again, this time beneath the shade of a large oak tree. "Where did you go?"

"Back to Missoula for a while. Right after graduation, I drove out to Virginia and I never looked back."

She leaned against the tree trunk and thought back

over everything he'd just told her. "So Monty didn't always disagree with what you wanted?"

"Not always."

"Then there's hope that you really can reconcile with him?"

"I'm counting on it."

She wanted it for him. She wanted Monty to relent. She wanted Helene to completely forgive him. She wanted his family to heal, and she wanted to see him smile without the shadows of heartache in his eyes.

That realization brought her up short. Why did she care whether or not Gabe smiled? Why should she worry about the shadows in his eyes? She could feel things shifting around inside of her, whether she wanted them to or not. "Well, I wish you the best of luck."

"Thanks. And what about you? When are you going to make some changes and let yourself live again?"

Siddah drew back sharply. "My husband is dead."

"But you aren't, and neither is Bobby. You seem like a warm, caring and generous woman, Siddah, but you also seem a little lost. Don't you think Peter would like to see you move beyond the moment of his death?"

"I have moved."

"Not far." Gabe touched her shoulder before she could move away. "It's not just you, Siddah. My parents are the same way. I know you loved Peter. Everybody did. But don't you think he'd rather see you all enjoying life again?"

Siddah glared at him, but she waited to speak until a couple on the sidewalk had passed them. "You don't know what you're talking about," she said when they were alone again.

"I know my brother. I know how much he liked to laugh. I know how much he enjoyed life. Of the two of us, I was the serious one. So I know how much he'd hate seeing my mother so sad and my dad so angry. I'm sure he'd feel the same way about you and Bobby."

"We're trying," Siddah snapped. "Helene's already different since you've been back. But I can't just flip a switch on my feelings."

Gabe's expression remained kind. Too kind. "I'm not suggesting that you should. But you wouldn't be betraying Peter if you rejoined the human race."

Siddah opened her mouth to argue, but the words wouldn't come. Much as she hated what he said, there was a ring of truth to it. But he was the last person she wanted advice from, especially since she knew Peter would have told her the same thing.

She fought to hang on to her irritation, but she had missed Peter's optimistic outlook on life, and there was one small part of her that wanted to find pleasure in life again. She just didn't know if she could, and the thought of trying terrified her. Already, Peter's memory was fading, and the thought of losing him completely sent her into a panic. And more to the point, she was terrified of what she might feel if she stopped resenting Gabe. If he wasn't the family ogre, then who was he?

Siddah was afraid to answer that question.

By TWO-THIRTY the next afternoon, Siddah knew she was in trouble. Evan had assigned her to complete the revisions on a pleading that was due in court, along with courtesy copies for the judge, his clerk and opposing counsel, before five o'clock. It should have been easy. She'd modified a hundred pleadings just like it in the past year. But computer problems had thrown her behind schedule. Not only that, but the phone had been ringing off the hook all day, and Bobby had called no less than four times to share something he'd just done with Gabe.

As the clock inched toward three o'clock, Siddah polished off the last of the sandwich she'd eaten at her desk and tossed the garbage into the can at her feet. She saved the work she'd done so far to a disk and flipped to the next page, where Evan had scribbled between the lines and in the margins in such tiny handwriting she wondered if she'd be able to read it.

A shadow fell over her shoulder, and she looked up to find Evan scowling at the thick pile of unrevised pages still beside her keyboard. "How's it coming?"

"I'm getting there," she said, trying to sound confident. "I have the first section finished if you want to look it over."

Evan waved off the suggestion. "I would, but I'm out the door for that order-to-show-cause hearing. It shouldn't take long, though. Do you think I'll be able to look at the whole thing when I get back?"

"I hope so."

"Great. Just leave it on my desk." He started to turn away, but caught himself and turned back. "I almost forgot. Chris wants to go over a few things with you on the Whitman case. Three-thirty okay with you?"

After checking the wall clock, Siddah nodded. "If I don't have any more interruptions. Amanda's fielding my calls, so I should be fine."

"Do you need help with the revisions?"

Some assistance would be a lifesaver, but Siddah would never convince Evan and Chris that she deserved the promotion if she started passing off her work. Trying for another confident smile, she shook her head. "I'll have it done, Evan. Don't worry."

Evan had barely stepped through the door when the telephone on her desk rang again. Siddah thought about ignoring the call, but Amanda wouldn't have put it through without a good reason. Maybe it was Judge Allen's clerk returning the message she'd left earlier. Or opposing counsel on the Whitman case calling to schedule the first of their depositions.

She picked up the handset, propped it between her chin and shoulder, and turned back to her computer. "Evan Jacobs's office. How can I help you?"

"Guess what, Mom. Guess what me and Gabe did."

Call number five. Holding back a sigh, Siddah searched the document for the next revision she needed to make. "Can it wait, sweetheart? I'm in the middle of something important."

"But it's cool, Mom. You'll never guess."

"I can't right now, Bobby. You'll have to tell me later."

"Okay," he said, his voice small and quiet again. "Will you call me when you're done? I need to ask you something."

Guilt inched up Siddah's spine. "Sure, honey. But I

just found out that I'm supposed to be in a meeting at three-thirty, so if I can't call before that, I'll call right after, okay?"

"But you have to call before. I can't ask you if you don't, and after will be too late."

"Okay, then, why don't you just ask me now?"

"Are you sure?"

"I'm sure. What do you need?"

"Well, first I have to tell you what me and Gabe did."

This time, Siddah couldn't hold back her sigh of impatience. "Just ask the question, Bobby. I don't have time to listen to the story."

She regretted her harsh tone immediately. She regretted it even more when Bobby fell silent.

"Bobby? I'm sorry. I didn't mean—"

"It's okay, Mom. I'll just tell you later."

"No! Bobby..."

But the click in her ear told her she was too late. Feeling about an inch high, she found a dial tone and started to punch in Helene's number, but the sound of Chris's voice in the hall outside her door changed her mind. Evan didn't mind personal calls as long as she kept them to a minimum, but Chris wasn't so understanding. She'd have to wait until he went back into his office or left for court.

Forcing her attention to the job, she studied Evan's notes for a few seconds. When she was satisfied that she'd read them correctly, she began to type. Before she'd even finished the first sentence, the cursor froze in the middle of her screen and the computer made a sick, beeping sound.

Frozen again! She'd never finish at this rate.

Chewing her lip in frustration, she tried every trick she knew, but she couldn't get the computer working again, nor could she get the disk she'd been using to save an extra copy of her work out of its drive.

Finally, in desperation, she rebooted the computer and checked the pleading she'd saved to the hard drive. When the file opened without a glitch, she breathed a sigh of relief. But as she scanned down to where she'd left off, she realized that all the changes she'd made in the past half hour were gone. Holding back tears of frustration, she compared the document to the rough draft on her desk and finally located the last place where her changes had been saved. But as she began typing again, she hoped Bobby would understand why she wasn't able to call him.

And for the first time, she wondered if she was asking her son to pay too high a price for their security.

WITH ONLY A COUPLE of minutes to spare, Siddah printed a clean copy of the pleading, left it on Evan's desk and sprinted down the hall toward the conference room, where Chris was waiting for her. He sat at the long table, surrounded by thick file folders, stacks of documents and a library's worth of law books. His suit jacket lay over the back of a chair, and he'd rolled up his shirt-sleeves so he could dig in to work.

He looked up impatiently as she breezed into the room, his pale brows knit in consternation, his light eyes icy. Chris was a good attorney—bright, ambitious and honest—but as different from Evan in personality as a fence post from a tree. While Evan made a point of looking at the employees' family photos from time to time and even absorbing a few details about their personal lives, Chris made no secret of his disdain for individual touches within the office, and he resented every interruption caused by family and friends.

"I was beginning to think you weren't going to make it," he said, motioning Siddah toward an empty chair at the conference table. "Why don't you sit there? I've been sorting documents, and those are the ones I want you to start with."

Trying to catch her breath, Siddah slipped into the chair and pulled her pen from behind her ear. "What am I doing with them?"

"I want you to create a time line for the night of the stabbing. All the testimony we've gathered so far is there. I want to know where Asa Whitman was from the minute he got up that morning until the moment his wife and her friend were killed outside the Timberline. I've got a dozen witnesses who'll testify that he was at the bar shortly before the stabbings occurred. I've also got two women who are prepared to swear that he was with them across town when Cheryl Whitman and Dallas Trimbull were killed. I want to find a hole in their stories before the depositions."

Nodding, Siddah pulled the stack of documents toward her. "I can do that. When do you need it?"

"By morning. If there's so much as five minutes unaccounted for, I want to know about it."

By morning? Bobby would never understand this. Siddah kept a smile on her face and hoped the stack wasn't as large and confusing as it looked. "Anything else?"

"Not at the moment."

Chris turned his attention to another file folder on the table, but Siddah decided to take advantage of this rare moment alone. "I wanted to thank you for considering me for the paralegal position. I appreciate the chance more than you'll ever know."

He frowned up at her as if she'd spoken gibberish, and it seemed to take him a few seconds to process what she'd said. "I guess we'll find out if the job's too much for you, won't we?" Gesturing toward a sort stack of manila file folders, he shifted subjects without taking a breath. "When you finish with the time line, I want you to go over the police reports until you know them as well as you know your own name."

"Tonight?"

"I have a meeting with defense counsel in the morning. Is there a problem?"

Siddah's heart dropped, but she shook her head quickly. "No. That's fine. You want the time line first?"

"I do. I spoke with both women yesterday," he said, still focused on what he was doing. "I'm convinced they're lying, but I couldn't get anywhere with either of them."

Nervous sweat moistened her fingers, but she resisted the urge to wipe her hands on her pant legs. "Maybe someone else should try." At Chris's sharp look, she added quickly, "You know how sometimes people respond to one person and not another?"

His lips thinned. "I know how to do my job, Siddah."

"I know you do. That's not what I meant. I only thought—"

"Well don't, okay?" Chris tossed something onto the

table and planted his hands on his hips. "Evan might think you're right for the paralegal position, but I don't."

Gasping as if he'd punched her in the stomach, Siddah tried not to let him see that he'd just devastated her. "May I ask why?"

"Do you need to?" When she didn't say no, he launched into a list, ticking off points on his fingers as he spoke. "You're a single mother. You're doing the work of two people at home already. You're a recent widow, and I don't care what you say, you're not ready for a job this demanding."

"Don't you think I would know if I'm ready or not?"

"No. Frankly, I don't. And I haven't even gotten to the most important strike against you. Your son."

Siddah sat up sharply. "How do you consider my son a strike against me? You have children, and so does Evan."

"Yes, but neither of us is a single parent, and Evan's children are grown."

"No matter who you put into the paralegal position, they're bound to have a life," she argued. "Mine might be different from yours, but that's no reason why it should work against me."

"It has nothing to do with your life," Chris said with infuriating calm. "It's just a question of the time and attention you can give to the office and our caseload. Your life requires too much of your focus, Siddah. Surely, you aren't going to deny that."

No, but she sure wasn't going to admit it. If she did, she could kiss the promotion, and her chance to pay off Peter's debts goodbye. "I do deny it," she said, hating how weak she sounded and trying to conceal the fear and anger in her voice. "Yes, I occasionally take a break to talk to my son, but any good parent would do that. And yes, maybe being a single parent does require a lot from me, but I'm still capable of doing the job."

Chris shrugged and turned back to his work. "We'll see. Evan wants to give you the chance, and so we are. I just thought you should know where I'm coming from, that's all. If you can prove me wrong, I'm sure the job will be yours."

Still shaking, Siddah pulled the stack of files he'd assigned her and began reading. But she couldn't make sense of the words swimming on the page in front of her. The realization that Chris felt so strongly against giving her the job rolled around with the thought of Bobby waiting for her call. He'd be growing more disillusioned and hurt as the minutes ticked past, and knowing that made it hard to concentrate.

What if she couldn't prove Chris wrong? What if she couldn't save the house and get the growing stream of creditors off her back? What if she couldn't give Bobby a better life than the one she'd had? The need to escape her life had driven Siddah to make some desperate choices. She didn't want that for Bobby. But would she be able to prevent it?

CHAPTER EIGHT

JUST AFTER SUNRISE, Gabe stood, stretched and opened the door of the guard shack to let in the morning. He'd passed another uneventful night at the sawmill with nothing but newspapers, a good book and his own thoughts to get him through. He sure hoped Carlos was right and Monty would move him into another position soon. Something that required the use of his brain might be nice.

He wasn't going to hold his breath, though. He'd been back in Libby for nearly two weeks now, but he had yet to hear a good word out of the old man, or get more than a dip of the head when Monty drove through the gates in the morning.

But Gabe wasn't going to quit trying.

As he did every morning, he put coffee on to brew and strolled around the mill's yard to make sure everything was secure. He walked slowly, taking his time and relishing the cool breeze that blew into the valley from the canyons. Two weeks of breathing clear, dry air had made a little difference in his physical health—at least he thought it had. He hadn't had a recurrence of the fever in days, and last night he'd made one complete circuit of the mill's perimeter without getting winded.

On the mountaintops, the rising sun draped a golden

web across the treetops, and Gabe realized again how much he'd missed this valley. He'd have to make it a point to get back here more often. If he was honest with himself, he'd admit that it wasn't just the scenery that made him want to come back. He found himself looking forward to the hours he spent with Bobby, and he couldn't deny the rush of anticipation he felt in the evenings when Siddah came to pick the boy up.

He finished his circuit just as the coffee finished dripping, and he carried a steaming mug into the warming sunshine to wait. Just like clockwork, the old man's truck rolled into view a few minutes past six-thirty and Gabe unlocked the gate to let him into the yard.

As he had every morning, Monty gave the barest dip of his head to acknowledge Gabe's presence, then turned his eyes straight ahead and drove toward the office. Knowing that the morning crew would start arriving soon, Gabe secured the gates open. But instead of heading back to the guard shack as he usually did, this morning he strode toward the office.

He'd been cooling his heels for a week now. Biding his time. Waiting for the old man to get used to having him around. But he couldn't wait much longer or Monty would read his silence as weakness.

Gabe left his cup on the ground near the door and let himself inside. Joan hadn't arrived yet, so Gabe hurried past her desk and into his father's office. He found the old man sitting, eyes closed, hands linked together on top of a stack of paperwork. The sadness that had become so much a part of his expression seemed even heavier this morning.

Suddenly uncertain, Gabe knocked softly. "Do you have a minute?"

The old man's eyes flew open, the sadness disappeared, and the rigidness that seemed reserved for Gabe replaced it. "You got a problem?"

"Not exactly." Gabe stepped inside then nodded toward an empty chair. "I'd just like to talk to you."

"What about?"

"Peter."

A mask of anger covered Monty's face. "No."

"Why not? We're going to have to talk about him sometime."

"I don't see why."

"Because he's standing right here in between us, and we're never going to resolve anything until we do."

Monty stood abruptly. "Peter was never the cause of our problems."

"I didn't mean to imply that he was. But you're still angry with me for not coming home sooner. Until we can get past that, we can't even begin to work on the rest." Gabe took a few steps into the office, moving closer to his father's desk. "Carlos told me what happened the day of the accident. Why didn't you tell me that other people had been injured?"

"Why should I? It's not as if it's anything to do with you."

Gabe didn't want to argue that point right now, so he ignored it. "How did it happen?"

"How does any accident happen? Something went wrong."

"Was it human or machine error?"

Monty assumed a look of irritation. "Why do you want to know?"

"Because my brother was killed and other people were hurt," Gabe said, purposely keeping his voice low and even. "And because you and mom are obviously still deeply affected by it."

"Well, don't let it worry you. We'll get over it."

"Will you?"

"Sure. Why not?" Monty returned to his desk and shoved a stack of paperwork out of his way. "Let it rest, boy. Your mother may believe this act of yours, but I don't."

"It's not an act."

A smirk crossed his father's face. "Really? You're ready to stay home? Step into the business and take over where Peter left off? You're going to stick around, be an uncle to that boy, a son to your mother?"

"I never said I was here to stay."

"Then we have nothing to talk about."

"Why? Because *you* say we don't?"

Shoving away from the desk, Monty glowered across its expanse. "I'm not talking about this with you."

"Why not?"

He jammed his chair under the desk so hard, a stack of papers slid onto the floor. He ignored it and started toward the door.

In frustration, Gabe went after him. "What's your problem, anyway? You're acting like you have something to hide."

His father's step faltered. He recovered quickly, but not before Gabe noticed his hesitation.

"Is that it? You're hiding something?" Gabe grabbed his father's arm and pulled him around to face him. "What's going on around here? Why are you suddenly drinking in the middle of the day? What's going on with Mom? I want to know."

"It's none of your damn business."

"The hell it's not."

Jerking away, Monty wrenched open the outside door. "Drop it, Gabe."

"I can't."

"I don't see why not," Monty said as he started down the stairs. "You were able to forget about us before."

"I never forgot," Gabe shouted after him. "I just didn't come back because I was afraid you'd do this. And I was right." He took the stairs two at a time behind his father. "You're so eager to lay the blame for this at my feet. Why don't you look at your own part in it? Maybe if you didn't treat me like some kind of leper, I'd want to come around more often."

Monty reached the bottom of the steps, but he didn't turn around. He didn't stop walking. Didn't even acknowledge that Gabe had spoken.

In frustration, Gabe slammed his hand against the metal stair rail. Pain shot through his hand and up his arm, but he barely noticed it. He set off toward the parking lot where he'd left the Jeep, wondering if he was on a fool's mission. Maybe the fever had scrambled his brain. Why had he ever thought he could get the old man to accept him just because Peter was gone?

IT WAS LABOR DAY WEEKEND before Siddah could carve a few minutes from her schedule to take Bobby school shopping. After dragging herself out of bed on Saturday morning, she nursed a cup of coffee, threw together a quick breakfast and ran a batch of laundry so she and Bobby would have clean jeans to wear.

Last night's dishes sat on the counter, waiting for her to wash them, and a huge stack of newspapers teetered in the corner, reminding her that she hadn't been to the recycling drop-off in far too long.

The past couple of weeks had left her so exhausted she would have preferred to stay at home in her pajamas all day, but school would be starting on Tuesday, and she already felt guilty enough about making Bobby wait. With the holiday weekend stretching out in front of them and three days off in a row, she planned to make up for her recent lack of attention.

Yawning hard enough to bring tears to her eyes, Siddah stepped over a pair of shoes Bobby had left in the living room and scooped up an empty candy wrapper from the couch. Hard as it was to admit, she wasn't handling the extra responsibility at the office well.

By midmorning, she and Bobby were on their way to the Ben Franklin store. Bobby sat ramrod straight, staring out at the town as they passed. Temperatures had soared for the past week, and today's forecast called for a high in the upper nineties—unusually hot weather for Montana in September. The heat only added to Siddah's fatigue.

She had to circle the block twice before she found a parking space. She stifled another yawn as she followed Bobby along the shaded sidewalk. When they reached the Ben Franklin, he stopped with his hand on the door and looked back with obvious impatience. "Come *on*, Mom. How come you're so slow?"

She grinned at her eager young son. "I'm slow because I'm not the one getting new clothes, I guess. How come you're in such a hurry?"

Bobby pulled the door and held it open with his back while she stepped inside. "I want to get to Grandma's before Gabe leaves. He said he'd wait for me, but maybe he won't."

"But honey, you're not going to Grandma's today," Siddah reminded him. "It's Saturday. Our day to spend together."

"But Gabe said he'd show me the spot where him and Dad used to go fishing."

"Can't he show you on Tuesday?"

"No, because on Tuesday I go to school."

"But I'm off work today," Siddah pointed out. "I was hoping that we could spend the day together."

Bobby sidled past a display of school supplies and turned toward the clothing department. "We still can. You can talk to Grandma and Grandpa while Gabe and me go fishing."

"That's not exactly together is it? Besides, I had other things planned for us today."

His freckled nose scrunched in concentration. "Like what?"

"Well…like shopping for school clothes and then having a special lunch together." Even as she talked, she knew her plans couldn't hold a candle to time with Gabe and a secret fishing hole. And the expression on Bobby's face let her know that she was right. "I even thought we could stop by and watch a peewee football game," she said, hopefully. "The Falcons are playing this afternoon."

Bobby's expression went suddenly flat. "I don't care."

The fact that he responded at all gave her hope. "But the Falcons are your team."

"Not anymore."

"They could be again, you know. Coach said you could come back anytime."

Bobby lifted his shoulder in the old, lifeless shrug that had all but disappeared since Gabe came to town. "I don't want to."

"You might like it if you'd just give it a try. It's been a while. You've probably forgotten how much fun you had on the team."

"I haven't forgotten."

"Well, then, why don't we check out the game? Maybe if you see the other kids—"

Bobby rounded on her, his eyes flashing, his mouth twisted with emotion. "I don't *want* to play football, Mom. I keep telling you that, but you won't listen to me."

Shocked by his outburst, Siddah drew him to one side of the aisle. "I do listen to you, Bobby. But you've always loved football, so it's a little hard for me to believe that you suddenly don't like it at all."

"I'm not lying."

"I never said you were," she assured him quickly. "Maybe it would help if you'd tell me *why* you don't like it."

Something flickered in his eyes, but it disappeared too quickly for her to read it. "I just don't."

"All of a sudden?"

"No."

"So you were only pretending to like it before?"

"No." He shifted his weight from one leg to the other and focused on his hands as if he suddenly found them fascinating. "But I don't like it now. I'd rather go fishing with Uncle Gabe."

Siddah didn't want to do or say the wrong thing and send him into a back slide, so she swallowed her personal disappointment and sent him a cheery smile. "Okay, then, if that's what you want, that's what we'll do. But let's get your school clothes first, okay?"

The relief on his face was palpable. "Sure. How many shirts do I get?"

With her hand on his shoulder, Siddah started walking again. "That will depend on whether or not we can find a sale."

"And if we can?"

"Then it will depend on how good the sale is." She tried to regain her earlier optimism, but she didn't believe for a minute that Bobby had suddenly discovered a dislike for the game or for his team. So what was going on with him? And why wouldn't he tell her what it was?

She wondered if Gabe knew, and hated the flash of envy that tore through her when she thought he might. This wasn't about her, she told herself firmly. This was about Bobby. Besides, she was almost positive Gabe would have told her if he knew. And whether she liked it or not, Gabe was the person most likely to bring her son back to her.

A FEW HOURS LATER, Siddah pulled off the highway onto the lane that led to her in-laws' house. On the seat beside her, Bobby leaned forward, straining against his seat belt in his eagerness to get there.

"I hope Gabe's still there," he said. "I hope he hasn't gone without me."

The look on his face and the eagerness in his voice both pleased and frightened her. What if he invested too much in this new relationship with Gabe? Siddah knew how it felt to be left behind, and she didn't want that for her son. "He's still there," she assured him. "I called while you were in the dressing room trying on jeans."

"And he said he'd wait for me?"

"He said he'd wait." Working up a smile, she lowered the visor to block the sun. "You like Gabe a lot, don't you?"

"Sure. He's cool. You should come with us sometime, Mom. I'll bet Gabe could even teach you how to fish."

Siddah laughed and shook her head. "I think I'll pass. Fishing isn't really my thing."

"I'll bet you'd like it the way Gabe fishes. You could sit on a rock or something and read. That's what Grandma used to do when she went with him and Dad."

"Did she?" Siddah didn't remember Peter ever talking about that. "I might enjoy the reading part," she admitted, "but I'm not sure about the sitting on a rock bit—unless the rock is cushioned."

"Rocks don't come with cushions," Bobby said, his little face serious. "But I'll bet you could bring one with you."

"If I ever decide to go fishing with you and Gabe, I'll definitely do that." The house came into view between the trees, and Siddah slowed the car slightly. "I'm really glad you like Gabe," she said, "but you do know that he's going to be leaving again, right?"

"Someday, probably. But he'll come back to visit. He said so."

"Did he?" Could they count on that promise? Or would he forget once he got out there in the world again? "Well, I hope he does," she said, keeping her voice carefully even, "but he's a busy man with important things to do. He might not have a lot of time for us once he gets back to work."

Bobby's smile evaporated. "Yes he will. He's not gonna forget about me. He told me so."

"I never said he'd forget," Siddah assured him. "Just that…well, he might get busy and he might not be able to get back here very often."

"Nope." Bobby shook his head firmly and lifted his chin defiantly. "That's not going to happen. He promised."

"People make promises all the time," Siddah warned as she parked and turned off the engine. "They don't mean anything."

"Maybe not to you," Bobby said, his voice strangely quiet, "but they do to some people. Not everybody likes their work best."

Siddah sucked in a stunned breath. "Is that what you think? That I like my work more than you?"

"Well, don't you?"

"No! I'm only working so many hours to make things better for us. I don't want you to do without."

"Without what?"

"New school clothes, for one thing. Food on the table

and a roof over your head for another. Those things don't just happen by magic, you know."

"But you didn't used to work."

"I didn't have to when Daddy was alive." But her dreams of staying home and being the mother she'd always wanted for herself had been lost with everything else.

Bobby sent her a sidelong glance. "So are you gonna work from now on?"

"I think I'm going to have to. But we're adjusting, aren't we?"

Bobby nodded, but Siddah could tell that he wasn't convinced.

"It's going to be okay," she assured him. "Things will settle down at work, and we'll get used to our new schedule. We'll catch up at home, and pretty soon this will feel like it's the way life is supposed to be."

"But I don't want life to be like this," Bobby lashed out. "I don't like it when you go to work all the time. I want it to be the way it was before."

"I understand that," Siddah said evenly, "but sometimes things change and there's nothing we can do about it. I felt the same way you do when my mama died and I had to go live with my aunt." She unbuckled her seat belt and reached for Bobby's hand. "She didn't really want me there and I was miserable, but I couldn't change it. And I can't change this. We're just going to have to get used to it."

He jerked away from her as if she'd hurt him. "Well, I don't want to. I want you to be home. You're no fun anymore." Before she could stop him, he threw open the door and staggered out into the clearing.

She scrambled to catch him, but he'd slammed through the screen door into the kitchen before she was even halfway across the yard. Tears burned her eyes and she couldn't get her breath. Turning away, she wrapped her arms around herself and fought for control before she went inside. She didn't want Gabe and Helene to see her like this. If Monty and Helene knew that she and Bobby were struggling, they'd pressure her to quit her job. Exhausted as she was, she didn't know if she could resist. But exhaustion was only temporary. The shame of accepting handouts lasted a whole lot longer.

Behind her, the screen door closed quietly, and she turned, hoping that Bobby had come back outside. Instead, she found Gabe watching her from the shaded porch, his eyes narrowed, his expression kind. He jerked his head toward the house and stepped off the porch. "What's wrong with Bobby?"

"He didn't tell you?"

Gabe shook his head and closed the distance between them. "He didn't have time. He just went flying through the kitchen and upstairs to Peter's old room."

The stress of the past few weeks must be getting to her, because she couldn't seem to stop the trembling of her hands. Nor could she stop herself from responding to the worry in his eyes. She didn't want him to worry about her.

Clasping her hands together tightly, she tried to smile. "Maybe you should go talk to him."

"Mom's doing that. I came to see if you were okay."

She should have known she wouldn't be able to keep Helene from finding out. The urge to fling herself into Gabe's arms hit Siddah sharply. Probably because he was too close. Invading her personal space. Looking calm and reasonable and concerned.

She pulled away to put some distance between them. "Of course I am. Why wouldn't I be?"

"Bobby's upset. You're standing in the yard crying. Let's just call it a hunch."

A reluctant smile tugged at her lips, but his sense of humor only made him more attractive, not less. For safety's sake, Siddah took another step away. "I'm not crying. Not really. I'm just frustrated. Tired. Over-whelmed. And you're not helping."

"Me? What have I done?"

Unbidden, Bobby's last accusation raced through her mind. No fun. Was Gabe right? Had she locked herself in the moment of Peter's death? Was she letting life pass her by? Without warning, the urge to smile and laugh, to wake in the morning filled with anticipation instead of dread rose up within her.

"It's not you," she admitted with a sigh. "It's me. He tells me I'm no fun anymore."

"Ouch."

She laughed softly. "Yeah. Ouch. You, on the other hand, are all kinds of fun."

"Do you want me to stop? Turn into some kind of jerk?"

She laughed again and shook her head. "No, of course not. Bobby wants me to quit working and stay home with him. I guess so I can take him to secret fish-ing holes and teach him how to split firewood. But that's just not going to happen. It can't."

"So you have to work," Gabe said with a shrug. "That doesn't mean you can't still have fun with him."

"Right now it does. The only way I can get this promotion is by putting in long hours. That doesn't leave a lot of time for fun."

"Maybe this isn't the best time to go after the promotion."

The muscles in Siddah's neck tightened. "I know you mean well," she said, "but you just don't understand. The world is filled with families who are barely getting by on two incomes. We're living on one. I have to get that promotion. It's the only way we're going to survive."

The confession surprised her as much as it seemed to surprise him. "That's a bit drastic, isn't it?"

She could have kicked herself for admitting so much aloud, but Bobby's accusations had unsettled her and the urge to unburden herself was too strong to resist. "The situation *is* drastic," she said. "I'm in debt up to my eyeballs. Unless we find a miracle, we'll be lucky to hang on to the house."

Gabe glanced back at the house and lowered his voice. "Do Mom and Dad know about this?"

Siddah shook her head firmly. "No, and I don't want them to. They're so kind. So generous. But I can't let them support us."

"They wouldn't see it as a burden," Gabe said gently. "You're family."

"I won't let Bobby grow up feeling like a charity case."

"That's better than letting him end up homeless, isn't it? Do you mind me asking where this debt comes from?"

Siddah hesitated, but she'd gone this far already and sharing the worry with someone else actually made her feel a little better. "Peter took out some loans before he died, but your parents don't know, and I don't want them to."

Gabe dipped his head. "Will you be able to repay them?"

"I've put his life insurance toward some of it, and if I can get this raise, I'll be able to pay off the balance in time."

"With all that on your shoulders, it's no wonder you forget to have fun. So you're looking for more money. Is that all?"

He seemed so nonchalant about the disaster that had her in knots, she felt herself smiling. "You want the whole list?"

"Why not? What are friends for?"

Friends. She liked the sound of that. "School is starting on Tuesday morning, and I still don't have a permanent baby-sitter."

"What are you going to do about that one?"

She liked that he didn't try to solve the problems for her. "I don't know. Look harder, I guess. Pray that I can think of someone I haven't thought of before."

"What about Mom? I know she's enjoyed having Bobby around the past few days. Maybe she'd be willing to keep watching him."

Siddah shook her head firmly. "She's been great. She always is. But I don't want to take advantage of her."

"Bobby's her grandson. I don't think she'd feel taken advantage of."

"Not at first," Siddah agreed. "But having a ten-year-old around isn't easy. Helene has already raised her family. She deserves to live her own life. Besides, she already does way too much for us."

"So your biggest worry is that you're going to take advantage of someone."

"I've been in that position before," Siddah said, forcing herself to look away. "I've seen the desire to help turn into annoyance and resentment. I've heard the things people say when they start feeling as if they're being used. Helene and Monty are the only family I have. I couldn't bear to lose them that way."

"I don't think that would happen with Mom, but even if you don't want to let Mom baby-sit permanently, it might at least buy you some time."

"Yes, it might. But—" She broke off and shook her head again. "It's an alternative if I can't find anything else," she said, "but that would mean asking Helene to run to town twice a day to drop Bobby at school and then pick him up again. It may not seem far when you make the trip now and then, but two round-trips into town would mean a hundred miles every day. I'm afraid that would get real old, real fast."

"Okay then, what about friends?"

"I've already tried everyone I know, but things have been tough around here for the past few years. It seems that everyone's doing what they can to get by. There are very few mothers staying home with their kids these days."

Nodding, Gabe looked out at the tops of the trees that towered behind the house. "There's one more alternative," he said after a long silence.

"And that is?"

"Me."

"You?"

He shrugged casually. "My shift at the mill doesn't start until eleven. Once Bobby is at the school, you don't need a sitter until what? Three? Four?"

"Three-thirty."

"I get off work at seven every morning. I'll come home to grab a few hours' sleep, then head back to town and stay with Bobby until you get home. No running back and forth, no money out of your pocket."

Siddah gaped at him. "You can't be serious."

"Sure I can."

"You're offering to be my baby-sitter."

He pretended to think for a moment, then nodded. "I'm pretty sure that's what I just said."

"That's not a whole lot different than asking your mother."

"Sure it is. For one thing, you've already agreed to let me spend time with Bobby. He's a great kid, Siddah. I like being around him. For another, I already have to drive to town every day for work, and I'm not as busy as you are. Not even close. I can easily make sure that Bobby gets out here to see Mom once or twice a week, and that would make them both happy. And last but not least, I *need* to do something good for somebody, so there's no way you could take advantage of me."

He was so much nicer than she'd expected him to be. So generous and warmhearted. His smile lit something soft inside of her. It had been such a long time since she'd felt anything like this, she spent a few seconds enjoying it.

"That's a good argument," she said at last, "but I don't want to have this same problem again in a month."

"I told you, I'll be here for six."

She stopped walking and waited until he turned back to face him. "What if you change your mind?"

"What if I promise on my honor—and I *do* have some—that I won't do that? I'll stay here for six months, at least."

"Are you serious?"

"Absolutely." He shrugged and touched her arm almost shyly. "Come on. Give me a shot. What do you have to lose?"

Looking into his eyes in that moment, Siddah realized that she had far more to lose than she wanted to think about. She stared at him for a long time, weighing her options. "I can't believe I'm even considering this."

"Once again, that makes two of us. I've gotta be honest with you. This didn't even make it onto the short list of things I thought I'd be saying to you today. But you need help, and I'm here. What do you say?"

"You *swear* you'll stick around for six months?"

He held up a hand. "As God is my witness."

"And you'll be careful with Bobby?"

"If you look up 'careful' in the dictionary, there'll be my picture."

It had been a long time since she'd wanted to believe anything so much. "Will you help me try to find out why he won't play football? He's come alive again since he met you, but he still won't consider going back to the team. I'm worried that something else is bothering him, but he won't talk to me about it."

"I'll do what I can."

She couldn't ask for more than that, but it still seemed

like such a risk. Not just for Bobby, but for herself. Having Gabe in her house? Coming home at the end of each day to find him there? Could she handle that?

What a question! Of course she could. It wasn't as if she *felt* anything for him. At least, that's what she told herself. "All right," she conceded at last. "I guess it'll work. I know it's what Peter would have wanted me to do. But if you let me down—"

"That's not going to happen," Gabe said again. "I promise."

I promise. Siddah's smile faded and some of her earlier anxiety returned. He seemed sincere, but she'd been on the receiving end of too many broken promises in her lifetime. And this promise was perhaps the most important of all.

CHAPTER NINE

SIDDAH CAME INTO the kitchen a few minutes later. She'd watched Gabe and Bobby set off toward the river, fishing poles slung over their shoulders. It had been nearly two years since she'd seen Bobby so excited about anything, and her heart had melted a little as she'd watched him skipping to match Gabe's stride, chattering eagerly as they disappeared into the trees. No matter what else Gabe did, she'd always have a soft spot in her heart for the changes he'd brought about in Bobby.

"They're off?" Helene asked.

Siddah nodded. *Like two peas in a pod.* "How far away is this secret fishing hole?"

"Not far. Half a mile, maybe." Helene put something away in a cupboard and turned back with a sigh. "Siddah, sweetheart, I'm so glad you decided to come out and spend the day. Monty's gone to the mill for a little while, so that will give the two of us time to chat without him. And I do hope you and Bobby will stay for supper. I'd so very much like to have the whole family together."

How could Siddah say no to that? Or to the expression of hope on Helene's face? The air was filled with the rich aroma of a beef roast slowly cooking in the Crock-Pot, and the pile of new potatoes on the counter waiting for parsley, butter and garlic completed the picture. It had been too long since she'd had one of Helene's home-cooked meals. Too long since she'd had time to do more than stir together a few canned ingredients for supper at her own house. Besides, maybe Ivy was right. Maybe Siddah had been pushing Helene and Monty away.

"I'd love to, and I don't have to ask what Bobby would want." Siddah tossed her purse and keys onto the table. "What can I do to help?"

"Absolutely nothing." Helene waved her toward a chair. "You've been working too hard lately, and I'm just glad to have a little female company. So sit and talk. There's iced tea in the fridge if you're interested, and a couple of cinnamon rolls left from breakfast."

Siddah was still comfortably full, but she filled two glasses with tea and carried both to the table. "I haven't thanked you yet for suggesting that Gabe spend time with Bobby. I'll admit I wasn't convinced in the beginning, but Bobby seems to be responding to him."

"He does, doesn't he? And Gabe seems to be responding to Bobby, as well."

"I guess he is. Gabe has just offered to baby-sit Bobby after school."

Helene turned to look at her. "Did he? When did that happen?"

"Just a few minutes ago." Siddah pushed at a piece of ice in her glass with one finger. "I said yes."

Helene sat across from her. "You look uncertain. You don't think it's a good idea?"

"I don't know." She glanced out the screen door toward the spot where Gabe and Bobby had disappeared into the forest. "I'd feel better if things moved a little more slowly, I guess. But their relationship seems to be taking on a life of its own."

"That happens when Gabe is around. He's always had a knack for knowing what he wants and making sure he gets it."

"And what does he want now?"

Helene shrugged. "I think he really does want to make amends for the past."

"Bobby's not part of that."

"But of course he is." Helene smiled sadly. "It's only natural that he should do what he can for his brother's family."

"I suppose so," Siddah said, "but it was your idea that he spend time with Bobby, not his."

Helene waved off the suggestion with one hand. "Maybe technically, but Gabe would have gotten there by himself. I just prodded him to get there a little sooner. And what does it matter whose idea it was? This friendship between Bobby and Gabe is real and right. You can see that, can't you?"

Siddah nodded slowly. "As long as Bobby isn't hurt when it's over."

"Who says it's going to be over?"

"I didn't mean that," Siddah said quickly. "I only meant when Gabe leaves to go back to his real life. He won't stay here forever, you know."

"I suppose not, but you can't blame a mother for hoping." Helene took a long drink of her iced tea and shifted gears. "Bobby's doing fine. It's you I'm worried about."

"Me? Why me?"

"You're working yourself too hard. You're exhausted all the time and you're never home. That can't be good for you or for Bobby."

"It's temporary," Siddah said. "It won't last forever."

"Really? If you're having to put all this time in now, won't that continue once you get the promotion?"

"I'm sure I'll have to work longer hours than I did before," Siddah said, "but we'll eventually settle into a routine, and then everything will be fine."

Sitting back in her chair, Helene searched Siddah's face. "I know how much you want to believe that, but do you believe it really?"

"Of course I do. I wouldn't say it if I didn't."

"You could solve all of these problems if you just accepted our offer. You could stay home. Be there when Bobby needs you—"

"No!" Siddah realized how sharp her voice sounded and tried to soften it. "You know how I feel about that, Helene. I appreciate the offer, but I can't take charity."

"It's not charity, it's help. We're family, Siddah. Monty and I want the best for both you and Bobby."

"I know you do. I just wish you could understand that doing for ourselves *is* what's best. I can't teach Bobby to have self-respect if we take handouts. And you know how important security is to me."

"Yes I do, but you don't really have it now."

"Maybe not, but there's *no* security in relying on other people."

"We're not other people, Siddah. We're family. We'll make sure you have everything you need."

"And if something happens to you? If the mill closes? If your money disappears?" Siddah shook her head firmly. "I have to be able to rely on myself, Helene. Otherwise, it could all be snatched away."

Her mother-in-law smiled gently. "You're so stubborn."

"Maybe, but I don't think I'm the only one in this family that term could apply to."

"Well, you're right about that," Helene admitted with a laugh. Her smile faded almost at once, and she drummed her fingers on the table. "Stubborn pride has cost this family a heavy price over the years. I don't want to see you making the same mistakes."

"The same mistakes as Monty and Gabe? I don't think that's going to happen."

"Oh, I don't mean the very same mistakes, but you're a lot like Gabe, you know."

Siddah nearly choked on her tea. "I don't think that's true."

"You don't see it?"

"Not at all."

"Siddah, honey, you left Arkansas on a bus with an infant and only a little cash in your pocket. You decided to carve out a life for yourself and your son, and you've done that. Peter could never have done something like that, but Gabe..." Helene smiled and shook her head. "It's very much like what Gabe did when he left here."

Stung by the unfair judgment against Peter, Siddah

said, "I think you're wrong. Peter could have done the same thing if he'd wanted to."

Helene shook her head. "He wasn't like Gabe. Gabe and Monty have been at loggerheads since Gabe was young. Peter somehow always knew what Monty wanted, and he was always able to give it to him. Gabe couldn't, or wouldn't."

"Peter didn't go into the business just because Monty wanted him to," Siddah protested. "He worked at the mill because he loved it."

"He loved working with wood," Helene said. "And he loved his father. But I'm not convinced that he loved the sawmill."

The conversation was making Siddah uncomfortable. "Of course he did. He wouldn't have gone to work there every day for ten years if he'd hated it." Nor would he have mortgaged her house and left her nearly drowning in debt for that damn mill's sake.

Helene turned her glass in circles on the table. "I wish I could agree with you, but I don't think Peter liked working at the mill any more than Gabe did."

"Peter wasn't that weak. If he'd been unhappy at the mill, he would have said so."

"Do you really think so? Gabe was gone, and Monty needed help. Peter was a peacemaker, Siddah. You know that as well as I do."

Siddah felt her throat closing. She couldn't deny that, but it sounded so wrong when Helene said it. So…weak. "He was a peacemaker," she agreed, "but he wasn't a pushover."

Helene lifted her glass but stopped short of drinking.

"The hardest thing in the world is to look honestly at the people you love, especially once they're gone. I adored Peter. You know I did. But he always needed approval more than Gabe did."

A niggling voice in the back of Siddah's mind insisted that Helene was right, but she didn't want to think less of Peter, and she definitely didn't want to start thinking that he fell short in comparison to Gabe. She stood and crossed to the pile of potatoes by the sink. "I think it would be better if we didn't talk about this now."

"I've upset you."

She whirled back to face Helene. "Yes, you've upset me. How dare you start comparing Peter to Gabe? How dare you hold Gabe up as some kind of paragon? It was Peter who stayed here in Libby while Gabe was running around God only knows where. It was Peter who devoted his life to the family business after Gabe turned his back on it, and it was Peter who spent every birthday and holiday making sure the two of you were happy while Gabe couldn't even be bothered to send a card."

"You've been listening to Monty."

"No! I've been here, watching. I know how often Gabe called and wrote home. I know how much he didn't do for you." She raked her fingers through her hair in agitation and sank against the counter. "I understand why you're doing this, Helene. Peter's gone, and Gabe is here now. You want to believe the best of him, and maybe you can. Maybe he has changed. But don't run Peter's memory into the ground to do it."

"Admitting that Peter wasn't perfect is hardly running his memory into the ground," Helene argued. "I'm merely acknowledging that maybe Monty and I were selfish when it came to him, too."

"And saying that Peter wasn't strong enough to stand up to you."

Helene left the table and came toward her. "Siddah, sweetheart, you're misunderstanding me. I'm not saying anything negative about Peter. I'm just observing that he didn't have the same temperament as Gabe." She smiled sadly and ran her knife through a mound of fresh parsley. "It's funny how you can have two children, same parents, same home, same upbringing, and end up with two people so very different. That's all I'm trying to say. Gabe made his decisions. Peter made his. I'm not sure that either one was better than the other. Just don't judge Gabe too harshly, that's all I'm asking."

"I'm not judging him harshly," Siddah protested. "I'm letting him spend time with Bobby, aren't I?"

"Because you're worried about Bobby, not because you trust Gabe."

"That's not entirely true." Siddah took a knife from the drawer and began cutting potatoes into quarters. "He and I have talked a few times, and he seems like a good guy. My only concern is what will happen to Bobby when Gabe leaves again."

"And I'm saying that maybe Gabe won't leave if there's a reason for him to stay."

"Bobby?"

"Family."

"His family has always been here," Siddah said flatly.

"But Gabe is different now. I don't know why, exactly. He hasn't said, and I haven't asked, but there's something in his eyes that wasn't there before." Helene propped her hands on the edge of the sink. "You want to help your son. I want to help mine."

"Helene…"

"Just hear me out, Siddah, please. Gabe seems drawn to the two of you. Why else would he offer to sit with Bobby after school?"

"Because you want him to."

Helene shook her head. "Gabe might think he's doing it because I asked him to, but Gabe doesn't do anything he doesn't want to do. You're all of Peter we have left, you know. That's why Monty and I want so much to be part of your lives, and I'm sure that's what Gabe is feeling, too."

There was no reason for Siddah to feel let down by that…and yet the sinking sensation in her stomach almost felt like disappointment. "Even so—"

"He could use a friend, Siddah."

The idea was certainly tempting, but it could lead to big trouble. "He has friends in Libby. People love him around here."

"He has acquaintances. He needs a friend."

And Helene thought *she* should be that friend? Siddah's stomach turned over. "I don't know, Helene." Siddah quartered another potato and dropped it into a bowl at her side. "Don't you think that Gabe and I suddenly becoming friends would be a little strange?"

"Strange?" Helene's raised an eyebrow. "Absolutely not. I think it would be the most natural thing in the world. You share something in common—your love of

Peter. No matter what Monty thinks, I know how much Gabe loved his little brother."

Even if Gabe's story was true and Monty had kicked him out, that didn't excuse the years he'd ignored Peter. "He had a strange way of showing it."

"Siddah, darling, you didn't know them when they were younger. Until the day he left home, Gabe was always Peter's champion. Gabe left to protect himself, but it was the only selfish thing he ever did."

Siddah stopped working. "I don't question the decision he made when he left. It's the ten years that came after that cause me trouble."

"And it's the choice he made three weeks ago that gives me hope." Helene sighed heavily and a sad smile flickered across her lips. "Monty can't seem to find forgiveness, Siddah, but I can. And I hope you can, for all our sakes. The family needs it. I need it. Holding grudges and nursing anger will only cause more hurt, and Bobby is the one who will suffer most."

"I'm doing my best," Siddah whispered.

"Good. So will you do one more thing for me?"

"If I can."

"I want you and Bobby to join us on Monday. We're inviting a few friends and family over for a barbecue, and it won't feel right unless you and Bobby are here."

It would be the first family get-together Monty and Helene had hosted since Peter's accident, and Siddah knew what a monumental step it was for both of them. The thought of a barbecue without Peter made her throat burn, but maybe Gabe was right. Maybe it was time.

She smiled and touched her mother-in-law's hand,

and she turned a corner she'd been too afraid to face until now. "We'd love to, Helene. It sounds great."

She meant it. She just didn't know whether it was the family tie or the chance to spend more time around Gabe that interested her most.

SIDDAH WOKE EARLY on Sunday morning, suddenly desperately aware that her house was a mess. She couldn't seem to find time to vacuum as often as she wanted, she hadn't deep-cleaned anything in months, and she couldn't remember the last time she'd been caught up on the laundry. But somewhere deep under the panic, there was something that disturbed her even more—the unmistakable tickle of anticipation.

She didn't want to look at the reason for it, so she dragged herself out of bed, found a light T-shirt, a pair of old jeans so faded they were almost white, and tugged on socks to protect her feet from the early-morning chill. The temperature would soar again in the afternoon, but evenings were always cool in the valley, even in the middle of summer.

While she drank her first cup of coffee, she attacked the week's accumulation of clutter in the living room and tossed a load of towels into the washer. Over her second cup, she unloaded the dishwasher, scrambled eggs for breakfast, and switched loads of laundry.

With a sinking heart, she surveyed the living room. Yes, the clutter was gone, but the furniture still needed dusting, and the carpet needed more help than the vacuum cleaner could give it. She set Bobby to work on the tangle of PlayStation cords and controllers in front of the TV, then grabbed her furniture polish and a rag from the hall closet.

She bustled from one table to the next, but Bobby moved slower than a coon dog on a summer day. After just a couple of minutes, he stopped working completely and frowned up at her. "Why do I have to put all this stuff away?"

"Because we want the house to look nice when Gabe gets here on Tuesday."

"Why?"

"So he doesn't think we're slobs." Carefully, Siddah put the glass figurine Peter and Bobby had given her on their last Mother's Day on a freshly dusted table. "Don't you want to make a good impression?"

Bobby rolled his eyes and plucked at a game-stick. "Yeah, but I thought we were going to have fun today."

"And we are," she said firmly. "But first we need to make sure the house looks respectable. We still need to get our regular weekend chores done, especially if we're going to the barbecue tomorrow."

"So we have to mow the lawn?"

Sighing, Siddah shoved a couple of paperbacks into place on the bookshelf. "Yes, we do. Now, will you please get started? It will take less time to do the work than it will to argue with me."

Bobby actually picked up the game-stick, but that's as far as he got. Scowling a little, he cocked his head to one side. "How come you don't like Gabe?"

"What makes you think I don't like him?"

Bobby shrugged. "Well, it's kind of easy to tell. You never smile at him or anything."

Siddah wiped the bookshelf with her cloth and tried to decide how to respond to that. "I don't know Gabe very well," she said carefully, "but you and Grandma think he's pretty special, so he can't be all bad." She grinned at Bobby, who suddenly looked little and lost. "Right?"

He hitched one shoulder. "I guess. Do you think he really likes me?"

"Well, who wouldn't?" Siddah abandoned her dusting and sat on the couch where she could be closer to her son. "You're a great kid. You're smart and funny, and handsome as all get-out, if I do say so myself."

A pleased smile tugged at the corners of his mouth, but only for a second. "When Whitney was baby-sitting me, she said freckles are ugly."

"She said *what?*"

"Freckles are ugly."

"She said that to you?"

"Nuh-uh," Bobby said again. "She said it to somebody on the phone, but I heard her."

"Well, Whitney was wrong." Siddah traced one finger along her son's dear little cheek. "Don't you remember what I told you? Every one of those is an angel's kiss. How could an angel's kiss be ugly?"

"She said I'm gonna grow up to be a dweeb."

Siddah's initial disbelief turned into protective maternal anger. "You are certainly not going to be a dweeb when you grow up," she said, struggling to keep her voice sounding normal for Bobby's sake. "Whitney didn't know what she was talking about. There's not a thing wrong with freckles."

"You don't have freckles."

"I did when I was your age."

"As many as me?"

"Not quite, but I had a lot. If anybody should have grown up to be a dweeb, it would have been me. I was born in a little-bitty town in the Arkansas hills, ran around barefoot all the time, had buck teeth and freckles, and my mama had a horrible time trying to get my hair to behave. But I grew up. Grew into myself, I guess you could say, and so will you. You, my handsome little son, are going to be a heartbreaker. I guarantee it."

Bobby squinted at her through one eye. "Are you sure?"

Unable to resist any longer, she slid onto the floor and pulled him close. "Oh, Bobby, I can absolutely guarantee it. You are going to be a knockout when you get older, and I'm gonna need a big old broom to keep the girls away."

"Mom!" He struggled against her embrace for a few seconds, then grudgingly held still until she released him, which she did sooner than she wanted to. "I thought you wanted me to put my things away," he groused.

"Yes, I do."

"Well, I can't when you're doing stuff like that!"

"No, you're right." Siddah pushed to her feet and reluctantly returned to her dusting. But she wondered how many other self-doubts were churning around inside her son's mind, and she couldn't help but miss the days when he'd willingly snuggled up to her and stayed on her lap when she gave him a hug.

For the first time in years, she let herself acknowledge a tickle of baby hunger. This wasn't the first time she'd felt it by any means, but she'd learned to ignore it as the months passed and her hopes for more children had slowly died. Month after month, she'd held her breath as her time of the month approached, and month after month she'd grieved when she started her period.

She and Peter had undergone a few tests, most of which had come back with inconclusive results. Peter's sperm count had seemed healthy, so the problem must have been with her. Maybe having Bobby when she was so young had been too hard on her. For a while, Siddah had hoped they could get help through a fertility clinic, but Peter had convinced her that it would be too expensive.

Now, she knew the truth and anger chased away the longing. The cost of a baby would have been too great for Peter, but he'd borrowed all that money for the mill. Apparently, their priorities hadn't been as in sync as she'd once thought. And she wondered, just for a moment, whether their marriage would have survived the truth if she'd known about the loans while Peter was still alive.

But like so many other questions, she wasn't sure she wanted the answer to that one.

CHAPTER TEN

THE HOUSE SEEMED to come alive on Labor Day. Relatives began arriving early in the morning—aunts armed with platters full of food, cousins carrying coolers filled with soda and beer, and his two uncles, broad-shouldered and barrel-chested, who claimed chairs in the shade and visited with his father while kids Gabe had never met raced around the yard.

When the noise in the kitchen began to float upstairs to his bedroom, he left his sanctuary and came down the stairs, unbelievably nervous to see them all again. What kind of reception would they give him? Would they be happy to see him, or had they just gathered here today out of morbid curiosity?

Time would tell, he supposed. Might as well find out.

First stop, the kitchen.

He found his mother zipping from fridge to stove to counter to sink, calling instructions to his aunts Jodie and Teresa as she worked. Jodie, a tall woman with streaked blond hair and a warm smile, saw him first. She'd been married to his Uncle Keith as long as Gabe had been alive, and he couldn't imagine a family get-together without her.

Her mouth fell open when she saw him. Shrieking with delight, she stopped chopping onion, set the knife aside and raced around the table with her arms held wide. "Gabriel Douglas King! I could hardly believe it when Helene called to say you were home." She managed to gather him into her arms for a hug he was powerless to resist. Not that he wanted to. The welcome filled him with warmth and hope.

After several minutes, Jodie pushed him away and held him at arm's length. "You look wonderful," she said as she ran her eyes over him. "Just wonderful."

Before he could respond, Teresa nudged Jodie out of the way and pulled him into another hug. "Don't you *ever* stay away that long again, do you hear me?"

Surprised, humbled, and so grateful he was nearly speechless, Gabe chuckled and grinned down at his diminutive aunt. "Yes ma'am."

"There's absolutely no excuse." Teresa stood about five-three and probably weighed all of a hundred pounds, but she glowered at him as if she thought she could still turn him over her knee. "If I had a nickel for all the sleep we lost worrying about you, I'd never have to worry about money again. What were you thinking?"

The question was asked with such love, Gabe couldn't be offended. But today wasn't the day for telling the whole story about why he left, so he merely grinned. "Long story, Aunt Teresa. Let's talk about something else. How many of those juvenile delinquents out there are your grandkids?"

She grinned, just as he'd known she would. "Five. The other three are Jo and Keith's."

"Quality, not quantity," Jodie called out from the table behind them.

How could he have forgotten the teasing banter that had always taken place between these two? He glanced at his mother, who looked on with a fond smile, and he wondered whether she ever longed for a grandchild of her own, or if Bobby filled that need well enough.

Years ago, when he was young, Gabe had thought he might marry and have a family. That dream had been lost along the way, but the realization that it might never happen, that he might never contribute to the large, noisy brood racing around the yard outside, made him suddenly sad.

With a pat on the shoulder, Jodie nudged him toward the door. "You might as well get out there. Your uncles are waiting to see you."

Gabe nodded. He had to face them, but it would have been easier to deal with them one at a time. The three King brothers all at once were a little much for any mere mortal.

"Just don't let them talk nonsense to you when you get out there," Teresa muttered. "You know how those three are."

"They're lots of bluster," Jodie said over her shoulder. "But they're harmless."

"Harmless?" Gabe gave a little laugh. "Are we talking about the same three guys?"

With a roll of her eyes, Jodie turned around, linked arms with him, and steered him relentlessly through the living room toward the porch. "Your Grandpa King was an ornery old thing. Everybody knows that. But the boys grew up all right in spite of everything old Calvin dished out."

"He wasn't exactly a cuddly grandpa," Gabe said with a wry grin.

"Let's be honest," Jodie said, her voice low. "He wasn't cuddly at all. I never did know what caused him to be such a grump, but Monty got the worst of it. I guess that's because he was the oldest, but Keith and Andrew got their fair share, as well."

She spoke matter-of-factly, but Gabe was having trouble following what she said. "What do you mean Dad got the worst of it?"

"Oh, you know…" She waved one plump hand in the air between them. "Monty was never quite good enough for his dad. Calvin didn't think he was dedicated enough to the business, and he rode that boy something fierce. We were all just kids then, but everybody knew how Calvin treated him. Calvin pulled Monty out of school so often to help at the mill Monty almost didn't graduate."

Gabe looked out the window. "Are you sure about that?"

"I was there."

"Why didn't I ever hear about it?"

"Oh, you know Monty." Jodie lowered her voice and shut the door to keep their conversation from carrying outside. "Pride is his greatest downfall. He was mortified that he came so close to failing in school. He wouldn't have graduated at all if his mother hadn't dragged him down to talk to the principal. She stood her ground with Calvin, got your dad back into school and kept him there, but it was tough on Monty. I don't think he wanted you boys to know about it."

Gabe struggled to take everything in. "So why are you telling me now?"

"Because it's time. Monty hated the way old Calvin treated him, but he does the same thing with you. I don't know why. Maybe he doesn't know any other way to act. Maybe he still resents the fact that he's had to dedicate his entire life to that damn mill, although nobody forced him. He could have walked away at any time, just like Andrew and Keith did."

"Andrew and Keith? When did they work at the mill?"

"All the time they were growing up." Jodie patted the cushion beside her and Gabe sat. "Sounds like there's a lot you don't know."

"I thought they didn't want to work at the mill."

"That's right. They didn't. But that doesn't mean old Calvin didn't put them to work before they were old enough to tell him so. Those boys didn't have a lick of fun when we were in school. They were too busy working. Not one of 'em ever played sports or joined a club or went anywhere much with the group. Monty went straight to work after high school, just like Calvin wanted him to, but Andy and Keith weren't having any of it. You'd have thought World War Three had broken out the way things were around here for a while."

That certainly sounded familiar, but Gabe still felt as if he'd come in on the middle of something. "So my dad didn't *want* to work at the mill? Is that what you're saying?"

"That's exactly what I'm saying. He just didn't have

enough gumption to walk away when his dad threatened to kick him out."

Gabe could only stare at her for a long time. "Old Cal threatened to kick my dad out?" he asked at last. "When?"

"Shortly after he graduated from high school. So Monty didn't go. And he eventually adjusted all right. People usually do. But he sure wasn't happy about it at first." Jodie smiled gently. "I suppose he thought you'd cave in just like he did if he put enough pressure on you. He was furious when you didn't, but I think he was angrier with himself than with you."

"You sure could have fooled me."

"It's that pride of his. It's not always a good thing, and the King boys have got way too much of it. Present company included. But all that bluff and bluster is really hiding a deep sense of insecurity that's plagued your dad his whole life. My advice to you is to learn from his mistakes. Don't let your pride keep you from making peace with him or you'll regret it the rest of *your* life."

A burst of laughter drifted inside, and Gabe recognized his father's among them. For the first time in his life, he thought about what the old man's childhood had been like. If Jodie was right, it shed a whole different light on Monty's actions.

"Why didn't my mother ever tell me about this?"

"Because Monty didn't want her to. She wanted you to know, but you were too volatile back then. We were all afraid you'd have used the truth to hurt him, not to make things better."

And they were probably right. "I want to make peace with him," Gabe agreed. "I just don't know how."

"Stop looking at him as the dad who hurt you and try seeing him as a human being. Look beyond that mask he holds up to the world and find out who he really is. And most of all, stop bristling whenever you're around him." Jodie smiled and slid an arm around his shoulders. "You know what the definition of crazy is, don't you? It's someone who keeps doing the same old thing in the same old way, expecting to get different results."

"Yeah?" Gabe said with a laugh. "Well, that pretty much sums up the past twenty years."

"So give your dad something new to respond to and see what happens."

"You really think that will work?"

She shrugged and stood again. "Why wouldn't it? He wants to be loved and appreciated just as much as you do."

"Yeah, but— It sounds so simple. Almost too simple."

"Give it a try. What do you have to lose?"

Shaking his head in wonder, Gabe stood to face her. "That's a good question. Aunt Jo."

WANDERING ONTO THE PORCH a few minutes later, Gabe drew a deep breath for courage. He couldn't put off talking to his father and uncles forever, but they looked so foreboding sitting there on the other side of the lawn. The last thing he wanted was to ruin the day with an argument, but he wasn't sure he could keep his cool if all three of them got started.

He walked slowly, giving them time to see him coming. His uncle Keith had grown old in the time Gabe had been away. His hair was more silver than brown, he'd gained a good fifty pounds, and the skin on his face sagged. Andy, the youngest brother, looked as if he hadn't aged a day. He was still tall, lean and wiry, with a face weathered by years spent outdoors. How had these remote men ever managed to marry three such warm and caring women?

Gabe didn't expect a warm welcome. They were, after all, his father's brothers, raised by the same cold father who hadn't known how to love. Keith saw him coming and said something under his breath to the others.

Andy actually smiled as Gabe drew near. "Well, look what the cat dragged in." He half stood, held out a hand for a quick shake, and dropped back into his chair. "Monty tells us you're back working at the mill."

"In a manner of speaking. He's got me working as his night watchman."

"Good place for you," Keith muttered. "You've been out of the business too long to be safe on the equipment."

That was no doubt true, but Gabe couldn't tell if Keith was concerned about Gabe's safety or everyone else's. Knowing he couldn't escape yet, he dragged a lawn chair over and sat. "It's honest work," he said. "Nothing to be ashamed of."

Gabe was aware of the startled look on his father's face and tried to steer the conversation onto neutral ground. "So how've you been, Uncle Keith? Still working at the hardware store?"

Keith shook his head and leaned forward, resting his arms on his thighs, studying the ground beneath his feet. "Retired a couple of years ago, just before the store closed down. I'm an old, lazy horse in the pasture now."

"He always was an old lazy horse in the pasture,"

Andy said straight-faced. "Never could get him to do anything, much."

Keith made a noise of disapproval and shifted position in his chair. "I carried my own weight. Took care of my wife. Raised my kids." He shot a look at Gabe. "What's the story with you, boy?"

"The story?" Gabe shrugged and tried to keep his voice light. "I don't know yet, but I'm here for a few months."

"What for?"

"Excuse me?"

"I understand coming home for a visit," Keith said, "but six months? What happened? You lose that fancy-ass job of yours?"

He couldn't have asked for a better opening to tell them about his illness, but it seemed wrong to share it with the uncles when he hadn't even told his parents. "I'm taking some R & R."

"Rest and relaxation?" Andy snorted a laugh. "Hell, if I'd known you could get six months off whenever you want it, maybe I'd have gone off to do…whatever it is you do. How 'bout you, Monty?"

The old man shook his head, but instead of looking at Gabe or his brother, he kept his focus locked on a group of kids who were gathered around something near the back porch. "I'd have stayed here. Done my duty to my family."

Monty had made similar remarks over the years, but Gabe had always assumed they were directed at him. Today, the look his uncles exchanged left him with no doubt that Jodie had been telling the truth. He'd taken the road he thought most honorable, and now, with Peter gone, it would all have been for nothing. Triple Crown would either fold or go to someone else when Monty died. The sting might not be so bad if one of the cousins stepped up to the plate, but would they?

Triple Crown was still in business when so many others had gone under. That alone ought to earn the old man a little praise. For the first time in his life, Gabe saw his father as someone who made a contribution to the community rather than someone who sucked the life out of it.

Remembering Jodie's advice, Gabe decided to take a chance and change his approach with the old man. "Dad's provided a good living for a lot of people over the years because of his sense of duty," he said. "There are a lot of folks in town who've been able to take care of their wives and raise their kids because of the mill."

The old man looked away from the kids and straight into Gabe's eyes. "Damn right."

Uncle Keith leveled Gabe with an expression reminiscent of old Calvin King. "Wasn't good enough for you, though, was it?"

"We all made our choices," Gabe said evenly. "Dad chose the mill. You chose the hardware store. Uncle Andy chose the farm. Who's to say which choice was best?"

The corners of Keith's mouth turned down even more. "Andy and I stayed home, close to family. So did our kids."

"Seems funny, doesn't it?" Andy grunted. "Monty here has this thing about family and obligation, but he got the kid who runs off and spends his whole life away. Kind of ironic, don't you think?"

Growling with displeasure, Monty pushed to his feet and glared down at his younger brother. "Why don't you leave the kid alone? He's come back to see his mother. He doesn't need any guff from the two of you."

With that, he ambled off, leaving Gabe and the uncles staring after him. Andy huffed out a breath and Keith rolled his eyes as if he suspected his older brother had lost his mind. But Gabe felt a slow curl of surprise and gratification spreading through him. It was the first time in years he could remember the old man taking his side on anything, and he wasn't sure how to respond. But as he watched his father cross the lawn, an unexpected rush of affection overshadowed everything else.

Maybe they really could make peace.

"SIDDAH, HONEY, you just sit right down here and put your feet up." Aunt Teresa put her hands on Siddah's shoulders and guided her toward a chair deep in the shade behind the house. A few feet away, some of the kids and their parents were playing volleyball. Their shouts of laughter echoed across the lawn. The scents of hot coals and grilling meat filled the air, and pleasant memories of other barbecues floated all around her.

When Peter was alive, she'd looked forward to these family get-togethers almost more than he did. At every one, she'd been acutely aware of Gabe's absence, even though no one had ever mentioned his name above a whisper.

Today the tables were turned. Gabe was here. Peter was the one missing. But somehow, with the sun streaming across the lawn, the sounds of nature and laughter all around her, and Bobby playing with the kids, just like old times, the pangs weren't quite so sharp today.

Scowling up at the determined older woman, Siddah tried to rise. "I'm not going to sit around while the rest of you are working."

"You will if I say so. We've already got more hands in the kitchen than we know what to do with." Teresa pressed her back into the chair and planted her fists on her hips to show she meant business. "Helene's been telling us how hard you've been working lately, and we all agree that you need a break. So you sit right here and keep an eye on the volleyball game. Referee if you think you need to do something useful."

In all the years she'd been a member of this family, Siddah had never met anyone who'd actually won an argument with Aunt Teresa, and she wasn't even going to try to be the first. "All right," she conceded, "but if you need me, you'll call—right?"

"Absolutely. If we need you."

"I won't hold my breath."

Teresa laughed, but she sobered again almost immediately. "Helene's worried about you," she said, sinking into a chair next to Siddah's. "She thinks you're working yourself too hard."

"She worries too much. I'm working some extra hours, but I'm fine."

"Are you really?"

"Of course! Don't I look fine?"

Teresa smiled halfheartedly. "You're adorable as ever, but you do look a bit tired." She put a hand on Siddah's knee. "Jodie thinks you're working to distract yourself from losing Peter. But driving yourself into an early grave isn't going to help."

"It's not that bad," Siddah said with a thin laugh. "I appreciate everyone's concern, but I'm fine."

Teresa gave her a skeptical look. "If you say so. Just promise me that you'll have a good time today. It would be lovely to see you smile again."

Without warning, Bobby's accusation raced through her head. *You're no fun anymore.* It seemed that no matter where she went, someone was accusing her of being too serious, of letting life pass her by. Had she really been that bad? Surely not.

As if she could read Siddah's thoughts, Teresa leaned closer. "You remember when my sister's husband died a few years back?"

Siddah was surprised by the abrupt shift, but she nodded. "Of course."

"Well, Melanie did the same thing you're doing. Withdrew from life. Threw herself into her career." Teresa settled back in her chair and watched the game for a minute. "It took her a while to realize that she didn't have to mourn forever to honor Jack's memory. We all know how much she loved him."

Siddah looked at her sharply. "And that's what you think I'm doing?"

"I don't know," Teresa said, pulling her focus away from the game and back to Siddah. "But I think it's a good idea to make sure it's not, don't you? There isn't a person here who needs to see you miserable to remember how you felt about Peter." Teresa stood and smiled down at her. "Bad things happen to all of us, Siddah, but life goes on. That's either the best thing about life, or the worst. The best tribute you can pay to Peter is to learn how to be happy again. Embrace life. Be grateful for every day you have with the people you love. Don't keep wasting the time you've been given."

"Maybe you're right, but how am I supposed to do that? It's not as easy as just deciding."

"Honey, sometimes you have to act the part first. When you do, little by little, even you will start to believe that it's true."

"That's easier said than done."

"I don't doubt that," Teresa said gently. "But that sweet little boy of yours shouldn't go through life without both of his parents, should he?"

The question sent a shaft of guilt through her, but the suggestion seemed a bit extreme. She knew how it felt to be abandoned, and she most certainly hadn't done that to her son.

As Teresa walked away, Siddah closed her eyes and tried to find some peace. And she asked the question she'd asked a thousand times before. Why did Peter have to die?

He'd loved playing horseshoes with the cousins, rounding up the kids for a rousing game of volleyball, teasing reluctant smiles out of his gruff old uncles. He'd been the first to come running if one of his aunts needed help, and his mother had rarely been left wanting for something before Peter made it happen.

If anyone had embraced life, Peter had, and before the accident, Siddah *had* been fun. She'd laughed readily, joined in any excursion or activity Peter suggested, and she'd put together a fair share of them, herself. If Peter had walked into the party today, he probably wouldn't recognize the shell she'd become.

With her eyes still closed, she imagined him walking around the yard, talking and laughing with the members of his family, serving the volleyball, jumping up to the net for a spike. She imagined him turning to look at her, but the face she saw wasn't Peter's. The image of Gabe and his grin made her heart turn over in her chest.

His laugh sounded from somewhere nearby, and her eyes flew open. She looked for him and felt an odd sensation of comfort when she saw him near the volleyball net, a gaggle of kids around him clamoring for the ball he held just out of reach.

His eyes met hers, and the breath left her lungs. What was wrong with her? It was Peter she loved. Peter she would *always* love. So why was she entertaining this attraction to his brother?

She tried to convince herself that she wasn't drawn to Gabe, but that was the funny thing about attraction. Once it happened, the thing was done. You can't undo your awareness of another person once you've found it. And Siddah wouldn't be able to turn off this feeling now that she'd really acknowledged it.

Was she just missing Peter? Seeking a substitute? She looked away quickly, but it wasn't so easy to still the beating of her heart or stop the trembling of her hands. She told herself it was just the exhaustion finally getting the best of her, that's all. Teresa and Helene were right. She *did* need to rest.

But Siddah had never been one to lie to herself, and

she couldn't do it now. It wasn't Gabe's resemblance to Peter that drew her. It was the quiet way he honored what she was feeling, the way he seemed to know what she needed without even asking. It was the way he stood up for what he believed, no matter what kind of pressure people put on him.

She was drawn to him, not because of his similarities to Peter, but because of their differences. But now that she knew, what on earth was she was going to do about it?

IN THE GATHERING TWILIGHT, Siddah picked her way along the path beside the river, careful not to trip over rocks or exposed roots. She'd laughed more in the past few hours than she had in the past two years, and her cheeks actually hurt a little from smiling so much.

All the fun had made her lose track of time, and only the rapidly approaching evening and a comment from one of Gabe's cousins had reminded her that school would be starting in the morning. Much as she hated to leave, she had to get Bobby into bed, or he'd never get up.

Relishing the cool of the evening after the heat of the day, she moved along the riverbank. Water splashed over rocks along the banks and the setting sun winked off the deeper water in the middle of the river. She'd never found the solace so many people seemed to enjoy in the forest or the side of a mountain but, then, the towering mountains had made her feel almost claustrophobic when she first came to Montana. Tonight, after a day filled with good company, with the gentle breeze stirring the tree-tops, Siddah began to understand the pull of this place.

Gabe's cousin Olivia had mentioned seeing a group of boys heading off in this direction, and Siddah had offered to find them. Her friend Ivy and Teresa had been right. She had needed to relax and let go. She felt better than she could remember feeling in a long, long time.

Humming softly under her breath, she rounded a curve on the path, realized Gabe was standing just a few feet in front of her and stopped abruptly. He stood with his eyes closed, his face lifted toward the sky, and the evening chill disappeared as she watched him.

There was something almost boyishly appealing about the expression on his face, but that was the *only* thing boyish about him. Broad shoulders tapered to a trim waist and narrow hips, and every inch was solidly muscled from the years he'd spent in the jungle.

She must have made a noise, because his eyes opened and he turned his head slowly toward her. When he saw her, a slow smile spread across his face. "Hey there."

His voice was low and strangely intimate, and made her warm all over. "Hey."

"Looking for the kids?"

She nodded. "Olivia said she saw them come this way with Jarrod, but that was a little while ago. Have you seem them?"

"I think they're just up at the fallen log. Want me to get them?"

"Thanks, but it's nice out tonight and I'm enjoying the walk." Noting the maze of fallen logs in the undergrowth, she smiled. "Just tell me, is there anything I need to know to find *the* fallen log?"

Gabe grinned and her heart gave another little skip. "How about I just show you where they are?"

"That might be easier," she admitted. "Is it far?"

"Not really, but it is a little way." He moved aside on the path and waited for her to join him. "I saw you playing volleyball earlier. I had no idea you were such a good player."

"It's the one sport I know something about," she said with a smile. "That and badminton."

"Ah…you're well-rounded." His gaze dipped to her breasts and back to her eyes. Even Siddah couldn't miss the desire smoldering in their depths. "In sports."

She smiled, surprised by how much she liked knowing that he found her attractive. "Yes. In sports."

Color flushed his cheeks and an embarrassed smile curved his lips. "Okay, so you're well-rounded in other areas, as well. I didn't mean to offend. That was completely uncalled-for. But you're an attractive woman, Siddah. And even more attractive when you smile."

Her breath caught and she felt her own cheeks grow warm. Maybe she shouldn't feel that slow coil of pleasure, but it had been a long time since she'd flirted with anyone. A long, *long* time since she'd felt like a woman. "It's all right," she said, and gave in to the urge to touch his arm. The feel of sun-warmed skin and bristly hair scorched her fingertips, but she didn't draw away. "I'm not that easily offended."

As if she was waking after a long sleep, she could feel parts of herself coming back to life. A tingle here, the sharp pinprick of pain there. Deep inside, guilt threatened to ruin the moment, but was it really wrong to move on with her life? To crave the attention of a man again and ache for the feel of someone's arms around her?

No. She knew it wasn't. But was it wrong to be drawn to *this* man?

When Gabe didn't speak, she decided to break the tension. "I told Bobby that you'd be watching him after school tomorrow. He's thrilled, of course. I hope you're prepared to spend some time playing video games. We don't have hiking trails and secret fishing holes in our backyard."

Gabe started walking slowly. "I'm sure we'll find plenty to do."

"You're really good with him, you know. Your mother was right."

"And you're surprised?"

"A little, maybe. But I don't know why I should be. Peter was a natural father, so it shouldn't surprise me that you are, too." She realized what she had said and blushed furiously. "Good with kids, I mean."

Gabe laughed and the sound warmed her clear through. "So we're even. One mortifying slip apiece. Does that mean we can start over?"

"I certainly hope so."

He stopped walking so suddenly she stumbled a little. His hand shot out to steady her, and a finger of heat traced up her arm. "I'm glad," he said, his voice low and almost intimate. "I'd like that."

There had been many different emotions racing between them since the day they met, but through every one they'd always been honest. She had to be honest with him now. "So would I."

His eyes locked on hers, and what she saw there sent excitement and anticipation skittering up her spine. Did he want to kiss her? Yes, she thought he did. Did she want him to? She'd be lying if she said no. But was she ready?

His eyes roamed her face, taking in every detail as eagerly as she studied him. He must have sensed her hesitation, because he stepped away and they started walking again.

After a few minutes, he nodded toward a hill, barely visible through the trees. "See that? When I was a kid, that's where I planned to build my house someday."

Siddah smiled softly. "It's a beautiful spot. I can see why you'd choose it."

"You should see the view from up there. It's magnificent." He grinned and kicked a rock from the path. "Had it all planned out in my head back then. Four bedrooms upstairs. A bright, sunny kitchen down. A wrap-around porch so I could see the view from every angle."

"And rocking chairs?"

"Absolutely. A porch without rocking chairs would be a crime."

She was suddenly vividly aware of the feel of her blouse against her skin, of the rush of blood through her veins and the whisper of the breeze against her cheek. It took effort to force simple words out of her throat. "So why don't you build it?"

He shrugged as they rounded a curve in the path and the hillside disappeared from view. "One person rattling around in a house that big? It would be a little lonely, don't you think?"

Was that regret in his voice? Longing? She couldn't tell. "I suppose you're right," she said. "But it's a shame."

He moved ahead on the trail to sweep the branches of a huckleberry bush out of her way. She walked on as if nothing had happened between them, but she knew she'd just turned a corner.

From this night on, her life would be completely different. She would always love Peter, but it was time to let him go. To move on, as so many people had been urging her to do.

CHAPTER ELEVEN

AT A LITTLE BEFORE EIGHT the next evening, Siddah pulled into the driveway of her small house and turned off the engine. Dusk was just beginning to settle over the valley, and long shadows stretched across the patio and onto the porch. On any other night, she'd kick off her shoes and race inside to get comfortable. But not tonight.

Tonight, Gabe was in there with Bobby, waiting for her to come home, filling her house with his energy, turning her life upside down and leading her relentlessly toward the future. She just couldn't afford to forget that it was a future he wouldn't be sharing with her.

Pocketing her keys, she crossed the driveway and let herself into the kitchen. Before she could call out to let Bobby know she was home, the sound of excited voices caught her attention. A second later, the lawn mower roared to life, drowning them out.

Siddah tossed her purse and keys onto the table and hurried through the house toward the back door. She found Gabe standing at the base of the steps, watching as Bobby pushed the mower along a stretch of lawn. Grass clippings and lawn tools lay piled in front of the garage door. Two long grass stains adorned Bobby's jeans, but her son beamed with pride at his accomplishment.

Gabe watched him like a hawk, shouting directions now and then, adding encouragement at a job well-done. Moments like this were precisely why Helene had suggested that he get to know Bobby. Her son needed this, and she wouldn't dream of taking it from him, but she battled a quick flare of jealousy as Bobby looked to Gabe for approval.

Telling herself to grow up, she kicked off her shoes, pasted on the brightest smile she could manage and stepped onto the back porch. Gabe motioned for Bobby to do another row and climbed the steps to stand beside her. "You're home early," he shouted over the racket. "We were hoping to be finished before you got here."

"You didn't need to do all of this," she protested. "I usually cut the lawn on Saturdays."

"That's what Bobby tells me, but I also know that you missed this week. That was my fault, I'm afraid."

Siddah didn't have the energy to argue with him, and a rebellious part of her whispered that she should be grateful for the help. It meant she didn't have to break her back fighting with the mower after a twelve-hour day at the office. She sat on the top step as Bobby negotiated another turn. "How did the day go? Are you having second thoughts yet?"

Gabe laughed and shook his head. "Not yet. Bobby's not half the trouble Peter and I were at that age."

She wondered if Bobby would be different if she'd been able to give him a brother or a sister. "Is that good?"

"You'd have to ask my mother about that."

"I already know what her answer would be." Siddah worked her shoulders to get rid of the knots of tension she'd brought home from the office. "I've heard a few stories over the years."

"I'm afraid to ask which ones."

"That's probably smart. From what I hear, the two of you didn't make her life easy."

"We were boys," he said with a shrug. "What can I say?"

Siddah laughed and stretched her legs out in front of her, tilting her face to the fading sun. "I should probably get inside and fix dinner, but this feels so good."

"It's already past seven-thirty," Gabe said. "Isn't it a little late to start cooking?"

"Not when you have a ten-year-old who's been doing yard work all afternoon. I'd be fine with a glass of milk and a piece of bread, but I'm sure that Bobby will feel differently."

Beside her on the step, Gabe leaned back on his elbows. "I have to eat before I head over to the mill. Why don't the two of you join me?"

"You want us to have supper with you?"

"Sure. What do you say to pizza? My treat."

"Offer Bobby pizza and he'll think you're some kind of god."

"What about you?"

"Will I think you're some kind of god?" She swallowed and shook her head. "I'm not sure I'd go that far, but this will definitely move you up a notch or two on my good list."

"You have a 'good list'?"

With a grin, she reached for the railing and pulled herself to her feet again. "Doesn't everybody?" Without giving him a chance to answer, she opened the back door and stepped inside. "I'm going to change out of these work clothes. I should be ready by the time you and Bobby are finished out here."

"Sounds good to me."

As Gabe strode toward the jumble of tools near the garage, Siddah indulged herself for a minute and watched him. His long legs chewed up the distance easily, his broad shoulders swayed as he walked. He shouted something to Bobby, but the words were swallowed up by the roar of the lawn mower.

Smiling, Siddah turned away and closed the door. It felt good to have a man around again.

Maybe too good.

GABE KNEW he'd made a mistake the second he set foot inside the pizza parlor. He'd followed Siddah and Bobby in his Jeep, giving them time to talk, giving Siddah a chance to find out about Bobby's first day in school. The short break had also given him a chance to figure out what the hell he was doing.

Granted, they all needed to eat. And Siddah had been working all day. And eight o'clock in the evening was no time to start fixing a home-cooked meal. But dinner? Together?

He must be crazy.

Holding the door for Siddah felt just a little too familiar. Standing together while they waited on a table for three felt strange. Worse than strange. Like he was stepping on his brother's toes. Moving in on Peter's territory.

He blamed Carlos. If he hadn't put the idea in his mind, Gabe wouldn't have given any of this a second thought. He wouldn't have noticed the way Siddah's eyes gleamed in the dim lighting of the restaurant. Wouldn't have paid attention to the musky floral scent she wore. Wouldn't even have thought twice about the way she smiled or the warmth of her laugh while she listened to Bobby chatter about their day.

Feeling decidedly uncomfortable, Gabe followed a middle-aged hostess toward a booth and tried not to care that people were watching them. While Siddah and Bobby sat on one side, Gabe slid onto the bench across the table and snagged a menu. Not that ordering pepperoni pizza required any great concentration on his part, but he needed a minute to pull himself together and figure out where to go from here.

He'd never been particularly worried about other people's opinions, but Carlos's asinine suggestions had made him paranoid. Would seeing them together put ideas in anyone else's head? Or was everyone else smart enough to see this for exactly what it was?

And what was it, anyway? He could deny it all he wanted, but the truth was, he *did* find Siddah attractive. He enjoyed spending time with her. Liked seeing her smile. She was the first woman in a long time who'd held his interest, and no matter how many times he told himself to get a grip on what he was feeling, he wasn't in control at all.

He admired her spunk and her fierce quest for independence. Her eyes intrigued him, and he could probably spend a lifetime trying to figure out all the emotions that flickered through them. Her mouth captivated him. When he was with her, kissing her was all he could think about.

And since last night by the river, he was in worse shape than ever. He wasn't a child any longer. He knew a few things about women. Siddah had wanted him to kiss her as much as he'd wanted to. He'd stake his life on it.

But wanting something didn't make it right.

He dragged his attention back to the table, the menu, the boy he was starting to care about more than he'd ever thought possible. The next few minutes were consumed with earth-shattering decisions like whether to order extra cheese and convincing Bobby that a second order of garlic bread was unnecessary.

For the first time in weeks, Gabe felt a part of something larger than himself, and the envy he'd felt at Carlos's house spiked sharply. Old dreams he'd been pushing aside rose up out of nowhere and threatened to choke him. A home of his own. A family. Children. Roots.

A wife…

With a start, he realized Siddah was watching him and tried to wipe away any longing or regret from his expression.

"Why so glum?" she asked.

"Do I look upset?"

"A little. Is something wrong?"

He couldn't very well tell her the truth, so he shook his head and told a little white lie. "It's just been a while since I went out for pizza. I'm not used to this."

"It's been a while for us, too," she said, her smile fading slightly. "The last time we were here was Bobby's eighth birthday." She found some energy for her smile and turned it on her son. "Remember that, Bobby?"

"Yep. Dad and I played on the pinball machine for, like, two hours."

"I don't think it was quite that long," Siddah said with a laugh, "but you were over there for a while." Looking back at Gabe, she explained, "Peter and Bobby loved their video games. It didn't matter where we went, the two of them were always at it."

And Gabe knew Bobby missed that. "I already warned you that I'm no good at video games," he said, "but pinball I can play. What do you say? Want to challenge me to a game?"

Bobby lunged forward eagerly. "Now?"

"Or after we eat."

"We could play now. Then we'll be through when the pizza comes."

No man with a heart could resist the eagerness on that small face. Gabe checked with Siddah. "Do you mind?"

"Of course not," she said, waving them away. "That's what you're here for."

"Are you going to join us?"

"Me? Oh heavens no. I don't play pinball."

It seemed wrong to leave her sitting alone in a booth crowded with memories. "Is that because you don't like it, or because you don't know how?"

"I know how. I just don't know how to do it well."

"I could teach you."

She laughed uncomfortably. "Peter tried. I'm not a very quick study."

"Peter was good," Gabe admitted, trying to keep the moment light, "but I'm better. Who do you think taught him?"

Siddah ran a slow, assessing glance across his face, and he wondered if he'd said the wrong thing. But after a long moment her lips curved into a smile and a sparkle danced in her eyes. "You really think you can teach me?"

He liked making her smile, far more than he should. But after everything she'd been through, didn't she deserve it? "I'd almost bet money on it," he said. "Besides, what else are you going to do while we're over there? Read the menu?"

She looked toward Bobby again, still obviously uncertain. "Is it okay with you?"

Bobby lifted one shoulder as if the question surprised him. "Sure. Why not?"

"It's just that this was your thing with Dad. I don't want to intrude."

Gabe slid from the booth and held out a hand toward her. "You're not intruding," he said firmly. "We both want you there."

Siddah hesitated, then touched his hand with her fingertips as she stood. There'd been many times in his life when Gabe had envied Peter, but this…well, this was the worst. What kind of man was he to envy his brother's wife and son?

Struggling to keep his expression neutral, he motioned Siddah and Bobby toward the pinball machine on the other side of the restaurant. But he found himself watching the gentle sway of her hips as she walked and he knew he was in bigger trouble than he'd thought.

She was family, he told himself firmly. His brother's wife. Absolutely off-limits. But no matter what his mind said, his instincts were telling him something else entirely.

He'd never seen her with Peter. Never had a chance to watch them together. He'd never witnessed them in love. Never seen them kiss. There wasn't even a child to show for their years together. Nothing except a few stories that felt more like fairy tales than reality.

But it *was* reality, and Gabe would be smart to remember that. No matter how hard it was.

HOLDING THE COFFEE TABLE aloft with one hand, Gabe slid the other toward Bobby. He'd been hanging around Siddah's house for a couple of weeks already, and it seemed that everywhere he looked, something else needed attention. "Looks like I'm going to need the Phillips screwdriver. Remember which one that is?"

"The one with the star on the tip, right?"

"That's the one. How about you hand it to me, then slide on under here so you can help me with this?"

Bobby slapped the tool into his hand and squiggled under the table, his little face awash with excitement. It would have been easier to tighten the table leg without him, but Bobby was so eager to help, so hungry to be included, Gabe couldn't leave him on the sidelines.

He jerked his head toward the loose screw. "That's the one. Think you're strong enough to get it back in there?"

"I think so."

"Okay then." Gabe moved over to give him elbow room. "Show me what you've got."

"I'm pretty good at some stuff. Dad said I was a natural."

"Well, if anybody would know about that, your dad was the guy." Gabe watched as Bobby fumbled with the screw, got it into place, and finally, grunting with each turn, got it slowly turning into the wood. His little arms bulged with the effort and his face was screwed up in concentration.

Not for the first time, tender warmth spread through Gabe. This boy might not have been the son of Peter's body, but he was for damn sure the child of his heart. No wonder his mother had been so eager for Gabe to step in. No wonder the old man thought the sun rose and set on the kid's little red head. If Gabe wasn't careful, he'd get caught, too.

He inched away, as if putting a few inches of carpet between them might insulate him from the growing affection he felt for the kid. "You do that pretty well," he admitted. "Want to do the others, too?"

"Sure!" Bobby turned a snaggletoothed grin in his direction. "I could have fixed this whole thing if Mom didn't think I was too little."

"She'll get over that. It just takes moms a little while to figure out that their boys are becoming men."

Bobby wiped sweat from his nose with his sleeve. "I guess. But she's gotten all weird since my dad died."

She had? Interesting perspective. "How has she gotten weird?"

"She works all the time, for one thing. I don't think she likes being home anymore."

"She's trying to get a promotion, you know."

"Yeah. But she's weird in other ways, too. Like she never goes places with her friends anymore."

"And she used to?"

"Her and my dad used to do all sorts of things." Bobby finished the first screw and they both shifted position so Bobby could tackle the next one. "Maybe you should go out with her. She might think it was okay if she didn't have to do things alone."

Gabe coughed uncomfortably. "Just where do you think we should go?"

"I don't know. Maybe you could take her to one of her dinners. She hasn't been in a long time."

"What dinners are those?"

"Progressive dinners. There's a whole bunch of people who get together to eat. They start at one person's house for, like, cheese sticks or something and then they go to the next person's house for salads, and somebody else's for roast or hot dogs."

Gabe bit back a smile. He seriously doubted cheese sticks and hot dogs were on the menu. "And your mom used to go to those?"

"All the time. You should take her to one."

It sounded so simple, but Bobby couldn't understand all the complications involved. "I'll think about it," Gabe said.

"Really?"

"Sure." Sensing an opening, he decided to bring up a subject they hadn't discussed before. "I'll think about that if you'll think about something. Your mom said your football team is having practice today. You want to go check it out?"

Bobby's expression went from eager to bland in a heartbeat. He lifted one shoulder in a listless shrug. "Not really."

"You don't like playing football anymore?"

"It's okay."

"Just okay? I thought you liked it. Grandma and your mom tell me you're pretty good."

"It's okay," Bobby said again, "but it's kind of boring."

"All right. No football. What would you like to do instead?"

"Nothing. Just fix stuff around here. That's all."

"Has to be something else," Gabe insisted. "You want your mom to get out with her friends, right? Well, she feels the same way about you."

"But I'm okay."

"She doesn't think so."

"Well, I am."

Gabe studied the boy's stubborn little face and tried a different approach. "I'll let you finish this table by yourself if you'll go with me to that football practice."

Bobby turned a suspicious eye on him. "Why do you want to go to that?"

"Why not? We've been hanging around here for the past two weeks. I'm in the mood to get out and do something. What do you say?"

Bobby gave that a moment's thought and Gabe was positive he'd come up with a great incentive. But it didn't take Bobby long to hand back the screwdriver and slide out from under the table. "That's okay," he said. "You can finish it."

"Wait!" That wasn't how this was supposed to go. Gabe fumbled for the right thing to say. "I thought you wanted to work on the table."

Bobby flopped on the couch and reached for the remote. "I changed my mind."

"Because I wanted to go to football practice?"

"Naw. I just don't feel like doing it anymore, that's all." He pressed a button and the television blared.

But Gabe had his answer. Something was keeping Bobby holed up in this house, and it wasn't just Peter's death. There was something else at work here. He just had to find out what.

ON EDGE AND EXHAUSTED, Siddah let herself into the house at a little before ten o'clock. She'd had a rough day at work and she'd missed another evening with her son. She was going after the promotion to make things better in their lives, but tonight, with her eyes scratchy and tired, her head pounding, and that sick feeling still in the pit of her stomach, she wondered if she was only making things worse.

Peter would have hated the long hours she worked. They'd both agreed that having her home with Bobby and the other children they'd once dreamed of having was a priority. Even now, with her whole focus on the promotion, she wanted to stay home with her son, to be there when he came in the door at the end of the school day, to see his face when he told about his joys and disappointments.

The days were passing her by, and someone else was raising her son. Maybe some women could do it all, but Siddah wasn't one of them. If she gave Bobby the financial security she wanted for him, was she robbing him of something equally important? Even *more* important?

Aching with exhaustion, she let herself into the house, tossed her purse and keys onto the table, and dragged herself into the living room, where she found Gabe in Peter's favorite chair immersed in a mystery novel. He looked up as she entered, and a quick, warm smile lit his face.

His was the first friendly face she'd seen in hours, and her reaction both surprised and frightened her a little. She couldn't rush across the room and throw herself into his arms. She shouldn't even want to. But it had been too long since someone had held her. Too long since she'd been able to lay her worries at someone else's feet, even for a little while.

She dropped onto the couch and leaned her head back.

"You look tired," Gabe said.

"*Tired* isn't the word for it." She lifted her head off the couch cushion just enough to see him. "I don't remember when I've had such a long day."

Gabe set his book aside. "Want to talk about it?"

"Yes. No. I'm not sure." She let out a tight laugh and dropped her head back again. "How's that for a definitive answer?"

"Sounds like you *need* to talk about it." He stood and moved closer. "I have a few minutes before I need to leave. You might as well take advantage of it. What do you say I grab a couple of Cokes while you make yourself comfortable? Kick off your shoes. Put your feet up." He grinned and added, "You know the drill."

Internal warning bells urged her to be careful, but Siddah was too tired to listen. "Are you sure you have time? Don't you have to be at the mill by eleven?"

"Yeah, but it's only five minutes away, and I'm sure Slim will stay around for a few minutes if I ask him to."

Maybe she should send him on his way, but the allure of having someone to talk to, even for just a few minutes, was just too strong. With a grateful smile, she slipped out of her shoes and curled her legs under her. "If you're sure Monty won't mind, maybe I'll take you up on it."

Gabe disappeared into the kitchen and returned in a few seconds holding two soda bottles. He uncapped one and handed it to her, then sat on the other end of the couch and turned toward her. "So tell me about your day."

He said it so matter-of-factly Siddah couldn't hold back a smile. "Are you sure you really want to know?"

"That bad, huh?"

She shifted on the cushion to face him. "Worse. The day started out bad when the judge's clerk called to let us know that a pleading I was supposed to have delivered was missing, and it went downhill from there. I've just spent the past three hours copying the most boring documents you've ever seen in your life." She toyed with the label on her bottle and smiled sadly. "I'm not sure I can handle these hours. I told them I could do this. I swore that it would be okay, but I hate coming home this late, and I hate not even getting a chance to see Bobby."

"You're not this late every night."

"No, thank God. But even twice a week is too much." She ran her fingers through her hair and rested one cheek on the back of the couch. "All I want is to better myself. To create some stability for Bobby and give him what I never had. Is that too much to ask?"

Gabe shook his head slowly. "I wouldn't think so."

"Then why does it have to be so hard?" When she realized how pathetic she sounded, she laughed and drew her knees up in front of her. "Ignore that. I'm just feeling sorry for myself."

"We all do that from time to time." Gabe set his bottle on the table beside him and rested one arm on the back of the couch. "Life *is* tough at times, and you've had more than your share of hurdles to jump the past few years."

"I'm certainly not the only one," she said, trying to ignore the closeness of his hand and the comfort that seemed to emanate from him. "The thing is, I used to think I was so strong. I thought I could do everything on my own. But I'm not sure I can."

"I think you're doing okay."

"I'm not doing even *close* to okay. I don't know what we'd do if you weren't here."

"But I am here, so you don't need to worry about that."

For how long, though? That was the question that never seemed to get an answer, and it was the question that ran through her mind too often these days. She wanted to convince herself that she only cared for Bobby's sake, but it was getting harder and harder to make herself believe any part of that.

Silence fell between them, as if neither of them knew what to say next. At least, Siddah didn't have a clue.

If Gabe was bothered by uncertainty, he got over it quickly. "What about Bobby's biological father?" he asked. "You never mention him, but could he be of any help?"

There weren't many subjects Siddah wanted to talk about less than Cornell Beesley. She pulled back instinctively, but exhaustion and the concern in Gabe's eyes drew an answer from her. "I can't ask him. He's completely out of the picture."

"Where is he?"

"Still back in Arkansas...at least, I think that's where he is. I haven't seen or heard from him since the summer I turned eighteen."

"High-school boyfriend?"

"Not exactly." Maybe she should have let him think so, but they'd always been honest with each other, and she didn't want him assuming things about her that weren't true. "I met Cornell a couple of weeks before my high-school graduation," she said. "He was a few years older, out of school, and working with his uncle for the summer. He noticed me. Asked me out a few times. But I always said no." She tried to look as if she told the story every day, but she could hear the trembling in her voice, and when the last remnants of Gabe's smile faded, she knew he'd heard it, too.

"What happened?"

"I was living with my aunt Suzette at the time. My mother died when I was twelve, and Suzette took me in. Things were just fine until Suzette got married again."

Her breath caught and her hands grew clammy. Lord, but it was hard to relive that time. Harder than it should have been, considering how many years had passed. She could hear the drawl tugging at her words, but she couldn't seem to get rid of it.

Needing something to hang on to, Siddah pulled her knees to her chest and wrapped her arms around them. "Long story short, my new uncle took a liking to me. Nothing happened," she said quickly, "but I wanted out of there before something did. Aunt Suzette was nice enough, but she wasn't the strongest woman in the world, and she changed a whole lot when Forrest moved in. I didn't figure she was going to protect me, so I started looking for a way out on my own."

"And you chose Cornell?"

Heat rushed into her face, but she forced herself to nod. "Looking back, I know it was a stupid thing to do, but at the time it seemed like my only option. I didn't have money. I didn't have much education. I was a nobody from George's Creek, and I didn't figure to ever make anything of myself."

He was watching her closely, his eyes filled with something too kind to bear. Only one other person in the world had ever looked at her that way, and she missed it suddenly with an intensity that took her breath away.

It had been too long since she'd been with someone who cared. At least in the beginning Peter had treasured her. He'd wanted to protect her from everything he considered rough and harsh and negative. He'd cared when she hurt, and there'd even been times when she felt as if she could lay her worries out for him and he'd take them over for a little while.

But it was so wrong to want Gabe to fill those shoes. It wasn't fair. Not to Gabe, not to Peter's memory, not even to herself.

She dragged her thoughts back to where she was supposed to be. Cornell Beesley. Standing to put some distance between them, she moved toward the window overlooking the backyard. "I thought Cornell loved me." She smiled ruefully and added, "After all, he said he did. But lesson learned. Some guys will say anything to get what they want."

"They're the ones who give the rest of us a bad name."

She managed a thin smile. "I guess that's probably true. It wasn't long before I figured out I was pregnant, and Cornell lost interest so fast after that I think he probably set a world record." She tried to laugh, but the sound caught in her throat. Not that it hurt anymore, but it was just so embarrassing to admit she'd been that naive. "Once Suzette's husband figured out that I wasn't a virgin anymore, he got brave. I knew I had to get out of there, so a couple of months after Bobby was born, I gathered up all the money I could and bought a one-way ticket as far as the bus would take us. We landed in Great Falls."

Suddenly anxious, she studied Gabe's reaction. Was he disgusted? Put off by her naiveté? Amused by what a child she'd been? Or worse? Though she'd come a long way since those days, Forrest's leering suggestions that *she* was somehow responsible for his interest in her hadn't entirely faded. There was, deep inside, a young girl who feared she was to blame, or that other people would think so.

Gabe stood and came to her. "That took a lot of courage, Siddah."

"I didn't feel brave," she admitted. "I just felt scared and alone."

"And that's when you met Peter?"

She nodded slowly. "He came to Great Falls on business. I'd managed to get a job in a restaurant, and he stopped in there for lunch. The rest is history, I guess. I was scared to death of him at first, but you know Peter. It didn't take long for him to convince me he was a different kind of man than the others I'd known."

"I'm glad."

"So am I." The sadness threatened to envelop her again, but she didn't want to feel sad tonight. For the first time in months, the burdens she'd been carrying felt manageable. Just having someone to talk to helped more than she could ever have imagined. Shaking off the melancholy, she tried to lighten the mood. "In the beginning, I thought Peter and I would have several more children together, but maybe it's for the best that we didn't. I don't know how we'd survive if I had more mouths to feed."

"Was that by choice?"

She shook her head. "No. We wanted a big family, but it just wasn't meant to be. I've wondered if something happened when Bobby was born. I was so young, and he was a big baby." A little embarrassed by how much she'd shared, she steered the conversation back on topic. "Anyway, you can see why I'm in no rush to ask Bobby's biological father for help. And it leaves me in my current predicament—taking advantage of you."

Gabe took her hand in his. "Why do you think that accepting help is taking advantage?"

"Isn't that what I'm doing? You're here with Bobby all afternoon and evening. You're seeing to his homework, making sure he has supper most of the time—even taking care of me. That's far more than you bargained for."

"Have you heard me complain?"

No. Never. And that, along with so many other things, was making her feelings dangerously complicated. "Not yet."

"But you're certain I will."

"Not one-hundred percent, but it seems likely."

"What would you say if I told you I was enjoying this?"

She laughed and tried to look away. "I'd say that sooner or later the novelty is bound to wear off and you'll start asking yourself what the hell you're doing."

"I suppose that could happen," he conceded, "but what if it doesn't?"

"You'll probably be more surprised than I am." His eyes were too deep, his voice too warm. He was close enough to smell his soap and see a tiny scar on his chin, another below his ear. Everything suddenly felt too close and far too intimate and, worse, she felt the desperate, urgent desire to feel his arms around her and his lips on hers.

He must have sensed something, because his expression changed in that moment. The kindness was still there, but something new joined it. Something Siddah recognized and, God help her, welcomed.

With his eyes locked on hers, he took a step closer and Siddah's breath caught. "I'm not Cornell Beesley either," he said, his voice barely above a whisper.

Delicious, heady, wonderful, frightening desire licked at her. She didn't want to feel it…or did she? Her head swam and the exhaustion that had been almost painful a few minutes earlier evaporated. All at once, she felt energized and alive, but that was probably only because it had been so long since she'd felt like this.

Gabe's eyes darkened with longing and Siddah gave up arguing with herself. Slowly, slowly, he moved closer, put both hands on her shoulders and pulled her toward him. She went to him with an eagerness that embarrassed her, and when his lips finally grazed hers, longing exploded inside of her.

Somewhere in the dim recesses of her mind, a warning sounded. She shouldn't do this. But for the life of her, she didn't know why.

His lips were soft and warm, and he tasted faintly of cola and barbecue sauce. When he realized she wasn't going to fight him, he slid his arms around her with a tenderness that both surprised and touched her.

Lost in the moment, she wound her arms around his neck. He was so strong, so solid, so…male, and she felt small, fragile and beautiful in his arms. His tongue brushed her lips and she opened them to him eagerly. Slowly, as he'd done everything else, he met her tongue and caressed it with his own.

That internal warning grew louder, but she ignored it. She knew he wasn't here to stay. Even if he did stay, this thing between them could never be anything more than it was right now. She wasn't even sure she wanted it to be. It was simply a moment stolen out of time. One she wanted to savor for as long as it lasted.

CHAPTER TWELVE

GABE PULLED AWAY first. Lord knows, it wasn't because he wanted to. He was on fire. Pulsing with desire he couldn't satisfy here, and nearly sick with wanting. And if he wanted to completely screw up his life and guarantee that the old man hated him, he'd hang on to Siddah and never let go.

He'd been waiting for Siddah, intending to tell her about his conversation with Bobby. But now didn't seem like a good time to add another burden to her shoulders. Later, he told himself. When she wasn't so fragile.

It took more willpower than he knew he had to release her and step away, and the look in her eyes, that glowing, passionate glimmer of desire, almost had him saying to hell with all of it. Let the mill fail. Let the old man hate him. Let the future die. Let his mother's disappointment in him grow. If Siddah had reached for him, he'd have given it all up in that moment without batting an eye.

But Siddah was a practical woman. She might have enjoyed their kiss, but she knew as well as he did that it couldn't lead to anything more. It had been a fluke. The result of one weak moment. One of those things that you don't regret but you don't go out of your way to repeat.

He'd never envied Peter more than he did in that moment, and he wondered what would have happened if Gabe had met her first? Since he couldn't continue looking at Siddah without wanting much more, he glanced at his watch and tried to look surprised by the time. "It's nearly eleven," he said, his voice too loud and eager. "I should go."

Nodding, Siddah turned partially away and wrapped her arms around herself. "You don't want to be late."

He didn't want to go at all, but he didn't let himself say so. It didn't feel right to just run out the door without saying something, though. More ill at ease than he'd been since he was Bobby's age at a school dance, he tried to come up with the right words. "Siddah, I—"

"Please don't," she said, cutting him off. "Whatever it is you're going to say, please don't." She turned to him, and he knew she was probably as torn, as confused and as guilty as he was.

There was nothing more to say. And though kissing her had been one of the best moments in his life, he had the foreboding feeling that he would live to regret it.

She deserved so much more than he could give. She *needed* so much more than he could give. If he was any kind of man at all, he'd keep his distance from here on out.

SIDDAH'S ALARM didn't go off the next morning, thanks to a storm that had moved into the valley overnight and knocked out power while she slept. Not that she'd slept all that well. Gabe had drifted in and out of her dreams all night, and she was more confused by morning than she was before. But with just half an hour to get behind her desk, she didn't have time to think about Gabe or the future.

She woke Bobby and rushed through her morning routine, throwing on an old standby outfit and running a brush through her hair, then sweeping a little blush and powder onto her cheeks before rushing out the door to drop Bobby at school.

She'd just slid into her chair when Chris came to the door of her office, and she knew at once that something was terribly wrong.

Wearing an expression as dark as the clouds outside, he wagged a pink message slip in front of him. "You want to tell me what this is?"

"I don't know," she said uncertainly. "What does it say?"

He made a show of looking at the message, clearing his throat, and finally reading, "Judge Benson's clerk called. Exhibits B-one through B-nine are missing from the packets you had delivered this morning." Looking away from the message, his cold eyes pierced Siddah. "You want to explain how that happened?"

The blood drained from Siddah's face. "That can't be right. Amanda and I went over everything with a fine-tooth comb before we finished last night. I'm sure we included everything. We checked three times."

"Apparently you didn't check well enough." Chris tossed the message onto her desk. "They're not only missing from the original set of exhibits, they're also missing from the courtesy copies we delivered to the judge's chambers. I'm guessing that means opposing counsel didn't receive them either."

With her mind racing as she tried to figure out how she could have made a horrendous mistake, Siddah reached for her master list and began thumbing through it. "B-one through nine?" She found them on the list and her heart sank. "Every one of the deposition transcripts? That's impossible. I'm sure they were there."

"*Not* there," Chris insisted. "And not in the files on my desk. I've already checked."

"But they were there last night. They couldn't have just disappeared. I certainly didn't throw them out, and I'm sure Amanda didn't."

"Well, they're gone somewhere," Chris snapped. "We've checked every inch of the office."

Siddah kneaded her forehead frantically. Those transcripts hadn't just walked out the door on their own, but she couldn't even begin to think of where they'd gone. "Can we order new copies?"

"Do you have any idea how much they cost?"

"Yes, but—" She broke off, sick with worry and having trouble forming coherent thought. "I just don't understand how this happened. I know those transcripts were there. I know we copied them."

"I think the problem is, your focus isn't on the job. We've talked about this before, but the situation isn't getting better."

Siddah shook her head firmly. "That's not true. I'm one-hundred percent focused when I'm here." But that *wasn't* true. Last night she'd been thinking about coming home to Gabe and Bobby.

Chris picked up the message slip from her desk and

held it out to her. "This isn't a hundred percent, Siddah. We both know that."

"No, of course not." Her stomach turned over, and she thought she might be sick. "I don't know how this happened, Chris, but I swear I'll make it right. I'll find the transcripts and I'll take them to the court myself. I'll stand there and watch the judge's clerk every second to make sure they get in the right place. It was a mistake, and I'll fix it. It won't happen again." Not if her life depended on it.

Chris stared at her without blinking for an uncomfortably long time, and Siddah had to force herself not to slink down in her chair like a child who'd been chastised. After what seemed like forever, he turned away.

Tears filled her eyes, but she blinked them away. She wanted so desperately to create a safe, secure world for Bobby, but what little security he had in his life came from Gabe, Helene and Monty. Instead of shoring up her son's world, Siddah felt as if she was knocking the foundation out from under him.

"TASTE THIS." Ivy shoved a spoon filled with something that smelled of almonds under Siddah's nose. "I'm thinking about making this for the progressive dinner on Friday. What do you think?"

Siddah pulled back sharply and wiped her juice-stained hands on a towel near her elbow. She'd been helping Ivy preserve cherries all morning, but she'd been so distracted thinking about work and Gabe, she'd hardly noticed that Ivy had stopped working to throw lunch together.

It took some effort, but she managed to put on what

she hoped was an enthusiastic expression as she took the spoon from Ivy. Though she hadn't spared a thought for food all day, one bite of Ivy's chicken-rice salad made her stomach growl with hunger. "It's great," she said, passing back the spoon. "Where did you say you got the recipe?"

"From a friend I used to work with." Smiling with satisfaction, Ivy reached for the foil she'd left on the counter. Even after working over a hot stove all day, her hair looked as if she'd just finished styling it, and her makeup was flawless. "I've had it in my recipe book for years, but I've never made it before. Do you think there's too much almond?"

"No. I think it's perfect." Siddah shook off her odd mood and took advantage of the break. "What course are you preparing this time?" .

"I have the salad," Ivy said over her shoulder as she carried the bowl to the refrigerator. "I thought I'd put a mound of this on a bed of lettuce, but I can't decide what I should offer to drink with it. Lemonade wouldn't really go, would it?"

"I don't think so. Too sour."

Ivy closed the refrigerator and came back to the table. She pushed aside the bowl of cherries Siddah had been pitting and put her feet up on an empty chair. "I thought about apple cider, but that doesn't feel quite right, either."

"That chardonnay you bought last month would be nice."

"It would be great," Ivy agreed, "but this is just the second stop. I need to keep this course dry so we don't have anyone driving under the influence. We don't want any trouble like that time Bruce and Melanie got pulled over."

Siddah frowned at the memory. "I haven't seen Bruce and Melanie in a while. How are things between them?"

"About the same. You know Bruce. He refuses to admit that anything's wrong, and Melanie can't talk about anything else." Ivy swept sugar from the table into her hand. "So have you made up your mind yet? Are you coming to dinner?"

Siddah hadn't given it much thought, but she didn't need to. "I don't think so."

"And the reason for that would be…?"

"Work, for one thing. I barely have time to breathe as it is, and I don't spend nearly enough time with Bobby."

"How's the job going?"

Siddah started to give a pat answer, but stopped herself and forced out the truth. "Not well," she admitted. "I made a mistake with some exhibits the other day that left the County Attorney's office looking sloppy and inept. Chris was embarrassed in front of the judge, and he wasn't happy. I can't even say I blame him. I found the documents and got them delivered where they needed to go, but if that had happened on a different case, the news media would have made hash out of Evan and Chris over it." She propped her chin in her hands and sighed heavily. "I feel like everything is falling apart around my ears. The harder I work, the worse it all gets."

"All the more reason you need to relax."

"If I'm lucky enough to be off work that night, I really should stay in with Bobby."

"You need to have fun, too," Ivy said firmly.

"I'm not in the mood for a lecture, Ivy. I'm doing what I need to do for Bobby's sake."

"Seems to me, Bobby might be happy just seeing you once in a while."

The observation stung. "Which only makes my argument stronger, not yours. Besides, I don't want to come alone. I'm trying to move on like everyone says I should, but if I go alone, all I'd think about was how Peter wasn't there. I just don't want to put myself through that."

"The first time is bound to be tough," Ivy agreed. "But we'll all be there for you, and it will get easier with practice."

"I don't want to practice." Suddenly desperate for some air, Siddah crossed to the back door and stood in front of the screen where she could see Bobby and Rebecca playing in the weak autumn sunlight.

"He's made a lot of progress in the last little while," Ivy said from behind her. "Gabe must be good for him."

That was another subject Siddah didn't want to discuss, especially since all she could think about was kissing him again. "I think he is. He's good for both of us, actually."

"Oh?"

"He's nothing like I thought he'd be," Siddah admitted.

"So why don't you invite Gabe? If he came with you, you wouldn't be alone."

The smile slid from Siddah's face. "Are you kidding?"

"Not at all. The two of you are getting along, right?"

Siddah's heart began to race, but she looked away so

Ivy wouldn't see how much the suggestion intrigued her. "We are, but I can't ask him to the dinner. What would people think?"

"Who cares?"

"I do, and I'm sure he does, too." Besides, things had been strained between them since that kiss. Gabe still showed up every day, and there was nothing she could put her finger on to prove that things had changed, but she could feel the difference.

Ivy waved away her concerns with one careless hand. "What *can* they think? You'd be having dinner with a group of mutual friends. What of it? It would at least give you a chance to get out of the house and see people, and you wouldn't have to be alone. I think it's a great idea."

"Of course you do. You suggested it." Siddah wondered what Ivy would think if she told her the truth, but she wasn't ready to take that step. "I'll think about it."

"Do more than think. Ask him. I'll ask my mom if Bobby can stay at her house that night with Rebecca while we're out."

"Don't start making too many plans," Siddah warned. "Gabe probably has to work that night."

"If you ask him soon enough, maybe he'll have time to change his schedule."

"Maybe."

Ivy huffed in frustration. "Come on, Siddah! If you don't want to ask Gabe, fine. But you've been hidden away in that house for too long. If you want Bobby to be interested in life and the people around him, maybe you should try showing him how it's done."

Siddah forced a laugh to lighten the mood. "Wow. All this because I'm not sure about asking Gabe to the progressive dinner?"

"I'm very passionate about the idea."

"I can tell." Sobering, Siddah gave the idea some thought. Maybe it wasn't such a bad idea after all. It would give them some time alone, away from Bobby. A chance to talk about this thing between them and decide exactly what it was. Right or wrong, the thought of an adult evening with Gabe was awfully appealing. "So, okay," she conceded. "I'll ask him. Better?"

Warmth crept into Ivy's smile. "If you mean it."

"Are you kidding?" Siddah held out both hands and pretended to weigh her options. "Ask Gabe to dinner. Get steamrollered by Ivy." She tilted her head, considering. "Yep. I'll ask him."

"When?"

"The sooner the better."

"Really? And if he says yes, you'll come to the dinner?"

"Well, it's either that or stand him up. So, yeah. If he says yes, I'll come to the dinner."

Ivy pumped one arm into the air. "Yes!"

"I said I'd ask," Siddah reminded her. "He hasn't said yes."

"Oh, he will."

"I wouldn't be so sure." But now that she'd decided, Siddah couldn't deny the seed of excitement budding inside her. She just hoped she wouldn't regret this decision.

THE SUN WAS CRESTING the mountains when the alarm on Gabe's watch dragged him reluctantly from dozing to wakefulness. His body clock had adjusted to being back in Montana, but he'd always been a morning person and working all night still played havoc with him at times.

Yawning, he stepped out of the guard shack into the cool of the morning. A stiff wind blew into the valley from the mountains, and the songs of birds on nearby utility poles brought back memories of other mornings so clearly he might have been twelve again, standing on the bank of the river, hair spiked from sleep, eyes blurry, but filled with contentment as his father rooted around in the supplies and started a fire for breakfast.

Smiling, he crossed the yard toward the front gate, his senses filled with sunlight and sawdust. In the distance, the song of a meadowlark split the morning and Gabe realized between one step and the next that he'd miss this when he left again.

He pushed that thought from his mind as he kicked himself into gear and jogged the rest of the way to the gate. After working the key in the massive lock, he pushed back the gate so that the yard stood ready for the morning shift to arrive.

He turned back just as his father's pickup loomed over the hill and into view. Since Labor Day, Gabe had been watching, waiting…wishing for something different than the usual noncommittal stare as the truck rattled into the yard. But day after day passed with no change in the old man's greeting.

Maybe it was the memories of long-ago summers that got his feet moving. Maybe it was the impatience he'd been known for his entire life. Whatever it was,

Gabe pounded up the steps into the office a minute after Monty did.

The old man must have heard him coming—nobody could sneak up those stairs—but he didn't even look up from the coffeepot when Gabe walked through the door.

Gabe didn't let that deter him. He shut the door behind him, blocking out the sunlight and the birdsong. "You got a minute?"

His father shrugged and turned toward his office. "What for? You gonna quit?"

Did he have to make this so damn hard? Gabe balled his hands into fists and struggled to keep his voice even. "No. I'd just like to talk to you about the mill."

That brought the old man's head around with a snap. "What about it?"

"I've been hearing talk. I want to know how true it is."

Monty dropped into the chair behind his desk. "What kind of talk?"

"About the mill being in trouble." Gabe sat across from him. He noticed his father's raised eyebrows and ignored them. "People are saying that you've been having trouble making payroll since the accident."

"And you believe that?"

"It came from a credible source."

His father's face became a mask. He turned away, grabbed something from the credenza behind him and began working as if Gabe wasn't waiting for an answer.

"Peter wasn't the only person involved in that accident," Gabe pressed. "I've also heard that you had to pay a big settlement on a lawsuit. Are you really having trouble?"

His father looked up, his expression bitter. "What's it to you?"

"You're going to punish me, is that it? I don't deserve to know what's going on because I left for a while? Doesn't the fact that I'm here now count for *anything?*"

Slowly, his father set aside the invoices he'd been thumbing through. "What do you want from me, Gabriel? You want me to fall at your feet or something? You're here. God only knows for how long, but you're here. It counts however you want it to count, does that make you happy?"

Gabe closed his eyes and tried to hang on to some control. But if he *ever* acted like the old man, he wanted someone to shoot him and get it over with. "Tell me about the mill," he said when he trusted himself to speak again.

"There's nothing to tell."

"I think there is. I think you're in trouble, and I'm worried about you and Mom."

"And you think I should tell you about it."

His father's face was so smug Gabe lost the battle. "Yes, I think you should tell me about it. I'm your son, dammit. I've been waiting my whole life for you to remember that."

"*You've* been waiting?"

Gabe turned away and mopped his face with one hand. "I know it's probably conveniently escaped your memory, but *you* sent me away. You told me not to come back, and God help me, I believed you. I missed everything that happened in the family because of that, but you can't keep laying all the blame for it at my feet. I just did what you told me to do."

The mask slipped, but Gabe couldn't tell what the emotion was in his father's eyes and the things he didn't say rang out loud in the space between them.

"All I ever wanted was for you to approve of me," Gabe said, his control slipping. "That's it. It would have been nice, just once, to feel as if you liked me one-tenth as much as you liked Peter. But you couldn't give it to me then, and you can't give it to me now. Well, I've got news for you, Pop," he shouted, thumping himself in the chest with both hands and then spreading his arms wide. "I'm all you have left. Like it or not, this is it. Peter's gone. I'm here. You damn near didn't have me around, but I don't suppose that would have mattered, would it?"

"What the hell does that mean?"

"I nearly died in that damn jungle, Pop. That's why I didn't find out about Peter until just a few weeks ago. I spent months recuperating enough to just get out of there, and the only thing I wanted when I got back to civilization was a chance to make things right between us. But that's not going to happen, is it? I could spend the next twenty years of my life playing night watchman for you, and it still wouldn't make any difference."

Unable to hold back the anger and hurt any longer, he wheeled away and wrenched open the door. Even then, some part of him wanted the old man to call him back. But it didn't happen.

He narrowly missed plowing into Joan as she rounded the corner, and ignored her when she called after him. She was his father's friend. Let her talk sense into him.

Still boiling, he passed the crew as they gathered for

their shift. He was furious with himself for caring, but even ten years away hadn't been able to quiet the kid inside who'd been hanging around all these years wanting something he was never going to get.

When he walked into the employee parking lot and saw Siddah standing beside his Jeep, he stopped cold. The early-morning sunlight caught her hair and gilded it with golden highlights, and she looked uneasy and vulnerable standing there waiting for him.

His heart skipped a beat, and for one split second he thought that at least one thing was right in his life. But their kiss had been a mistake. One he didn't regret, but a mistake nonetheless. He couldn't walk around indulging in fantasies about his brother's wife.

Determined to get his thoughts back in line, he took his time closing the distance between them. She looked up and their eyes met, but Gabe did his best not to acknowledge the way those eyes made him feel.

"Morning," he said, as if finding her there was part of an ordinary day.

Her lips curved slightly, and she shivered in the cool morning breeze. "I hope you don't mind me waiting here. I need to talk to you, and I didn't want to do it tonight when Bobby could hear."

He shrugged and tossed his jacket into the back of the Jeep. "No problem. Is something wrong?"

"No. It's not that." She broke off with an embarrassed smile and twisted her hands together. "I need to ask a favor."

"Of me?" That surprised him. "Sure. What do you need?"

"It's not something I *need,* really." She laughed uneasily, then seemed to pull herself together with a shake of her head and a lift of her chin. "This is silly. I'll just come straight out with it. Peter and I were part of a group of friends who got together for progressive dinners once a month. I haven't been to one since the accident, but there's a dinner coming up at the end of the week, and I've been thinking of going." She slid a glance at him and rushed on. "I just don't want to go alone. It would be awkward, I think. I wondered if you'd go with me."

Her question wiped away all the leftover irritation after the argument with the old man. "You want *me* to go with you?"

"If you don't mind. It wouldn't be a date," she added quickly. "Just…well, I don't know who else to ask."

"Ah. I see."

Her eyes flashed to his face and lingered there. "I didn't mean it that way. I'd really like for you to come with me. You've become a good friend, and I enjoy your company. I just didn't want you to get the wrong impression after…well, you know."

"The kiss?" He didn't need to ask, but he kind of liked the way color crept into her cheeks when he said it.

"I don't think we should talk about that right now."

He would have said the same thing a few minutes ago. Now he didn't want to talk about anything else. "I think we need to talk about it."

"Really, Gabe, there's nothing to say. It was a mistake—"

"Was it?"

"You know it was. You've been avoiding me ever since it happened. I understand why. You're my brother-in-law, for heaven's sake—"

"I don't feel like a brother-in-law." He shifted so that he was standing in front of her, leaning in, knowing it was the last thing he should be doing and this the last place on earth he should be doing it, but he couldn't seem to help himself. "I've been trying to convince myself that we made a mistake, but the truth is I'd like to do it again—often."

"We can't," she said quickly, but he could see the desire in her eyes, and that gave him courage.

"Why can't we? Is there a law against it?"

"I don't think there's a law. It's not as if we're related. But it's still not right."

"Why?"

"Because…it just isn't."

He touched her arm gently. When she didn't pull away, he moved to her shoulder and made a slow lazy circle on her neck. Big mistake. He felt a rush of desire and told himself to stop, but he'd never been good at taking advice. "Do you really believe that, or are you just saying that because you think you should?"

"I—" She broke off, eyes wide. When she spoke again, her voice was so low he almost didn't hear her. "I don't know."

"Fair enough." Gabe pulled his hand away and leaned against the Jeep, shoving his hands into his pockets to keep from pulling her into his arms in front of the whole crew. "I don't know either. But I don't think we're doing anybody any favors by pretending something we don't feel, or by ignoring what we do. I'm attracted to you, Siddah. That's the long and short of it. I'm more than attracted, in fact. I've never met a woman like you, and if you'd never been married to Peter, I'd be in hot pursuit. You might as well know that."

Letting out a heavy sigh, she sank against the Jeep beside him. "You're going to make me be honest, too, aren't you?"

"I don't plan on twisting your arm, if that's what you're asking."

She smiled without looking at him. "I know that. You're not like that. You're not at all like I thought you'd be, and I like the fact that we're honest with each other. So okay. If you're going to be so damn honest, I should be, too. If I'd never been married to Peter and you were in hot pursuit, I wouldn't run very fast."

Joy exploded in his chest and brought a laugh to his lips, but he stayed exactly where he was, hands in pockets, one foot crossed over the other as if they were talking about the weather. Admitting that they each found the other attractive didn't open any doors for them. But he more than admired her unfailing honesty and courage. If he wasn't in love with her already, he was damn close. "Well, so now we know. What are we going to do about it?"

From the corner of his eye he could see her looking out over the cars again and shaking her head. "What can we do about it? People still think of me as Peter's wife. You're still Peter's brother, and you're still leaving one of these days. Even if the other things weren't a problem, there's Bobby. He's doing much better since you've been around, but I don't want him to start thinking there's something permanent in the works. I'm quite sure your parents would be less than thrilled to find out how we feel, and there's no reason to upset them when nothing's going to come of it anyway, so I'd say there's not a whole lot we *can* do."

She was right, but that didn't stop him from feeling bitterly disappointed. Lifting one shoulder, he turned his face toward her. "So I guess we remain friends?"

"Seems like the only option."

Some perverse part of him wanted her to be as disappointed as he was. Not that he'd expected any other outcome. He knew the drill as well as she did. Why cause the old man to have a fit about something new? Why cause Bobby to hope for something that could never be? Why stir the water in the pond if he wasn't going to be around to smooth it again?

But leaving had never seemed less appealing.

CHAPTER THIRTEEN

GABE WAS STILL too agitated to sleep when he heard the phone ringing a couple of hours later. He lay on his childhood bed, one arm over his eyes in a vain effort to block out the light. He could hear his mother moving around the house, wielding the vacuum while daytime television shows kept her company.

The ringing of the phone stopped abruptly and his mother's footsteps on the stairs soon took its place. He was halfway across the room by the time she knocked on his door.

"Oh!" she said, when he yanked open his bedroom door. "I wasn't sure you were awake."

"I heard the phone," he said, stepping out onto the landing. "Is it for me?"

She paused there, looking at him for so long he knew his father had told her about his illness. With a muffled sob, she gathered him into her arms and held on for a few seconds, then turned around and started back downstairs.

"It's that Randy again. I wouldn't have disturbed you but he said it's urgent, and since he's calling from the university…" Her voice trailed off and she turned back to look at him. "I hope he's not calling to take you away from us. I'm not ready to let you go yet."

"I wouldn't worry about it, Mom. I'm not going any-where for a while."

She reached up to touch his face briefly before nod-ding him toward the kitchen. "Good. That's what I wanted to hear. Now go. Get your phone call. Find out what's so urgent."

Surprised by her reaction, and even more surprised to discover that his father had cared enough to phone her, he hurried into the kitchen and lifted the receiver from the counter. "Randy? What's up?"

"Just calling to see if you're surviving up there."

Gabe laughed, poured a cup of coffee and carried it to the table. "Hard as it is to believe, yeah, I am. I have a dandy job as a night watchman and everything."

"Night watchman?" Randy's voice grew serious. "You couldn't find anything else?"

"I'm working for my old man. Long story."

"Well, maybe I can help out. I'm actually calling to see if you've heard about the Westmoreland Grant."

Gabe cradled his coffee mug in both hands and notched the phone between shoulder and chin. "I thought that had been put on hold."

"It was. It's not any longer. Word is, you'd practically be a shoe-in if you get your name in."

He'd been too far out of the loop. Two years ago, he'd have known about this before Randy did, and his appli-cation would have been in the running before anyone else's. But two years ago, he could have done something about it.

"That's nice to know," he said, swallowing disap-pointment, "but it's not an issue. I have at least four months before the doctor says I'm clear to go back out into the field." And, strangely, he wasn't as antsy to get back as he'd once been.

"You wouldn't need to get back out there immediately," Randy said. "And your work with the Zapara makes you more than qualified. More qualified than anyone else, actually." He paused and then went on in a rush. "As a matter of fact, I'm hoping to piggyback onto your project. I think that together we stand a good chance of getting the grant. I could do the legwork here, you could do some of the behind-the-scenes stuff from where you are. I might need you back here by the end of November, but I think I could get along without you until then."

The old excitement began to stir. "Are you serious?"

"Absolutely. What do you say?"

"I don't know. Things are up in the air around here."

"So take the next few weeks to sort them out."

After the morning he'd had, the offer certainly was tempting. Whatever progress he'd made with the old man was destroyed now, and the longer he spent around Siddah, the more dangerous that situation became. The easiest thing—the smartest thing—would be to grab Randy's offer and run.

But he'd made promises. If he broke them now, he'd just prove the old man was right about him. "Wish I could, but I'm committed to being around here for a while longer."

"Don't say no," Randy pleaded. "You must be climbing the walls. If not now, you will be soon. So get your name in the running so we don't lose this opportunity. I'll handle everything I can for as long as I can."

Gabe rubbed the back of his neck and weighed the options carefully. But why shouldn't he get something in the works? It wasn't as if he planned to stay here forever. Why shouldn't he have something lined up and ready to go when he was healthy again?

His conversation with the old man had shown him that nothing was ever going to change around here, and staying had never really been an option. Not a serious one, anyway. Whatever fantasies he'd indulged in during his private moments were just that. "Okay, I'll do it," he said. "Let me grab something to write on and you can give me the details."

He jotted down everything Randy told him and tried to find some excitement in the prospect of winning the Westmoreland Grant. After all, research and travel, spending time in remote areas of the world, living in grass huts and sleeping on dirt floors—that was his life. But for the first time, that life seemed empty and uninviting.

The life he wanted was one he couldn't have. The life he had, he didn't want. How in the hell had this happened?

GABE WAS SURPRISINGLY NERVOUS as he approached Siddah's front door the night of the progressive dinner. He'd seen her every evening, but they'd both been extremely careful around each other since that morning in the parking lot. Siddah had phoned each day before leaving the office, and Gabe had walked out the door almost the minute she walked in. Neither wanted to cross the line again.

But tonight, everything would be different. They'd be together all evening long. A couple. He'd picked Bobby up after school as usual, but Ivy had come by to pick him up and take him to her mother's before Siddah even got home from work. That had left Gabe time to drive home, shower, shave and change.

Without Bobby to provide a buffer, anything might happen. Then again, nothing might happen. He knew how the evening *should* turn out, but he also knew how he wanted it to end and the anticipation was killing him.

He stepped onto the porch and pressed the doorbell. She answered almost immediately, her eyes wide and dark, her cheeks flushed as if she'd been running the same possibilities through her mind as he had. She'd dressed in a pair of black slacks and a formfitting green sweater that hugged her curves and made his heart hammer in his chest.

Smiling softly, she stepped aside to let him in. He'd been through the door countless times in the past few weeks, but tonight everything felt different. Special. Filled with meaning. The soft scent of her perfume filled the air between them and made it hard to breathe, and Gabe knew in that moment that he'd never be satisfied by a life without her in it.

She shut the door behind him, and they were alone. Away from the world and truly alone for the first time. He swallowed nervously and took in the length of her— her soft curves, the gentle swells that made him long to touch her. How would she feel beneath his hands? How warm and soft would her skin be? Just the thought of it made him hot, and he reacted so strongly he was glad they were standing in the dim light of the foyer.

"You look beautiful," he said. All the longing he was

trying to hide was there in his voice. Damn the dinner. He wanted her.

He longed to pull her into his arms, hold her until their hearts beat to the same rhythm. He ached to sweep her from her feet and carry her into the bedroom. He wanted to make love to her until the sun rose. To demand something of her he'd probably never have. To claim her and make her his, to wipe Peter out of her mind forever and cement his own place in her heart.

But for how long? Much as he wanted her, it wouldn't be fair or right to pretend something that would never happen. There was still nothing in Libby for him. Nothing except the woman he'd grown to love and the kid he was beginning to wish was his own.

Siddah flushed and turned to look over her shoulder. "I'm ready if you are. Just let me grab my purse."

Gabe wasn't ready to share her with the world yet. He caught her hand and pulled her into his arms, knowing he shouldn't, but too far gone to care. "You look beautiful," he said again.

He thought she might protest, but she melted into his arms eagerly. She didn't speak, she simply lifted her mouth to his and wrapped her arms around his neck. If there was one ounce of common sense left in his brain, it evaporated at her touch.

With a little moan of pleasure, she parted her lips and invited more. He groaned and tightened his arms around her, giving his hands free rein to explore those inviting curves. Sliding his hands to her hips, he cupped her bottom and pulled her against him. Another tiny moan escaped her lips and the fire she'd ignited flamed fully to life.

Somewhere in the back of his mind, disjointed words of logic floated just out of reach. All the reasons he shouldn't make love to her were there, but he didn't want to hear them. Not while she was running her hands along his back. Not when she leaned back, exposing the hollow of her throat to his eager lips. Not when she trembled beneath his touch.

He shut down the arguments and let himself have the moment. Right or wrong, this might be the only time he could be with her, and he wasn't strong enough to turn away. He slid his hands beneath her sweater and found her breasts.

With a shudder of pleasure, he pulled the sweater over her head and tossed it aside. She stumbled backward, taking him with her, and they landed on the floor together. Her hands were under his shirt, exploring his bare chest, then stroking his back so softly and sensuously he thought he'd explode. His shirt was there one minute and gone the next.

She trailed kisses across his shoulder and down his chest. He could hear his own ragged breathing but the staccato pulse of his heart drowned out everything else. Words rose in his throat, but he couldn't make himself speak. And when she slid her hands down to his waist, then inched lower to fumble with his belt buckle, the time for talking was past.

With a cry, he found the zipper to her slacks and opened it. He slipped the slacks down her hips and gave himself one brief moment to look at her before she reached for him again. Even if the world had come to an end in that moment he wouldn't have been able to stop himself. He wanted her. She wanted him. Why did it have to be more complicated than that?

In his fantasies, he'd made slow, gentle love to her, but the reality was far different. Desire had been growing for weeks, and they were both too hungry to take things slowly. Oblivious to the time and the world around them, Gabe claimed her, and when they climaxed, unbelievably together, he knew he would never experience anything like that again. It didn't occur to him until afterward, as they lay entwined together on the floor in a tangle of clothes, that he hadn't even thought about using the condom in his wallet.

Suddenly thinking rationally, he levered himself up on one elbow and looked down at her. She lay with her eyes closed, her lips slightly parted, and she looked so utterly peaceful, Gabe hated to disturb her.

He brushed her cheek gently with the backs of his fingers, and her eyelids fluttered open. Aching, he pressed a soft kiss to her lips and whispered, "Hi."

She smiled up at him. "Hi yourself."

"That wasn't exactly the way I'd planned to start the evening. I'm usually...well, I had a condom. I hope—"

She cut him off with a kiss. "Don't worry about it. I'm sure we're fine."

"Really?" He couldn't decide if he was disappointed or relieved. "How can you be sure?"

"I told you, I don't get pregnant." She reached for her sweater and drew it across her bare breasts.

That same odd feeling zapped Gabe again, but this time he recognized it. He was disappointed. But why should he be? That didn't make any sense at all. If he wanted to upset his parents and prove what a screwup he was, ruin Siddah's life and create more confusion for Bobby—not to mention throwing a monkey wrench into his career—getting her pregnant was the way to go about it.

He should be relieved.

But Gabe had never been one for doing what he should.

"So?" Ivy asked an hour later as she followed Siddah into the kitchen carrying a load of salad plates. "Want to tell me what's up with the two of you?"

Siddah's stomach turned over, but she pretended nothing was amiss as she stacked dishes beside the sink. They'd been to just one house and eaten just one course, but already Ivy's nose was twitching. What had possessed either of them to think they could get away with this?

She pasted on a bright smile and reached for the dishes Ivy was holding. "There's nothing *up* with the two of us," she said firmly. "We're friends."

"Friends who showed up late and can't stop staring at each other." Ivy leaned so she could see into the dining room and lowered her voice to a whisper. "There are two things a man can't hide, Siddah. When he's drunk and when he's in love. Bruce showed up at the door three sheets to the wind, but Gabe is just as obvious. And so, might I add, are you."

"I'm not in love with him," Siddah whispered back, too quickly.

"In a pig's eye." Ivy turned on the faucet. "I've known you too long. You can't fool me."

"Well that's good, since I'm not trying to." Gabe's laugh sounded from the other room, and all of her senses flared to life. Siddah resisted the urge to look over her shoulder. Ivy would make something of it, and she wasn't in the mood.

From the minute she'd started dressing for dinner, Siddah had been at war with herself over what to wear, how to do her makeup, what scent to use. Everything seemed fraught with hidden meaning. The war had escalated when Gabe, looking way too handsome in a black Polo shirt and jeans, arrived to pick her up.

She'd lost one battle when she practically threw herself at him on the floor.

The *floor!*

Just thinking about it made her face burn—not just with embarrassment, but also with remembered pleasure. She'd had a healthy and active sex life with Peter, but they'd *never* done anything like that.

Peter had been a wonderful man. She'd never deny that. But he'd never had Gabe's easygoing nature or his ability to make friends. He'd never been as comfortable in a crowd, and though he'd been kind, he hadn't been as instinctively compassionate as Gabe seemed to be. Whether Gabe was asking after someone's aging mother or helping a very pregnant Celia Segretti up the stairs, Gabe's heart seemed to lie wide open, and Siddah couldn't imagine why anyone would think of him as cold or self-centered, or why they'd doubt his sincerity.

Realizing that she'd have to be even more careful, she set her expression and turned toward the dining room to finish clearing the table.

"What?" Ivy demanded. "You don't want to talk about it?"

"Not particularly. Besides, the others are getting restless to move on."

"Trying to avoid me?"

Rolling her eyes in exasperation, Siddah turned back to her friend. "Yes. But don't take it personally. There's just no point in talking about this. It's nothing. A momentary infatuation or transference of my feelings for Peter to Gabe." But that was a lie, and her feelings of disloyalty to Gabe were nearly as strong as the disloyalty she battled over Peter.

"Even if what I felt for him was real," she said, checking over her shoulder to make sure they were still alone, "he'll be leaving again in a few months. The last thing I need is to get all wound up over somebody who won't be around. The situation is just impossibly complicated and there's no point even wasting time thinking about it."

Hands dripping water, Ivy turned away from the sink. "Maybe he'll stay."

"I don't think so."

"You never know. Have you seen the way he looks at you?"

"His own family couldn't keep him here before. I doubt that a fleeting attraction could."

"What if you're more than a fleeting attraction?"

"What if I'm not?" Siddah tossed a towel to her and turned away. "Let's just forget about it, okay? We're here as friends, and it would be helpful if you'd play along." She didn't wait for an answer, but hurried back into the dining room and tried not to do anything that might raise questions in anyone else's mind.

She did her best not to look at Gabe, not to listen too attentively when he spoke, not to laugh too much when he said something amusing—which was far too often. She tried not to notice the glances he sent her way, and she did her best to ignore the tingle that jolted along her spine whenever he drew near.

But tonight was just a fantasy. Tomorrow, Bobby would be home and full of stories about his sleepover with Rebecca and her grandma, and the world would start spinning again. Neither she nor Gabe needed to act upon something that existed only in a fairy tale, no matter how much she might want to.

IT WAS NEARLY MIDNIGHT when Gabe pulled into Siddah's driveway and turned off the Jeep's engine. The minute he did, Siddah's hands grew clammy and her heart took up residence in her throat. She'd done a pretty good job acting as if he was just a friend all evening, but now, alone in the darkened car, all that flew out the window.

Crickets sang somewhere nearby, and a canyon breeze stirred the air, bringing with it the scents of cut lumber and sweet wild grass.

He loomed large behind the steering wheel. Large and solid and male. She could hear the sound of his breathing and smell the faint scent of the soap he'd used to shower earlier. The remembered taste of his lips and feel of his hands swept over her, and her breath caught.

Making love to him had been wonderful and exciting—and completely spontaneous. Now, if she invited him inside, she'd practically be suggesting a repeat performance, and that seemed a little too brazen.

Not that she didn't want to. Her body tingled all over and her skin seemed ultrasensitive to the brush of fabric as she moved. She could easily imagine being with him again, making love more slowly, taking time to explore each other's bodies…

But this was a small town. People would be sure to notice his car outside her house. Bobby could find out. Helene and Monty could hear gossip. Siddah wasn't ready to deal with that yet.

She didn't know if she ever would be.

She could feel Gabe watching her, taking his cue from her, and her gratitude made her weak with relief. "I'd invite you in—" she began.

"It's probably not a good idea," he finished for her. He grinned and leaned forward for a chaste kiss. "I'm sure Mom's waiting up to hear how the evening went. I'll stand a much better chance of pretending dinner was the highlight if I get in at a reasonable time."

Siddah knew he was giving her an out, but she grabbed it gratefully. "I hadn't thought of that. It must be strange, living with them again."

"Very."

"And for six months!" She shook her head in wonder. "You know, you still haven't told me how you managed to get six months away from work."

"Haven't I?"

"No, and I'm wildly curious. Maybe it would work for me."

Gabe laughed, but he sobered again almost immediately and his expression became almost grim. He took her hands in his and gently ran his thumbs across her knuckles. "I have six months off because I was sick. I managed to contract a fever while I was in a remote village in the interior. Luckily, the people of the village knew what they were doing. Without them, I wouldn't have made it out alive."

Siddah's smile froze. "How close were you?"

"To dying?" Gabe shrugged, but he didn't look away. "Closer than I want to be again for a long time. It was weeks before I was strong enough to sit up, months before I could survive the journey back to civilization. My doctor wants me to stay away from humidity and heat for at least six months and the university wants me to be a man of leisure until the doctor gives the all-clear."

"And that's why you're here?" She wasn't even sure how she felt about that. Disappointed that he'd come back only because he was sick? Frightened that she'd nearly lost him before she even found him? Or angry that he'd been carrying this secret around all this time?

"I'm here because I got Mom's letter about Peter. I could have avoided humidity and heat anywhere—at least the kind you find in the rain forest."

"But that's why you're staying so long."

"It was originally." Gabe turned her hand over and studied her palm for a long moment. "Now there are other factors at work."

"Like a silly little crush on your brother's widow?"

Even in the dimly lit car, she could tell that his eyes darkened with displeasure. "Is that what you think?"

"I don't know what I think," she admitted. "I don't know what I feel, either."

Gabe lifted her palm and pressed his lips to its center. "I'm confusing you."

"You're doing more than that." Half-convinced that she'd melt right there on the seat, she pulled her hand away gently. "I think you're a wonderful man, Gabe. I really do. But we can't do this. We can't act as if there's a future for us when we both know there's not."

"*Do* we know that?"

"Of course we do. Unless you've changed your mind and you're planning to stay around." It was by no means the only sticking point, but it was the first. Unless they settled it, they didn't even need to think about the others.

Gabe sat back in his seat and stared up at the dome light. "I have never been so tempted to stay around in all my life."

"But—?"

"But my life isn't here. We both know that."

It was nothing more than she'd expected, but it still hurt to hear it. "That's my point," she said, pulling even further into herself. "You won't be here."

"You don't have to stay," he pointed out. "There's nothing keeping you here. You and Bobby could relocate. Come to Virginia, since that's home base for me."

He made it sound so easy. "I don't have to stay," she agreed, "but I've worked too hard to find a place to call home, and I don't want to leave. I was uprooted too much when I was a kid and I can't bear the thought of moving Bobby around like that." She shifted in her seat so she could see into the shadows that hid his face. "Besides, let's pretend for a minute that I didn't have a problem with that. Where will you be? In Virginia, or in the rain forest?"

"I'd probably split my time."

"And I'd be doing what? Working? Waiting for you to come back? Hoping you weren't out there contracting another fever?"

He sighed and ran a hand along the back of his neck. "You make it sound worse than it is."

"Am I missing something?" she asked. "Didn't you just say you'd split your time between Virginia and the jungle?"

"Well yes, but—"

"And my choice would be to either pick up a machete and follow you—which I'm not about to do—or stay home while you're off adventuring and be there to welcome you with open arms when you come back."

His mouth quirked. "That's where it loses something in the translation."

She appreciated his humor, but this was too serious to laugh about. "You have a better spin to put on it?"

He smiled, but the humor didn't reach his eyes. "I'm not a nine-to-five kind of guy, Siddah. I never have been."

"And I'm not asking you to change. But security is very important to me, and I can't change that, either."

"So we have a stalemate?"

For some reason, she didn't want to leave it there. "My dad had a wandering spirit," she explained. "I don't remember him leaving, but I have very clear memories of my mother waiting for him to wander back into our lives. And he did, every so often."

"I think our situation is a little different."

"In some ways," she admitted. "But the problems would be the same. When my dad was around, things were good for a day or two, but even as a little girl I resented him showing up without warning and then telling me what I could and couldn't do. Mom was used to doing things her way, handling the problems that came up. Then all of a sudden Dad would be home, acting as if he belonged there. But he didn't, Gabe. No matter what explanation you want to put on it, he didn't belong. And neither would you. Bobby would begin to resent you, and so would I." She smiled sadly and hoped he understood that she wasn't trying to hurt him. "I'm not going to put Bobby through that, and I won't put myself through it, either. Maybe some women could live that way and be happy, but I don't happen to be one of them."

Slowly, he put out one hand and drew a finger along her cheek. "I guess we're just too different, you and I."

It nearly broke her heart, but she had to agree with him. "I guess we are."

He tried to smile but failed miserably. "Are we back to being friends again?"

"We don't seem to do that very well," she pointed out. "One of us is always forgetting. Or both."

He smiled sadly. "Is that such a bad thing?"

"It is when you think about all the other people who are involved. Decisions we make won't only affect you and me, and we can't play fast and loose with other people."

He looked away and leaned his head against the back of the seat. She ached to hold him, but she knew that would only make things harder for both of them. Tonight *had* been a fairy tale, and it was time to return her glass slippers.

Leaning up, she kissed his cheek and then silently let herself out into the night. But walking away from him was one of the hardest things she'd ever had to do.

CHAPTER FOURTEEN

GABE WOKE LATE the next morning with a splitting headache—the result of a nearly sleepless night while he thought about his conversation with Siddah. What the hell had happened? He'd come to Libby to patch things up with his parents, but he'd lost sight of that goal and gone sprinting after something else. Something he shouldn't want and couldn't even have.

Angry with himself, he showered, dressed, and hurried downstairs for breakfast, only to find the house empty and the kitchen bare. A note from his mother explaining that she'd driven to town for a women's auxiliary meeting sat in his place at the table, and coffee left too long on the burner filled the room with a scorched smell.

After dumping the old coffee and starting a fresh pot, Gabe wandered onto the porch to wait. Summer had vanished in the time he'd been back, and autumn had settled in. This morning, fog shrouded the valley, dulling the colors on the mountains and holding the chill close to the ground.

Shivering a little, he sat and propped his feet on the porch rail. Baskets of faded red petunias swayed from the overhang and somewhere in the fog, a meadowlark trilled.

Memories of long-ago days rose up from the forest floor. Hours spent running football plays with Peter and forays into the woods. Early-morning chores and late-afternoon cups of cocoa and warm gingerbread cookies. He heard his father's laughter, his mother's shouted warnings for them to be careful, and Peter's eager voice as he trailed behind Gabe on one of their adventures.

Leaving the porch, he strolled past Peter's shed and into the woods as he'd done so often when he was young. He and Peter had worn a dozen trails over the years, but this one had always been his favorite. Here, in a place no one else knew of but him, he'd dreamed of days gone by, and imagined what the land had been like before settlers arrived.

Though it was already almost nine o'clock, dew still lingered on the undergrowth, and the fog made the forest seem silent. When he was a kid, he'd imagined what it must feel like to be the only person left on earth. This morning, he thought maybe he knew.

He plucked a piece of wild grass from the ground as he walked, fitting the blade between his thumbs to make a whistle. The memories came with him, running the trails, shouting rules to this game or that, and always, always there was laughter.

He'd spent a decade focused on the bad times, but there had been good times, too. More good times than bad. And as he leaned against the towering trunk of a lodgepole pine, he had the sudden, sharp need to share this place with someone. His ancestors had created this incredible haven, his parents had perfected this piece of heaven on earth. Now Peter was gone, and unless Gabe made some radical life changes, there wouldn't be any future generations of King boys running through these woods.

Gabe felt a flicker of honest compassion for his father. Was it this longing for continuity that drove the old man to be what he was? This need to pass what he loved on to the next generation? Had it always been that?

He moved away from the tree and stepped into a small, quiet clearing, tilting back his head, and closing his eyes.

Home.

The word shot through him and brought his eyes open. Where had that come from? He hadn't thought of this place as home in years. Hadn't let himself. He wasn't even sure he wanted to now. He didn't belong here. He couldn't make a life here. But the thought of doing just that stirred an excitement he hadn't felt in years.

Suppose he decided to stay. What would he do? Work at the sawmill? Prowl the grounds at night for the rest of his life? Throw away the thousands of dollars he'd spent on his education? The years of experience in the field? Maybe, if his father would relent, if they could put the past behind them and move on. Maybe then he could carve out a future here in Libby. Without that, it could never be.

A rustle of leaves somewhere close by brought his head up again with a snap. He held his breath as a deer moved slowly into a clearing, its movements slow and cautious, ears pricked and eyes darting nervously. Its beauty made his heart slow, its grace filled him with awe.

There was so much here in Montana that held his heart. One thing had driven him from these mountains, and he'd allowed it to keep him away. But he'd been gone too long now to start over. His education, experience and skills all pointed toward a life far away from this place, even if his heart did tempt him to remain.

He moved and a twig cracked beneath his feet. The deer froze, alert, then bounded into the trees and left him alone again. Unbidden, the memory of Siddah's clear dark eyes filled his mind, the blush of her cheeks, the curve of her lips.

Might as well forget about her, he told himself. Mooning around after her would only make him miserable and distract him from his real mission here. He'd never regret their loss of control last night, but they both knew they couldn't repeat it.

Siddah wasn't like some of the women he'd met in his travels. Some people might call her old-fashioned, and maybe she was, but it didn't take a genius to see how she felt about her past. And only a selfish bastard would put her through that again.

Maybe someday he'd find someone he could share all of this with. In the meantime, he needed to focus on what he could change. From here on out, he'd move forward with the Westmoreland Grant and he'd spend the time he had left in Montana trying to get through to the old man.

Siddah—and Bobby—were a distraction he didn't need.

"GRAB YOUR COAT," Chris said, poking his head into Siddah's office. "I need you to come with me."

Surprised, Siddah looked up from the pleadings she'd been filing. "Okay. Where?"

"We have an appointment to meet with one of the witnesses in the Whitman case."

She closed the drawer and tossed the unfiled pleadings into a basket on top. "We?"

"Evan's idea. Are you coming?"

Siddah nodded, gathered her purse and headed toward the door. "Who are we meeting with?"

"Ricki Archuleta. Evan's still convinced we can break her story under the right circumstances."

Out of the two women who claimed to have been with Asa Whitman the night his wife and boyfriend were murdered, Ricki did seem the one most likely to change her tale, Siddah thought as she trailed Chris across the parking lot. And maybe a change of pace would help get her mind off all the things that had been distracting her from work the past three weeks.

She still saw Gabe every evening, but only for a few minutes. If anything, he seemed more remote now than he had when he first came to town. Bobby still wouldn't talk with her about playing football, and for the past couple of days she'd been fighting a slight case of stomach flu, no doubt brought on by stress.

"So why does Evan want me to go along?"

"He thinks she'll relax more if there's another woman around." Chris turned the key in his Bronco's ignition. "It's worth a try, I guess."

"What do you want me to do?"

"Take your cues from me. I don't know what kind of mood she'll be in, or how receptive she'll be to talking with us."

"Fair enough." Siddah fastened her seat belt and settled in for the ride, but within minutes, her stomach started to churn again. The Bronco was too stuffy, but she'd been walking on eggshells around Chris for so long, she hesitated to complain. She just prayed they weren't in for a long ride.

Luck was with her for once. Three minutes later, Chris pulled into the parking lot at the Timberline.

Siddah climbed outside quickly and gulped fresh air as she walked toward the door of the bar. "She's here?"

"Strange, isn't it? It seems that the scene of the murder also happens to be one of her favorite places to hang out."

"And yet she wasn't here the night of the murders?"

"So she says." Chris opened the door and held it while she stepped through.

Inside the nearly deserted bar, the strong scents of stale cigarette smoke and old grease hit Siddah's stomach like a rock, and the queasiness that had been plaguing her became worse all at once. Irritated with herself, she took shallow breaths and told herself to get it together. She finally had a chance to do something important, and here she was letting nerves get the best of her.

Chris approached a woman wearing tight jeans and a skimpy tank top that made Siddah shiver in the chilly autumn afternoon. She looked young and beautiful from a distance. Up close, she gained at least twenty years. The signs of a hard life became evident in weathered skin, overprocessed hair, deep lines bracketing her mouth, and a slight pucker of the skin around her lips.

She gave Chris a once-over and turned back to the beer sitting in front of her on the counter.

"Ricki Archuleta?"

"Yeah?"

"Chris Leta from the County Attorney's office. This is Siddah King, my associate. Do you have a minute?"

"What for?"

"We'd like to ask a few questions if you don't mind."

Ricki ran another slow appraisal of Chris and then nodded. "I guess. What questions?"

Chris motioned toward a nearby table. "Do you mind if we move over there?"

"What for?"

"It might be more comfortable and it's a little more private."

Ricki shrugged, lit a cigarette, picked up her beer and slid from her stool.

Siddah's stomach lurched, but she did her best not to show her reaction. Maybe a glass of water would help. She checked around for a waitress, but the only employee she could see was the bartender whose attention was riveted on the television over the bar.

"Siddah?" Chris called impatiently. "Are you coming?"

"Yes. Sorry." She sat on the chair Chris indicated for her and tried breathing through her mouth so she wouldn't be bothered by the noxious smells. Here, too, the room was overly warm and she could feel beads of cold sweat forming on her forehead.

"I understand you were with Asa Whitman on the night of July fourteenth," Chris said, his full attention on Ricki.

Ricki nodded, took a deep drag on her cigarette and exhaled in Siddah's direction. "Yeah, I was. Why?"

Siddah's stomach buckled again and the clammy

feeling spread through her. If she didn't know better, she'd swear that she was about to throw up. She focused on her breathing. In and out, nice and shallow, but it didn't seem to help.

What on earth was wrong with her?

She was dimly aware of Chris asking questions and Ricki dodging them, but her head was swimming and she couldn't even follow the conversation.

Another cloud of cigarette smoke hit her squarely in the face. Gagging, she staggered to her feet and looked around blindly. She had no idea where the restrooms were, so she bolted for the outside door. But even the fresh air didn't help. She barely had time to duck around the back of the building before she began retching violently.

Later, stomach empty, she staggered toward a cement parking buttress and cradled her head in her hands. The clear, cool air finally began to help, but it was too little too late. She was mortified, and she didn't even want to think about what Chris would say when she went back inside.

Moaning, she covered her face with her hands and wondered again what was wrong with her. The unsettled stomach had been bothering her for several days, and the exhaustion was so bad at times she could hardly move her limbs at times. The last time she'd felt like this…

She sat up straight and covered her stomach with both hands. The last time she felt like this, she'd been pregnant with Bobby. But that couldn't be. Not after everything she and Peter had tried. Not after the years of hoping.

Could it?

Her hands began to tremble and tears blurred her eyes. Could she be pregnant? With Gabe's child?

No. It was too coincidental. They'd only made love once. Of course, she reminded herself, if everything was working right, once was all it took.

But everything *didn't* work right. Not since Bobby.

Even so, one part of her was elated by the idea of a baby and the other part terrified. She was having trouble enough making ends meet with one child. How would she ever survive with two? She was barely hanging on to her job now—and after bolting from the bar, Chris would be furious with her.

She told herself not to jump to conclusions. If she didn't start her period soon, she'd pick up a home pregnancy test. If the test turned up positive, she could worry then.

But if it was true, how would she ever explain this to Monty and Helene? To Bobby?

To Gabe?

It had been years since she'd thought about the hurt she'd felt when Cornell disappeared out of her life, but the fear that Gabe might follow suit almost made her sick again. Gabe was a far different man than Cornell had been, but he'd never made any pretense about his intentions.

His future was not here in Libby.

WHISTLING SOFTLY and trying to look nonchalant, Gabe pulled off the street and into the parking lot of the city park. He had no idea how Bobby would react to this little bit of subterfuge, but he was at his wit's end.

No matter what he tried, the kid refused to talk about

his football team. But Gabe had promised Siddah and his mother that he'd find out what was bothering the boy. He'd vowed to the old man that he'd break through to the kid. And, by damn, he wasn't about to let any of them down. All of Siddah's gentle persuasion hadn't produced results, so Gabe had decided to try another approach.

Maybe if he could get Bobby playing football again and everything back to normal, they'd forgive him for leaving early. The end of November was only three weeks away, and Randy was moving full steam ahead on their joint project. He'd express-mailed several packages, but Gabe had done little more than skim the information. He just couldn't work up any enthusiasm for it.

He'd better find some, though. He couldn't stay in Libby for another eight weeks, seeing Siddah every day but knowing he could never be with her again. If someone wanted a definition of hell, that would be it.

He pulled into a parking space and turned off the Jeep, then shifted so he could look at the sullen little boy who glared at him from the other side of the Jeep.

He jerked his head toward the field, where a dozen or so kids were running through drills at the direction of the coach and said just one word. "Practice."

"What are we doing here?"

"We're going to watch. Let's go."

"I don't want to."

"Sure you do." Gabe swung to the ground, rounded the back of the Jeep and yanked open Bobby's door. "Let's go," he said again.

Bobby's frown deepened, but he didn't argue. He

walked across the lawn, head down, feet scuffing softly on the grass. Still pouting, he climbed onto the bleachers and stared straight ahead without blinking.

But it didn't take long before his little body began to strain as he watched the other kids running on the field. After a few minutes, he scooted to the edge of the bench and followed the action with eager eyes. Hardly the way a kid with no interest in the sport would act.

Gabe leaned forward, resting his arms on his thighs, watching the action. The boys were dwarfed by the safety equipment they wore, but he admired the coach for minimizing the chance for injury. "Looks like a lot of work."

Even that was too much. Bobby straightened and the shutters dropped over his eyes. "Yeah, I guess."

Strange. It was almost painfully obvious that the boy wanted to be out there on the field, so why wasn't he? Gabe decided to give him another nudge. "What are they doing out there?"

"Those are jump-squats. Coach makes us do 'em every practice."

"They look painful."

"Only at first. Once you get used to 'em, they're not bad."

Gabe shook his head in disbelief and nudged Bobby with an elbow. "Yeah, but you don't have to put up with that anymore, right?"

Bobby hesitated for a second, then nodded. "Right."

"It must feel great. You don't have to waste your afternoons getting all sweaty, don't have anybody telling you what to do and when to do it." Gabe stole a glance at the boy's face. "Don't have to spend your Saturdays at the game. I'll bet quitting gave you a lot more free time."

Bobby shrugged with his mouth. "Yeah. I guess."

A whistle blew and the coach barked orders for another drill. Instantly, the boys split into four groups and gathered at each corner of the field. Another whistle. Two groups dropped and started doing push-ups. The other boys jogged the perimeter.

"Can we go now?"

"Not yet. I haven't talked to the coach yet. Just give me a minute longer. I don't want to interrupt him." Gabe fell silent again until a group of boys huffed past. One or two waved at Bobby. A few sent looks Gabe couldn't read. "I'll bet those guys wish they were in your shoes," Gabe said as the last one chugged past. "You get to lie around the house all day playing video games while they're out here sweating their tails off."

Bobby shrugged, but this time he didn't say anything.

Come on, kid. Let me know what's going on inside that head of yours. Gabe decided to let the silence work for him for a few minutes. It didn't take long for Bobby to start squirming.

He shifted this way and that, then finally squinted up at Gabe. "So what do you need to talk to Coach about?"

"He's an old friend of mine. I haven't seen him for a while, and I was thinking about asking if he needs help coaching." Gabe could spare a few hours between now and November thirtieth to help Bobby get back in gear.

"You're going to coach?"

"If he'll let me." Gabe slid a glance and a grin in Bobby's direction. "You wouldn't mind sitting here and watching while I help out, would you? You could bring one of your video games along." Bobby's quick frown left no doubt in Gabe's mind that he would mind…a lot.

"That's not fair."

"What's not fair about it?"

"You want me to sit here and just *watch*?"

"Well, sure. It's not as if you want to play, right?"

Bobby glared at him and set one foot kicking the bench in front of him. "I never said I didn't want to play."

"But I thought—" Gabe tried to look confused, fearing that if Bobby even suspected that he was manipulating this conversation, he'd shut down again. "I thought that's what your mom told me."

"Well, that's what she thinks."

"But it's not the truth?"

Obviously agitated, Bobby shot to his feet. "What else was I supposed to tell her?"

"I don't know," Gabe said cautiously. "Why don't you tell *me* the truth and then we can figure it out together."

"We can't figure it out," Bobby shouted. "I can't be on the team."

This time Gabe didn't have to fake confusion. "Do you want to play?"

"Sure. But I can't, okay?"

The kid started away and Gabe had to scramble to catch up with him. Halfway to the parking lot, he managed to grab the boy's shoulders and turn him around. "Talk to me, Bobby. Why can't you be on the team?"

"Because. What if I get hurt?"

"You have safety equipment to protect you."

"That doesn't always work. Patrick McShea got a broken arm last year, and Tubby Wheatman got a concussion."

"You're afraid of getting hurt, is that it?"

"No! I'm not afraid."

"Then what is it, Bobby? Why won't you play football?"

The kid's chin quivered and tears filled his eyes. Angrily, he dashed them away with the back of his hand. "Football's stupid, that's why."

"Says who?"

"It's stupid! Stupid! And I don't want to play it ever again."

Bobby turned to run, but Gabe caught him easily. "Come on, Bobby. Talk to me. Tell me why you're so upset."

"Because I hate stupid football."

"Why?"

Bobby squirmed against the hold Gabe had on him, but he wasn't strong enough to break away. "Because," he shouted. "If it wasn't for stupid football, my dad would still be alive."

The words hit Gabe hard enough to knock the wind from him. His grip momentarily relaxed, and Bobby sprinted across the lawn. It took Gabe a few seconds to go after him, and again he caught up and tugged the kid around to face him. "What are you talking about? Your dad died at the sawmill. How was football responsible for that?"

Like a little wild man, Bobby threw everything he had into the fight to get away, but Gabe held on. "Talk to me, Bobby. Please. Why do you think football killed your dad? He was at work when it happened."

"At work because of *me*," Bobby shouted. "He was only there because he wanted to come to my stupid game." A sob racked his little body and grief contorted his face. "He went to work that day because I wanted him to come to my stupid game."

And he'd been carrying around the guilt for that all this time? Aching for the boy's pain, Gabe pulled him into his arms and held him tightly. "Oh, Bobby. It wasn't your fault."

"Yes, it was."

"No, it wasn't. You can't blame yourself. Every one of us probably feels the same way. I could say that your dad was at work that day because I decided to leave the country. I'm sure your mom could find some reason to blame herself. If your dad hadn't been working that day, Grandpa would have been dealing with that load, and Grandpa would have been the one—" The words froze in his throat as Gabe realized what he'd been about to say.

Grandpa would have been the one who died.

His heart hammered in his chest and the hair stood up on the back of his neck. Was that why the old man refused to talk about the accident? Did he blame himself?

Chills rushed up Gabe's spine, but he didn't have time to think about that. Right now, Bobby needed his attention.

Keeping one arm around the boy's shoulders, Gabe started walking toward a picnic table in the shade of a towering pine. "You're not the only one who feels guilty about your dad's accident," he said again. "It's too hard to make sense of something so awful, so we come up with ways we could have changed what happened. It makes us feel less helpless somehow. If only I'd been here. If only you hadn't had a game. If only Grandpa had taken care of that load instead, we could have changed what happened."

Bobby sniffed and wiped his eyes with his sleeve. "Maybe we could have."

"Maybe." Gabe sat on the picnic bench and waited until Bobby sat beside him. "But maybe it was just your dad's time to go. Maybe God needed him for some reason we don't understand. Maybe we couldn't have done anything. We'll never know. But the one thing we do know is that your dad doesn't want us to ruin the rest of our lives feeling guilty for what happened with his."

Bobby leaned forward, his arms on his thighs, his head bent. "He doesn't know."

"You don't think so?" Gabe matched his posture. "I've spent a lot of time traveling around the world, Bobby. I've lived with a lot of different people in the past ten years, and I've encountered a lot of different beliefs about death. You'd be amazed at how many cultures believe there's life after we leave here."

Bobby's face was filled with misery. "Do *you* believe it?"

Gabe nodded. "Yeah, I do. I believe your dad's still around when he can be, and I believe he's aware of what's going on in your life. I also believe that he wants you to be happy, but he knows you never will be as long as you blame yourself for what happened."

"But he switched his days off so he could go to my game."

"Because he wanted to. He was proud of you. He wanted to see you play." Gabe straightened and put a hand on the boy's thin shoulder. "You gave my brother something nobody else in the world did. Do you know that?"

Bobby sniffed again and looked skeptical. "What?"

"You made him a dad. You're the only kid in the whole world who can call him that. And from everything I hear, he was more proud of being your dad than anything else he did."

Bobby's eyes filled with tears again. "I wasn't his real kid."

"No?" Gabe forced a smile. "Do you think he cared about that?"

Bobby shook his head and a hint of a smile tugged at his lips. "I guess not."

"My dad was forced to have me as a kid," Gabe told him. "He didn't have any choice in the matter. Your dad, though. He picked you out. You can't wonder if they love you when they go to all the trouble of picking you out specially."

"I guess not," Bobby said again, sounding a little less distrustful. "Do you really think he's still around? Like...a ghost?"

"Not a ghost," Gabe said. "A spirit, maybe." He shook his head and plucked a blade of grass from the ground at his feet. "I haven't worked it all out in my head, so I don't know exactly what I believe. But I'll tell you what I don't believe." He slid a glance at the kid and warmed up his smile a bit. "I don't believe that he could be here alive and laughing one minute and then just stop existing the next. And if he is out there somewhere, I don't believe that he likes seeing you miserable and unhappy."

Bobby shrugged again. "Can't help it."

"Well, I'm not saying you can't still miss him. But don't you think he'd rather see you laughing and having fun than moping all day long? And what if he is out there somewhere? Maybe he'd like to take some time off from whatever guardian angel work he's doing to hang out at your games."

Bobby actually managed a short laugh. "You think he does that?"

"I don't know. But if he does, I'm pretty sure he doesn't come to watch all those other kids play." Gabe patted the boy's shoulder. "Why don't you try a game or two? If it doesn't make you feel better to be back doing things with your friends, you can always drop the team again. If it does make you feel better, then you'll know it's making your dad happy, too. What do you say?"

Bobby rubbed his face with the heels of his hands and nodded uncertainly. "I guess."

"You're willing to try?"

"I think so."

Eager to seal the deal before the kid could have second thoughts, Gabe stood. "Do you want to talk to Coach right now?"

"What about Mom?"

"Your mom will be thrilled. Trust me."

Bobby stood more slowly. "Are you still going to help coach the team?"

"If Coach Russert has a spot for me, you bet." Slinging his arm across the boy's shoulders, Gabe turned back toward the field. "If not, I'll just have to sit in the bleachers and cheer."

Bobby grinned and Gabe's heart did a somersault. One thing was for damn sure. Walking away from this kid, when the time came, was going to be harder than Gabe had ever imagined.

CHAPTER FIFTEEN

CARRYING TWO GLASSES of wine, Gabe stepped out of Siddah's kitchen and onto the patio where she was taking advantage of a rare warm evening and the opportunity to relax. He'd been biding his time for three days, waiting for a chance to tell her what was really troubling her son when Bobby couldn't hear them.

She glanced up as he approached, her face stunning in the moonlight, her eyes bright with an emotion he couldn't read. A smart man in his situation would have handed her a glass and taken a seat as far away as he could get. But Gabe had been fighting his feelings for her, and losing, for weeks.

He drew a chair close to hers and sat beside her. "I thought maybe we could both use this," he said, handing her a glass.

"Thank you, but I—" She broke off, accepted the glass and set it aside without drinking. "It seems I have a lot to thank you for these days."

"I wouldn't say that."

"You got Bobby back onto the football team, and he's more like his old self than I thought possible." She touched his hand. It was just a brush of fingers against his skin, but it sent a shaft of heat up his arm and into his heart. "I'd say I have reason to be grateful."

He wanted to take her hand in his, to talk about things he shouldn't even think, but this wasn't the time. "I've been wanting to talk to you about the football team," he said, struggling to keep the longing from his voice. "Bobby told me something the other day that I thought you might find interesting."

"Oh? What did he say?"

"Apparently, he's been feeling guilty about Peter's death. He thinks he's responsible for Peter being at work that day."

Siddah's eyes flew wide and the soft look on her face vanished. "He told you that?"

"He says Peter changed shifts so he could attend a game."

"Yes, he did, but Bobby wasn't responsible for that."

"I tried to explain that to him, but I'm not sure he really believes me. I thought you should know, but I didn't want to tell you while Bobby could hear. I wasn't sure how he'd take it."

"Thank you for that." Siddah rolled her head to one side and let her focus linger on his face. Again, the fingers of desire curled through him, and again he fought them off.

"Peter did change shifts that day," she said, "but Bobby's game wasn't the reason. At least, it wasn't the only reason."

"Maybe you should tell Bobby that. It might help."

"I can't." She sat up straight, and her expression changed again. "I haven't told anyone else in the family what Peter was doing."

Gabe didn't like the sound of that. "What do you mean?"

Siddah stood, and wrapped her shawl tighter around her shoulders. She stared out over the darkened backyard, gathering her thoughts. "Peter wanted to modernize the mill," she said after a long time. "He'd been doing some research, and he wanted to bring in new equipment and update the operation." She turned back to him, her face a mask. "He and your dad had been going the rounds for months. Monty said they couldn't afford to retool. Peter said they couldn't afford not to. He thought the answer was to test equipment for the manufacturer."

"He wanted to test equipment here?" Gabe asked, incredulous. "Was he crazy?"

Siddah shook her head. "Not crazy, just...enthusiastic. The mill has been losing money for the past couple of years. Peter thought that retooling could help move it into the twenty-first century and make the business competitive."

"And the old man disagreed?"

"That's putting it mildly. He argued that spending money now would be foolish and drive the mill into bankruptcy."

Gabe couldn't imagine Peter and his father disagreeing, but he didn't have time to sort through that now. He moved closer, dreading what she had to say, but needing to hear it anyway. "Go on."

Siddah shivered again in the chill autumn air. "He believed so much in what he wanted that he mortgaged the house and took out several large loans, but the money he got wasn't enough to refit the mill, and he spent most of it attempting to get more financing, flying experts in that he believed could convince Monty to make the changes he wanted."

No wonder she was frantic to get that promotion. "So the money's gone?"

"With nothing to show for it."

She looked so vulnerable, Gabe had to fight with himself to keep from taking her into his arms. "Why did Peter go to the mill that day?"

"He was going to try again to get Monty to listen to him. The mortgage was in trouble, the loans in default, and Peter was getting nowhere."

"How much money are we talking about?"

"A lot."

"Give me a ballpark figure."

"The amount of money isn't the issue," she said firmly. "Peter borrowed it, and he was determined to make your dad listen to him."

"That shouldn't have been a problem for Peter," Gabe said. "Dad thought the sun rose and set on him."

"And you think he would have gone along blindly with Peter?" Siddah laughed and shook her head. "You really don't know Monty at all, do you?"

"What does that mean?"

"Monty doesn't let anybody tell him what to do, and he doesn't like being contradicted. You ought to know that."

In spite of himself, Gabe laughed. "Yeah, I do know that."

"What you don't seem to realize is that it doesn't

matter who it is. You've been so busy nursing your own grudge, you haven't even paid attention to the way Monty acts with anyone else."

Gabe pulled back sharply. "Hold on a minute. I thought we were talking about the day of Peter's accident. How did this suddenly become about me?"

"It's always been about you," Siddah said, her voice soft. "You just never knew it."

Gabe laughed again, but the sound hurt his throat. "You've lost me."

"You really think Monty hates you, don't you?"

"It's pretty hard to think otherwise."

"Not for Peter." Siddah brushed a lock of hair away from her face and hooked her thumbs in the back of her waistband, inadvertently making her breasts press against the soft fabric of her blouse.

Gabe tried not to notice but he'd never been a saint, and the way his pulse thrummed with the memory of their one brief interlude convinced him that he never would be. "What does that mean?"

"Peter spent his whole life chasing after you. I don't mean literally, but you were the big brother and, in Peter's mind, you were the favorite."

Gabe barked a laugh. "You must have misunderstood him."

She shook her head. "But I didn't. He was convinced that's the reason Monty took your 'defection' so hard. He used to say that Monty would hardly have noticed if he'd been the one to leave town."

The smile slid from Gabe's face. "How could he think that? The old man doted on him."

"According to him, the old man doted on you." Siddah gave a weak smile and admitted, "That's one of the reasons I resented you so much. It didn't seem fair that Monty should prefer the son who turned his back on the family."

Gabe ran a hand across his face and struggled to take that in. "Peter wasn't serious."

"He was completely serious. Don't you understand? Both of you thought the other was your father's favorite, but your father never had a favorite. He loved you equally."

"If that's true, he sure had a strange way of showing it."

"Not so strange," Siddah said. "He's a lot like you, I think."

"Like *me?*"

"He's not entirely like you," Siddah said with a laugh. "Your personality is a *little* less abrasive. But you're both terrified of showing anybody how you really feel, and you'd rather break your necks than reveal your emotions."

"That's open for debate. And Peter?"

"Peter was more like your mother. A lot more open. More in touch with what he felt."

"You seem awfully convinced that I'm not in touch with what I'm feeling."

Her smile slipped. "I've offended you."

"You've underestimated me. I know exactly what I'm feeling. I just don't always choose to share it."

"What's wrong with letting people know how you feel?"

"I suppose that depends on what you're feeling, and who you're sharing it with." He gave in to the urge and touched her cheek with the backs of his fingers. "Not everyone would be sympathetic if I told them I'd fallen in love with my brother's wife."

He held his breath, waiting to see if she'd pull away, and half-expecting her to do just that. To his surprise, she pressed her cheek against his hand. "Not everyone needs to know that. Or that I don't seem to be able to control what I feel for you."

"Do you need to?"

She pulled away gently. "You know the answer to that."

"I know the logical answer," he agreed. "But it's not the answer I want."

"And what is the answer you want?"

It was his turn to smile. "You know the answer to *that.*" Giving up the fight, he leaned down and kissed her. The fire that had been smoldering all evening burst into flame as she moaned and leaned against him. The sound of her pleasure drove him to seek more, give more. He brushed her lips with his tongue and she opened to him eagerly. Her hands roamed across his shoulders and back, her fingers wound into his hair and held him close.

For this moment, there was no question of who needed more, who wanted more. There was no question of right or wrong. There was only desire and heat, and the longing to make the moment last forever that Gabe couldn't shake.

Siddah wasn't ready for the kiss to end when Gabe pulled away and smiled down at her. "That's what I want," he said, "and I don't want it to end when it's time for me to leave here."

But it had to end, and they both knew it. The pregnancy test had come out positive, but that had been no real surprise. She'd spent the past three days arguing with herself about when to tell him. Not telling him wasn't an option, but she didn't want to influence his decisions or make him feel trapped.

She didn't know how she'd get along with two children to raise alone, but she'd figure something out. The one thing she wouldn't do was move to a strange location and wait for Gabe's occasional visits.

She smiled sadly and answered him. "You know how I feel about that."

"Yeah, but you can't blame a guy for hoping something's changed."

"That hasn't changed. I can't follow you into the jungle, and you can't stay here."

"*Can't* is the wrong word," Gabe pointed out. "It's *won't*. Both of us *could* change, but neither will."

"I don't think I can change, Gabe. I have a child who needs me. I *can't* travel around the world and live in huts and eat grub worms."

"But you would if it weren't for Bobby?"

She sent him a grudging smile. "No. That's not the life I want."

"You never know until you try it."

This wasn't how she wanted to tell him, but then she didn't *want* to tell him at all. And she'd never get a better opportunity. Dredging up all her courage, she faced him squarely. "There's another reason I won't leave here and live the way you want to. I'm pregnant."

His mouth dropped for a split second before he shot

to his feet and pulled her into his arms so she couldn't see his face. He held her tightly, but she still wasn't sure whether he was happy or simply shocked.

After what felt like forever, he held her away from him and searched her face. "Are you serious?"

She nodded.

"But how—? Scratch that. I know the answer to that. It's just that—"

"Once is all it takes."

He let out a tight laugh. "I know that, too." He released her and paced a few steps away, shaking his head in confusion. "This is great. I'm just a little surprised, that's all. I never thought this would happen to me. I never expected—"

"I know that home and family and roots aren't big on your list of priorities," Siddah said, putting more distance between them. "And I'm not going to try to hold you here with this baby. I just thought you ought to know about it, that's all."

The smile slipped from his face. "What are you talking about?"

"What *we* were just talking about. You want a life out there somewhere, but I'm not going to drag my children all over creation with you. I'm staying here, and I'm giving my children the security of knowing where they belong."

"That's your final word? You won't even consider a compromise?"

"You can see them both whenever you're in town. I won't try to stop you." She couldn't believe how much this hurt. She'd grown to love him so much in just a few short weeks. She'd come to depend on him far too much. She'd been foolish and unwise, and now she was paying the price.

But once again, she wasn't the only one who'd pay for the decisions she'd made. First Bobby and now this baby. They would both carry the scars for her.

Gabe heard what Siddah was saying, but she wasn't making any sense. Or maybe he just wasn't hearing her right. He was stuck on the incredible news that he was going to become a father.

A father!

It was a miracle. An out-and-out miracle, no two ways about it. So why was she talking about staying in Libby and arranging visitation rights?

He tried to get his elation under control so he could make sense of her argument. "Does it matter at all that I'm in love with you?"

"Are you?"

"Of course I am. Marry me. I'll adjust my schedule somehow so that I can spend more time in Virginia. I'll get someone to help me with the more dangerous work…"

She began shaking her head before he'd even finished the first sentence. "It won't work, Gabe. I'd be miserable waiting around for you to come home, and you'd be miserable sticking around home just to make me happy."

"You don't know that. You're afraid I'd be miserable, and you won't even consider any other possibility."

"I know myself, and I know what it's like to live without the security of knowing what tomorrow's going to bring. I won't live that way again, and I won't ask my children to live that way."

Gabe rubbed the back of his neck in agitation. "This is crazy, Siddah. You've just told me that you're carrying my baby. This should be the happiest moment of my life. So how can you tell me something wonderful like that and then break up with me in the next breath?"

"I'm not breaking up with you."

"Really? It sure sounds like it to me."

"I'm not breaking up with you," she said again, "because we were never together."

We were never together. They were just four little words, but the pain they caused couldn't have been worse if she'd stabbed him.

He laughed harshly to keep her from seeing how much she'd hurt him. "We must have been together for a minute or two. Unless you're telling me that baby isn't mine."

He regretted the words the instant they left his mouth, but it was too late to recall them.

Her eyes flashed both anger and pain, and she whispered, "You're a heartless bastard."

"I didn't mean—"

But she was gone.

He went after her, but she was too quick for him. She slammed the door before he could get up the steps, and he heard the unmistakable sound of the key turning in the lock. He stood there for a full five minutes arguing with himself about what to do next. After all, he had a key. He could let himself in and sort everything out. But one thing kept running through his mind, and it was enough to get him turning around and walking away.

He'd obviously misread her signals. She wasn't in

love with him. She'd *never* been in love with him. He just didn't know why he hadn't seen it before.

Her heart still belonged to Peter, and it looked as if it always would.

HE'D JUST STARTED packing when the knock he'd been expecting sounded on his door. He'd come straight upstairs without speaking to his mother, but Gabe wasn't surprised that she'd sensed his anger. He'd never been able to slip anything past his mother.

Tossing the armful of socks he held into his open suitcase, he crossed the room and opened the door. When he saw the old man standing on the landing, he froze.

"You got a minute?"

"Um… Sure." Gabe couldn't remember the last time his father had sought him out like this, and he had no idea why he was doing so now. He moved aside to let him enter, and the old man took in the disarray.

"You leaving again?"

Gabe was in no mood for an argument, but he didn't have enough emotional energy to prevent one. "It's for the best, believe me. But if you want to say 'I told you so,' don't bother. I give in. You were right and I was wrong."

His father stuffed his hands into his pockets and rocked up onto the balls of his feet. "You want to tell me about it?"

Tell the old man what a mess he'd made of everything since he'd been back? Gabe nearly laughed. But why hold back? Sooner or later the truth would come out and everyone would know. Why not just face up to it now?

He shut the dresser drawer he'd just emptied and shrugged. "Sure. I'll tell you about it. I've screwed up, okay? I've done exactly what you thought I'd do, only I've done it bigger and better than you ever imagined."

"You never did do things halfway."

Gabe barked a laugh and ran a hand across his face. "There's no easy way to say this, so I might as well just come out with it. I've fallen in love." When the old man didn't react, he said, "With Siddah."

"Go on."

"You want more? Okay, how's this? She's pregnant. We were only together once, but that was enough."

"And you're running out on her?"

"Hell, no. I begged her to come with me. Even asked her to marry me. She's not interested."

"Never knew you to take no for an answer before."

"Well, there's a first time for everything." Gabe turned away and pulled an armful of shirts from his closet.

"You love her?"

"Yeah, I do."

"Well, then, do what you have to do."

Gabe crammed the shirts into his suitcase and met his father's gaze. "And what's that?"

"Get her to marry you."

"She doesn't love me."

"Horsefeathers."

Gabe planted his fists in the mound of clothes on his bed and stared at the old man. "She doesn't want me."

"You're the only person around who believes that. Keith and Andy saw it plain as day on Labor Day, and your mother's been buzzin' around here for weeks trying to decide what to tell them. So get Siddah to marry you."

Laughing uncertainly, Gabe sank onto the edge of his bed. He couldn't believe he was having this conversation at all, much less with the old man. "She doesn't want to marry me, Pop. That's the bottom line. I've already asked her. She won't leave here."

"So don't leave."

"I'd pretty much have to. Even if I could convince her to say yes, there's no way I could support a family of four on my night watchman's salary."

"There's no law that says you have to stay a night watchman forever."

He was in the *Twilight Zone*. Gabe was almost sure of it. "What are you doing? Offering me a promotion?"

His father turned to look out the window and stayed that way for a long time. "The mill's in trouble, Gabriel. I've been trying, but I can't pull it out on my own. I could use some help."

The admission came so softly Gabe wasn't absolutely certain he'd heard right. But the look on the old man's face when he turned back left no doubt. It had obviously cost him dearly, but Gabe couldn't remember many things that had ever sounded sweeter.

"You want me to help you?"

"I'm asking if you will. If we don't do something, we'll lose the whole thing. But I can't let that happen. There's too many folks relying on me."

"I don't know what to say."

The corners of his father's mouth tilted up. "I could give you a hand with that if you need one."

It had been so long since the old man joked with him, Gabe wasn't sure how to respond. "I'll bet you could," he said at last.

"Think about it," his father said. "Give me your answer later. And as for Siddah and the baby…it's not an ideal situation by any means. Somehow life works out a little easier when the baby comes after the wedding." He came near the bed, paused and put a hand on Gabe's shoulder. "But that doesn't mean you can't do the right thing. Sometimes we're lucky enough to make the right decision, son. And sometimes we've just got to make a decision right."

"But how do I know what right is?"

"You're a good man, Gabriel. If you love her enough, you'll know what to do."

CHAPTER SIXTEEN

A COLD GUST OF WIND WHIPPED around the bleachers, scattering dried leaves and dirt in its path. Low clouds hovered overhead, dark with the promise of snow. Shivering, Siddah pulled the knit scarf she was wearing tighter around her neck and dug into the bag at her side for the blanket she'd brought along. On the field Bobby looked toward her, and she held two mittened thumbs up for encouragement. But inside, she felt hollow, in spite of the new life growing there.

Gabe had been gone for nearly a month already, and though she suspected that Helene and Monty had heard from him, she'd had no word. Not that she expected cards and letters. She'd been through this before when Cornell found out she was pregnant. She knew the drill.

But that didn't stop her from replaying their last conversation and wondering. If she'd admitted how much she needed him, how afraid she was to have this baby on her own, or even just how much she loved him, might he have stayed?

She'd never know.

The sound of voices nearby brought her head around eagerly. So far she was the only parent here, and any conversation would be better than sitting here drowning in her own regrets. She wasn't surprised to see Helene approaching the bleachers, but she nearly fell off her perch at the sight of Monty all wrapped up in his sheepskin jacket and leather gloves.

Smiling uncertainly, she stood as they came near. "I didn't realize you were coming to watch the game."

"You know I wouldn't miss this for the world," Helene said, hugging her warmly.

Helene had taken over as Bobby's baby-sitter without a word of complaint after Gabe left, and Siddah had finally let herself accept the help with gratitude, but she still wondered how long that would last once she told them about the new baby.

She'd been seeking an opportunity to talk with Helene for weeks. Well…maybe not *seeking,* but at least wishing for an opportunity to present itself. But Bobby was always awake when she got home, and there never seemed to be a good time.

Tough as it would be to tell them about the baby, she dreaded telling them about the house even more. Reality had forced her to withdraw her name from consideration for the new paralegal position. Maybe she could have done the job under normal circumstances, but with a new baby on the way she simply couldn't devote that much time to any job. But without that extra money she wouldn't be able to save the house Monty and Helene had bought for them.

As Monty and Helene settled in, she checked around to see if anyone else had arrived. They were still alone, so maybe she should tell them now. Already, her clothes were getting tight, and she wouldn't be able to hide her pregnancy forever. But what if they got upset and Bobby found out why. Here, now, in front of all his friends.

If telling Monty and Helene was tough, try explaining to a ten-year-old why Mommy was suddenly having a baby, and why this baby would grow up without a daddy, too. She couldn't even explain it to herself.

She'd just have to tell them another time.

Monty sat on one side of her while Helene chose the other, and that surprised her even more than Monty's presence did. Obviously, Gabe's visit had brought about more changes than she'd thought.

She smiled over at him. "I'm glad you came. Bobby will be thrilled."

"That's my grandson out there. Of course I'm here."

Of course? She bit back a smile and decided not to remind him that he'd never been to a game before. "He's number twelve. There, on the other side of the field."

Monty looked to where she pointed and nodded. "Getting tall, isn't he?"

"Yes." Siddah wished Gabe could be here to see this. He'd be utterly amazed—just as she was.

They fell into a surprisingly companionable silence, which Helene broke a few minutes later. "Thanksgiving is next week. You and Bobby are coming for dinner, aren't you?"

She'd been dreading this moment, and had even let herself think that it might not come. "I don't know, Helene. I thought maybe we'd just have a quiet dinner together." Made up of whatever she could bear the smell of that day.

"Don't be ridiculous," Monty growled. "Of course you're coming. You're family."

"You certainly won't want to make a turkey and all the fixings just for the two of you," Helene said.

"I didn't plan on making anything elaborate."

"You're going to make that boy go without turkey?" Monty asked, his face incredulous. "On Thanksgiving?"

It took all the self-control Siddah had not to laugh. "I'm sure we'll survive."

"It's not a question of surviving." Helene tucked her arm beneath Siddah's and squeezed gently. "We know you'd both do just fine at home, but we want you with us. The holidays are a time for family."

Siddah was fighting a losing battle. With both Gabe and Peter gone, she and Bobby were the closest thing to an immediate family Monty and Helene had left. It would be tough for her, being back at the house, knowing that she'd lost both of the men she loved. But Monty and Helene had been through enough disappointment, and so had Bobby. She didn't have the right to be selfish.

"All right," she conceded. "We'll come. But only if you'll let me bring something."

Helene shook her head firmly. "You'll bring your-selves. That's all we need. Monty and I will take care of the rest."

A WEEK LATER, Siddah approached the door to her in-laws' house holding a bowl filled with mixed nuts. A light snow had begun to fall as they drove out of town, and a few soft flakes landed on her cheeks and eyelashes as she walked.

Bobby ran ahead of her, eager for the holiday to begin and completely oblivious to her uneasiness. But that's as it should have been. Bobby didn't need to carry the burden of her mistakes. He was doing enough of that already.

Before Bobby could knock, Monty opened the door and welcomed them both inside. But the instant Siddah stepped into the kitchen, she knew she'd made a serious mistake. Her stomach lurched at the scents of roasting turkey and cinnamon, and it was all she could do to deposit the nuts on the table before rushing into the bathroom.

When she came out a minute later, she found Monty bundled in his sheepskin jacket and wearing a hat. He'd obviously been waiting for her, and he held out her coat silently. Her mind raced as she took it, and she followed him outside wondering how to explain what had just happened. She didn't want to lie, but ruining Thanksgiving with her news didn't seem like a good idea either.

He led her to the edge of the porch, then stepped out into the snow and offered a hand to steady her as she joined him. Thrown off by his uncharacteristic behavior, Siddah followed his lead.

They walked for several minutes in silence, surrounded by the hush of nature, the only sounds the swish of their boots as they blazed a trail. Siddah didn't know what to make of Monty. She liked him this way. There was no question about that. But what had brought about this change in him, and would it last?

He led her to his truck, pulled open the door and spoke for the first time. "Take a ride with me?"

Siddah glanced behind her at the house, then nodded. "Okay. Where are we going?"

"Not far."

Once he was settled behind the wheel, he cranked the engine and set off carefully. "Feeling better?"

Siddah watched him adjusting the defroster and prayed he wouldn't turn the heat up too high. "Yes, thanks. I don't know what came over me."

"As I recall," Monty said, without taking his eyes from the road, "that's not uncommon when there's a baby on the way."

Stunned, Siddah tried to see if he was guessing or if he knew the truth. But he hadn't changed that much. His face was still an unreadable mask.

He took his attention from the road just long enough to make eye contact, and the truth hit her like a load of bricks. "How long have you suspected?"

He shook his head and turned off the lane onto a trail she'd never noticed before. "I don't know if 'suspected' is the right word to use. Gabe told me."

"Gabe?" That surprised her almost as much as the fact that Monty knew in the first place.

"When?"

"The night he left."

She sank back in her seat and stared out at the falling snow through the windshield. "Why didn't you say something?"

"We wanted to wait until you were ready. Thought it might be better that way."

"Then Helene knows?"

"Yep."

She felt small and foolish and embarrassed. "I don't even know what to say, Monty. Gabe and I were just together one time. It was a fluke. It should never have happened, but it did."

"You saying you don't love him?"

It would be so much easier to say yes. To leave Monty and Helene believing that she'd been loyal to Peter's memory. But she couldn't lie to him. Her stomach gave a weak protest, but she forced herself to tell the truth. "No. That's not what I'm saying."

"You do love him?"

"Yes. I know it's wrong. You probably think I'm the most horrible person in the world, and I'm truly sorry, but yes, I do."

"Why would we think you're horrible?"

"Because I was married to Peter. Because Gabe is his brother. Because—"

Monty chuckled softly and put a hand on her arm. "Helene and I love you, Siddah. Have done since the minute you joined our family. Why would either of us be upset to find out that both of our sons had good taste and common sense?"

He couldn't have surprised her more if he'd burst into song. She laughed uncertainly and felt the queasiness lessen a little. "Are you serious?"

"I'm not in the habit of lying."

She let out a breath heavy with relief and leaned her head back on the seat. It was one problem out of the way, but the road wasn't clear yet. "I suppose while I'm being honest, I should tell you the rest. I think I'm going to lose the house."

"Those loans of Peter's?"

She sat up sharply. "You know about those?"

"Didn't for a long time, but Gabe told me about them, too."

"I told him not to."

"Gabe's not famous for doing what folks tell him to. He thought I should know. He was right." Monty patted her arm and drew his hand away. "I've talked to the banks, and the mill will assume responsibility for all of them except the house."

"I can't let you do that."

"You can't stop me. Peter took out those loans to help the mill. That's where the money should come from to pay them back."

"But—"

"It's a done deal, Siddah, so save your breath."

"I don't know what to say except thank you." She couldn't even afford her pride anymore. "With the other loans out of the way, maybe I can save the house."

"Well, that's something to think about, I guess. That little house isn't good for much, though." He downshifted and began a steep climb up the mountainside. "Maybe you should sell it. Get yourself something better."

"Maybe I'll be able to afford that somewhere down the road," she said. "Right now, I'll be thankful just to keep it."

The truck rounded another curve, and Siddah caught a glimpse of something red through the trees up ahead. Below them, the river wound along the valley floor, and she caught a peek of the town in the distance. "It's a beautiful view from up here, but why—"

Her voice froze in her throat as they rounded another curve and a familiar red Jeep came into view. Beyond that, piles of lumber lay covered with tarp and her heart began to thump wildly.

Monty pulled to a stop and shifted in his seat to look at her. "Sometimes admitting you're wrong is less painful than living with the mistake," he said. "I learned my lesson the hard way. I also learned that life doesn't always give us second chances." He leaned across the cab and opened her door. "If you're lucky enough to get one, be smart enough to take it."

Her eyes blurred and she couldn't have gotten words out past the burning lump in her throat if her life had depended on it. Nodding mutely, she threw her arms around his neck and hugged him tightly before she climbed out into the snow.

She saw Gabe standing beside a pile of lumber in the next instant, his dark hair flaked with snow. Only the possibility of falling kept her from flying into his arms. She took a couple of steps toward him, but he was across the clearing and at her side before she could get far.

Wordlessly, he gathered her into his arms. She caught back a sob and wrapped her arms around him, hanging on for dear life. She lifted her head so she could look at him, but she could hardly see his face for the tears. "Oh Gabe, I'm so sorry. I—"

He touched her lips gently. "Don't," he said. She could hear the catch in his voice and she knew he was fighting tears of his own. "I don't want to waste time with the past. I want to start building our future—if you'll have me." Releasing all but one hand, he dropped to one knee. "I love you, Siddah. I want to spend the rest of my life with you. Marry me. Please."

Joy filled her and it was all she could do to speak. "Yes," she whispered. "Oh, yes."

EPILOGUE

Three Years Later

LOVE AND LAUGHTER FILLED the air as the family gathered for a Father's Day celebration at Gabe and Siddah's house in the mountains. Children chased one another around the yard, and Bobby, bent nearly double, followed little Peter around as he maneuvered his new plastic pedal car along the walkway.

Siddah lay curled at Gabe's side on the porch swing, her belly heavy with their second child. His father's truck rattled to a stop near the garage, and her eyelids fluttered open. But when she tried to rise, Gabe wrapped an arm around her and pulled her back onto his lap. She hadn't been as sick with this pregnancy, but she'd been more tired than usual. They were both hoping for a girl.

"Your parents are here," she protested.

"Teresa and Jodie have things under control in the kitchen," he said. "They'll skin me alive if I let you get up before they've given the word."

She laughed softly and snuggled against him. "Bobby was asking this morning how soon he can take Peter fishing."

Gabe shot a look of mock annoyance at the son he'd

adopted just the year before. "That kid's a King through and through. Once he gets an idea in his head, he won't let it go."

"He's focused."

"He's stubborn."

And he was theirs. Gabe bent to kiss her and waved at his cousin Jarrod, who pulled into the yard on his motorcycle. Lessons learned, he thought with a contented smile. Their way of life here on the mountain was every bit as worthy of protection as cultures around the globe. There would always be someone else who could travel the world to make it a better place. For now, Gabe was content taking care of his wife and raising his children. Making the world a better place from right here at home.

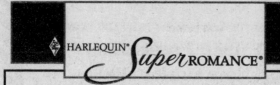

If you enjoyed what you just read,
then we've got an offer you can't resist!

Take 2 bestselling love stories FREE!

Plus get a FREE surprise gift!

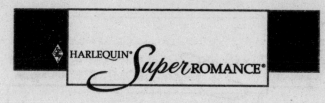

COMING NEXT MONTH